American Sadhu
Patrick Pfister

SPUYTEN DUYVIL

NEW YORK CITY

I am grateful to the following people who read and commented on the manuscript: Carmen Biarnés, Gabrielle Deakin, Pamela Field, Susan Hostetler, Sajid Maqsood, Merrilee Olson, Jeff Palmer, tt and Jil Windsor.

© 2021 Patrick Pfister
ISBN 978-1-956005-02-8
Cover detail from Francisco de Goya's
San Antonio de la Florida fresco.
Back cover © Lenny Silverberg

Library of Congress Cataloging-in-Publication Data

Names: Pfister, Patrick, 1949- author.
Title: American sadhu / Patrick Pfister.
Description: New York City : Spuyten Duyvil, [2021] |
Identifiers: LCCN 2021032362 | ISBN 9781956005028 (paperback)
Classification: LCC PS3616.F53 A82 2021 | DDC 813/.6--dc23
LC record available at https://lccn.loc.gov/2021032362

FOR CRAIG CARR

Eric Tyler still heard his daughter's rebuke echoing in his skull: "Dad, you're not some monk or Jesus crossing the desert. You're pathetic and crazy. Get hold of yourself."

Trembling, he paused by the dining room table where his family had enjoyed evening meals. Back when they were still a family. He stood in front of the fireplace where he and his wife, Kathy, had shared glasses of Pinot Noir and many intimacies. Back when they were still intimate. His home in Ashland, Oregon: the theater where he had performed and failed at his best roles. Husband, father, provider, householder, normal neighbor. He had just celebrated his 60th birthday and retired from DMT Worldwide. Now he would retire from his home, his wife, children, friends, society and identity in the world.

Nothing better symbolized his failure than the two central doors leading into the kitchen from the front and rear of the house. Unable to afford a divorce, he and Kathy had divided their home in half. Kathy got the front, Eric got the rear. One kitchen door always remained locked, splitting their dwelling, their lives and their marriage right down the middle. Three years had passed since he had last seen the opposite end of his home. He came and left by the garden door, the same door he was about to exit for the last time.

Every nerve end in his body burned. He already felt savagely detached from his car, his cell phone, laptop, the

Internet, email, two wearables, the supermarket, the Bright Day Café, his armchair, refrigerator, credit cards and money. Especially money. In his favor, he carried one fragile bit of knowledge. He knew he had created his own personality. Not a hastily painted self-portrait, but a day-by-day, year-by-year layering on of brushstrokes. He had created it. The whole mess. His bungled marriage, disturbed children and unhappy career were the dreadful result, not the cause. Ignore a vision and end up blind.

Staring at the bathroom mirror, he painted a green and yellow trigram across his forehead. Dead center, he dabbed on a bright red *tilaka* spot. He streaked his cheeks in gold, his jaws in gray and black, his nose orange, chin blue. He would shock others, but his intention was to shock himself, to jolt his being out of slumber. He took a last look at his wildly painted face. The mirror reflected back a grimace of desperation.

He entered his study, just off his bedroom. His desk stood free of pens and pencils, folders, documents and DMT project records. The window gave a view of the rear garden, the fuschia and eucalyptis trees. Rays from the rising sun thrust through the branches and fog, streaming in the window, falling onto the desktop, onto his hands as he reached for pen and paper. In shaky letters, he addressed a note to Kathy: "Eclipsed moon: no honey, no exit, no return." He read over his words. "Fall-flat spiritual poet," she had called him.

He signed his name and set the paper beneath his favorite Seattle Mariners coffee mug. Nearby, he left his house and car keys, his social security card, cell phone, bank book, credit cards, forty-two dollars cash, library card, driver's license and his marriage certificate. He resisted the urge to tear the certificate down the middle like the house.

He picked up his daypack and walked out the rear door. Not naked into the world, but damn close. The pack contained a bed sheet, a change of underwear, his glasses, a bottle of water, soap, toothbrush and a super-absorbent, quick-dry towel. He pulled the door shut. In the quiet morning the lock clicked loudly. Farewell to the empty half of an empty house. He gulped in the fresh garden air and tried to master his emotions. He should have been striking off brave and adventurous, but he felt disenchanted, fearful, empty.

Across from him near a eucalyptis stood the barbecue grill, rusted from disuse. Burgers and hot dogs in the backyard. Memorial Day, Father's Day, Fourth of July. The United States of Barbecue. It was the first time in years that he hadn't listened to the Monday morning news on the radio. So he had missed the weekend body count in Chicago, Detroit, Atlanta, and a dozen other murder zones. He wouldn't hear tomorrow's death toll either. What school shooting would set a new record? What far-off country would American bombs pummel and pockmark? He would journey beyond the radio. No more dawn reports on yesterday's sad slaughter.

He felt the autumn of animate life upon him, the season of benevolence. He had studied, worked hard, been a good if not always faithful husband, a good if not always stellar father, raised two children named Billy and Jessica, helped friends in need when and if he could, and in the end he had failed at it all. He wasn't sure if he had betrayed or been betrayed, but if the latter, he knew by whom: his wife, children, friends, boss, his lost and confused nation, divided like his home. Love goes astray and people betray each other. As simple and sorry as that. Though he also had to admit that poetry cannot betray; it can only be betrayed. Still, he had paid his debt to society and now he would become what he had never been: a beggar.

The day was cool and quiet, the sky foggy yet blue in patches. He left the garden, headed around the house and came out on Barbara Street, commanding himself not to look back. He took slow steps. The start of a journey into shadowland. No exit, no return. He felt surges of anxiety and bitterness. He felt the paint sticking to his face. Not a sadhu but a sadhu in reverse; not an Indian holy man, but a man full of holes. Maybe he had gone nuts, as Jessica had suggested, but there had been nowhere else to go. Now he had two hazy pilgrimage sites to visit and nothing to guide him there except a haunted life. No mantra to murmur, no prayer to pray. Time to summon the courage to meet his destiny.

Chapter Two

At twenty-five years old, Eric feels no hesitation when Kathy suggests they celebrate their honeymoon in India. Exactly the opposite: like her, he is eager to rule out the honeymoon havens of Hawaii, Tahiti, Paris, Bali, The Maldives. He and Kathy will go somewhere unusual, a special destination they will always remember. Not Taj Mahal India, but remote, exotic India.

In short order they find their honeymoon selves traveling through disease, poverty and suffering. They spend their first three days in tears. "It wasn't supposed to be like this," Kathy says. Only a day later, tears dry and vision clears. They see light, color, humility. Kathy is joyous. Eric enters euphoria.

How does the seed of emptiness take root in the soil of bliss? Very slowly. Eric feels it no more than the harmless sting of a non-malarial mosquito. He scratches for a moment and then forgets about it. But some single cell microorganism penetrates his bloodstream, plants in his consciousness. At first he pays no attention to the naked, ash-smeared beggars at the edge of every road, near the entrance to every temple. He drops a coin into a bowl and walks on. But Kathy says, "Look at their eyes," and in them Eric observes fire, worship, sacrifice. Dressed in rags, these strange mendicants rejoice in their own dirty skin. Before long he can't take his own eyes off them. Their fierce solitude, their painted faces, their courageous embracing of the unknown. "I have paid my debt to society," one saffron-cloaked holy man tells him. "Now I renounce worldy existence and seek the fourth stage of life: liberation."

At the time Eric still writes poetry. His self-published chapbook, Heart like a jewel, helped land him a job as a junior copywriter at a small Portland ad agency. The poetry of advertising, his boss told him and he believes it. Or wants to. Now, inspired by the holy man's words and the exotic landscape, he endeavors to compose a poem.

Safron-robed creature,
bare feet and tangled hair:
husk of blessing, cavity of calm.

His last act in India is to throw his failed poem onto a trash heap nosed at by an emaciated cow. Then he and Kathy return to Oregon and normal life.

Malaria symptoms usually begin ten to fifteen days after the bite of an infected mosquito. They often include headaches, fever, vomiting and extreme tiredness. Severe cases may result in yellowed skin, seizures, coma, even death. If not properly treated, victims may suffer recurrences of the disease months, even years later.

Eric still shows no external evidence of any malady. The emptiness in his bloodstream remains hidden. He continues to write clever ad copy, continues to rise in the company, eventually moves to a subsidiary of DMT Worldwide. Then symptoms begin to recur in small, inconsequential ways. One year he convinces himself that he has developed an interest in Hinduism and he purchases a book on its history. He reads verses from the Jayakhya Samhita:

"Who am I and in what really do I consist? What is this cage of suffering?"

He comes to a chapter on Sannyasa, the path of renunciation. Reading about the wandering holy men, the sadhus, he begins to understand why they so fascinated him. Owning nothing, they possess in abundance what he lacks.

"What's wrong with you?" Kathy asks him one night. "What're you always thinking about?"

She will repeat the same questions many times over the coming years. One autumn, Eric enrolls in an evening class at Rogue Community College and studies Sangam literature in southern India. Meanwhile, the emptiness in his bloodstream is spreading. A growing sense of disillusion. He is aware of it but he also sees that his life is no different from the lives around him. Everyone breathes the same air. They are all infected.

Malarial reinfection usually causes milder symptoms, but Eric's symptoms intensify. He craves more than books and evening college courses. One year he subjects himself to a Buddhist retreat of sitting hard-core meditation. Twenty-one days with a dozen other desperate souls in a remote valley of the Siskiyou Wilderness. Twenty-one days of backache, knee pain, itching, sleepiness and cramps while his enflamed brain goes through torment, desire, black thoughts.

Then the gauntlet of return. Welcome home Eric Tyler.

"I'm sick of your spiritual angst," Kathy tells him. "Everyday reality—shopping, paying bills, cutting the grass—doesn't vanish just because you do."

Her veiled warning and the venomous air at DMT Worldwide—rife with backbiting, harrassment, corrupt leadership—convince Eric he can endure no more metaphysical bootcamps. So he drops ad copy and abandons poetry and inveigles a change to the account department. Difficult at first, but he painstakingly struggles through various incarnations as an executive, supervisor, account director. In the process he finds the cure for spiritual angst: working fourteen hours a day. It leaves no time for cutting his toenails, let alone sanctifying his self. Beyond any doubt, the honeymoon has ended.

Chapter Three

As Eric continued down Barbara Street, a neighbor's cocker spaniel pranced after him, yipping at his heels, stubby tail wagging delightedly. Still emotional, Eric couldn't remember the dog's name. He scratched the tuft of fur behind her flappy ears, patted her rump, finally remembered. "Go home, Cookie," he said. "There's a good girl. Go home." He shooed her off and she scampered back down the street. The corner of Tolman Creek Road arrived, the first intersection of a thousand. Right or left or onto Old Mill Way? Direction no longer had meaning; nor did time or space.

Just then an elderly woman came stumbling down the center of the road, dressed in nothing but a flimsy nightgown and slippers. Her white hair stood on end and her boney arms flapped like broken wings. Her frantic gaze locked onto him. Onto his brightly painted face, he thought, but then he realized her gaze was frantic because she was.

"I think..." she said. "I think I'm turned around."

Her clear blue eyes were void of everything except panic and perhaps wonder. He guessed she was in her mid 80s, suffering from some form of senility. In the rainbow prism of her dementia, his painted face probably made sense. He took her by the arm and did what she had suggested, turned her around.

"Let's go back this way," he said, "and see if we recognize anything."

"Well, okay," she said doubtfully.

They had barely walked the length of four houses when he spotted a teenage boy trotting in their direction, a wooden cane in his left hand. The boy skidded to a stop in front of them.

"Hey, Granny," he said.

"Do we know you?" the old woman asked.

"He doesn't," the kid answered, nodding at Eric, "but you sure do. Come on, Granny." He placed the cane handle into her palm and she automatically squeezed it and set the rubber tip onto the asphalt. He took her arm out of Eric's grip and led her forward. "Thanks, mister," he said, and then called back over his shoulder. "Cool mask!" He pressed a button on a cell phone and spoke into it matter-of-factly: "I got her."

Eric continued on Tolman Creek Road. Farewell, goodbye Barbara Street. He passed Saratoga Lane, Grizzly Drive and Mistletoe Road. His neighborhood, his tiny world. Sweat formed beneath face paint. He felt bouyant but he tamped down the temptation to stride on vigorously. He was no longer in a hurry to get anywhere. From now on, he had all the time in the world to get nowhere.

A car or pickup passed by every few minutes. Houses stood in wispy fog. He stopped near a fence and rested as traffic trundled by, as a hawk circled overhead, as clouds circled above the hawk. He recalled that in India a sadhu was considered dead onto himself, legally dead to the country as well. Before vanishing from the world, a sadhu attended his own funeral. A ritual of withdrawal and abandonment onto an untrodden path, a Sadhu journey. He was still Eric Tyler but shadowland loomed ahead. The past would soon recede into nothingness.

He collected two windfall apples and stuffed them into his pack. He wandered empty streets, thinking he could roam circles around madness. Despair had been his religion. Hours later he arrived at a mall. The sun had vanquished the fog, rendering the sky intense blue. Tired, he sat on a bench and observed southern Oregon. Kids on skateboards, adults sipping from Starbuck cold cups, a pair of snow-white poodles pulling at leather leashes. He had never before begged and had assumed shame would pour down on him like flaming oil from a cauldron, but questions of form bothered him more. To stand, sit or kneel? Cupped hand or cup itself? His eye landed on one of the Starbuck cold cups brimming out of a litter basket. He washed it at a fountain, refilled his water bottle and selected a likely spot: a square of grass near a walkway where he would be neither hidden nor obtrusive.

He sat in the grass and held forth his cup. People passed by. He couldn't tell if they didn't see him or if they purposely ignored him, fearing his painted face belonged to yet another madman. The kid had called it a mask. Maybe instead of shocking others as he had thought, it rendered him invisible. He grew anxious. Now came the flaming oil. What was he doing? He had let despair push him into obsession, maybe over the edge into idiocy. He felt like a fool, ashamed of his clown act, his clown face, visible or not. A path not taken had haunted his life and now he was too spiritually crippled to walk it. Shiva and Chassors, his two hazy pilgrimage sites, were impossibly remote.

A construction worker dressed in worn bib overalls plodded down the way. He was big and muscular, bearded, beset by some worry creasing his large brow. He caught sight of Eric and scowled.

"Fuck you, asshole!" he said.

Startled, Eric fumbled for a reply. "What?"

"You heard me. Get a life! Fucking idiot."

His right foot twitched and for a second Eric feared the man was going to kick him. But he continued lumbering down the way. Ten steps onward he spat and Eric knew the discharge was aimed at him. Over the next two hours other passersby treated him to similar scowls and black looks. He overheard one woman mutter to another, "What's his trip?"

Finally, the obvious struck. It wasn't his painted face, at least not only his face. He might be invisible, but his clothes weren't. Top of the rack sportswear. Two hundred dollar waterproof jacket, convertible nylon hiking pants, high-end tennis shoes. Ignore his face and he looked like he was about to board a plane for a three-week Carribean vacation. He set the cold cup aside and took one of the apples out of his pack. He bit into it, sorry he had only carried off two.

Chapter Four

*E*ric rollercoasters through a decade of professional success and personal abuse. He rockets into the corporate stratosphere, crash-lands in dead-end bars, fathers Billy and Jessica, wheels and deals, spends whole days gazing at sports on TV and other days feverishly poring over thick books devoted to the "non-material self that never changes." The books ask him questions like, "When you eat an apple, at what point does the apple cease to be food and become you?" He is a soul who happens to have a body, the books say, eternal, unchanging, conscious. Sometimes he glances up from a page and finds that he has missed an inning and the score is now six to three.

Nonetheless he knows the score, knows that his life is in the process of decay. His marriage, his family, his friends not only surround but reflect a deteriorating self. He has a steamy affair and regrets it and then has another affair and doesn't regret it. If emptiness is truly empty, he thinks, how can I still ache so badly? Shouldn't my ache be empty as well?

Kathy no longer asks what's wrong or what he's thinking. She either knows or doesn't care. What she used to describe as his spiritual angst she now refers to as his delusional mania. He is a baseball fan who aspires to be a holy man. Eric realizes that he must take some action but no way can he handle another hardcore meditation retreat.

"I need to get away from myself," he says one night.

Kathy rolls her baby blues as in Not this again. "Who doesn't?"

"Well, maybe I need it more than most."

"Maybe you just think you do."

She pauses, then adds that she has received a promotion at the Health Center where she is a fitness instructor.

"That'll mean more time," Eric says. More time away from him.

"More pressure," she replies. "That's for sure."

An affair, absolutely no doubt. He wonders if she will move out, taking the children with her. That would create real ache, final decay, emptiness without bottom. He recalls Billy's long ago birth, Kathy's sweat-dappled face, the wonder in her expression. The feel of the tiny body in his trembling hands. The mess of tangled hair, the warm, oily, fishlike skin. Then the first emitted sound: a mewling of vulnerability that reverberated in the pit of his being. That was poetry, he thinks, eternal, unchanging.

He looks at his daughter, Jessica, now a teenager, her right hand perpetually poised near her chin, ready to cover any smile. Two years younger than Billy, she is a moody, clammed-up girl whose self-expression takes the form of bruxism. He and Kathy have tried a night guard, a mouth splint, bite plate and even a mandibular advancement device, but nothing stops her from clenching, cracking, pulverizing her teeth into tiny stubs.

"I need implants," she pleads.

His family is being chewed up and pulverized like his daughter's teeth. Terrified, he returns to his traditional cure for spiritual angst: fourteen-hour work days. Months of grind and stress follow. But they bear a result: single-handedly he lands the Pierce-Gladding account in Austin, Texas. A tour de force, smash-hit success. Big dogs at DMT stand up and take notice. The company awards him a fat bonus and rents him a luxury apartment in downtown Austin overlooking the river. He flies in every Sunday night, flies out every Friday afternoon. At the peak of his powers, he owns the planet. Austin has a great live music scene, well-kept parks, friendly people, teeming bars, an upbeat funky vibe. Better yet, five nights a week, he is now away from Kathy and his disintegrating family.

Then one Saturday afternoon, at home during a rain delay in a Mariners away game, he begins zapping channels and comes upon a PBS documentary on Indian sadhus. Sitting forward on his cushy armchair, he observes the naked holy men first seen on his barely remembered honeymoon. A moment later the camera shifts to Redding, California, just three hours south of Ashland, and Eric is astonished to see a stylized sculpture of a dancing Shiva. It stands gleaming on a pedestal in the center of town. Shiva the Supreme, who creates and protects the universe. Shiva who protects sadhus. Eric falls to his knees in front of the television. He does not even hear the narrator explain why the Shiva statue happens to be in Redding. He feels physically ill, as if poisoned by some evil drug. This isn't spiritual angst, he thinks, or even delusional mania. It's breakdown.

Back in Austin, he researches a variety of therapists, analysts, life coaches and clinical psychologists, and finally decides on a spiritual counselor named Walt Cummings. Walt's résumé includes a degree in clinical psychology and nine years as a Trappist monk at Chassors Monastery, by chance not so far from the Shiva statue in Redding. Eric arranges to meet him *every Wednesday evening. Walt is a bald fifty-year-old with a bushy white mustache and no-nonsense yet tranquil manner. In their first session, he asks Eric to choose five words which describe the emptiness he feels.*

"Chasm," Eric replies.

"Okay, that's one."

"Vacuum, lifeless, hollow, unfilled."

Walt's slow nod suggests recognition. Somewhere along the line, Eric thinks, in the monastery or out, the guy hit bottom.

"What you refer to as 'emptiness,'" Walt says, "might also be termed 'existential void.' A feeling of numbness, a sense of nothingness."

"You make it sound common," Eric replies. "Like everyday life."

"Well, common to modern life. People are thirsty. They crave water."

"I feel more like I'm thirsty and don't know where the water is."

"All we can do with emptiness," Walt says, "is learn to fill it or learn to live with it."

In ongoing sessions, he speaks of "unanswered spiritual impulse" and urges Eric to focus on his nakedness and injury. When Eric refers to his interest in sadhus as an obsession, Walt says, "Or perhaps a lifelong passion. A lodestar. Sometimes it's a fine line."

A black and white photograph hangs on the office wall to the left of Walt's head. It pictures Chassors Monastery behind a wrought-iron entrance gate. Observing it every week, Eric perceives mystery, solitude and prayer. The iron bars remind him of the question, What is this cage of suffering? *Life behind the bars: not a three-week retreat, but lifelong surrender. Refuge and redemption within the cage.*

"Tell me about your family," Walt says.

Eric hesitates but then pours out a torrent of emotion and Walt listens, moustache twitching. Finally, Eric runs out of words.

"Unfortunately," Walt says, "our children, spouse, friend, job, lover and, yes, even our family, are all designed to fail us. Just as we're designed to fail ourselves."

Eric looks at him closely. "To what purpose?"

"To leave us empty. So we can fill with something of greater worth."

"What's of greater worth than family, friends, profession, lover?"

"That's what we have to figure out for ourselves."

For a moment Eric remains silent, then he gestures at the photograph on the wall. "Is that why you left the monastery?"

Walt nods. "One of the reasons."

"And the others?"

"I felt I had more to offer than I was giving there."

"And how long did it take you to figure that out for yourself?"

"Longer than I care to admit."

Now it is Eric's turn to nod. He realizes he has been paying someone else to figure it out for him.

Chapter Five

He hiked out of Ashland on Green Springs Highway at the southern edge of Oak Knoll Golf Course. In good times, he used to play nine holes on Saturday mornings with his friends, Earl, Pete and Tony. Even when the bank threatened foreclosure, he managed to scrape up the cash to make a payment on the mortgage and also cover Saturday golf expenses. Then he began to talk about the possibility of a Sadhu journey and, one by one, Earl, Pete and Tony vanished from Saturday morning. That's how he learned the best way to lose your best friends: start figuring things out for yourself and get a wild idea.

Avoiding the racket and threat of I-5, he tramped the Old Siskiyou Highway into the Cascade-Siskiyou National Monument. Mother Nature awaited him in all her splendor. Unfortunately, he was no woodsman. Near a rushing stream he espied dried scat. Harmless deer or hungry mountain lion? He didn't know and he also couldn't identify an edible mushroom or invent a clever way to fish. Like it or not, he needed towns and people. Average citizens might not care much about homeless beggars, but trees cared even less.

Over the following days his clothes soiled and wrinkled, his flesh dirtied, his facial stubble turned to ragged whisker, and coins began to land in his cold cup. He ate a power bar, a tuna fish sandwich, a few bananas. On the fourth day he crossed the Oregon border and entered California. Twice that afternoon he was at the point of stealing food.

He resisted temptation, not out of virtue or integrity, but because store managers now had their eyes on him. If he wandered too close to a fruit bin or pastry display, a clerk appeared, snarling, "May I help you, sir?"

That night in the small town of Hornbrook, Eric huddled in a clump of trees behind a store called "All Star Liquors." Shooting pains ran through his sixty-year-old body and his stomach growled noisily. Hunched forward, he pulled his sheet tight around his shoulders. Tomorrow would make five days with little to eat. He had lost weight and he craved food, alcohol, pills, cigarettes. Bad enough, but he also felt torn out of his addiction to daily labor. Paperwork, files, folders, incoming mail, keyboard, important meetings, constant activity. Nothing to hold on to anymore. No cell phone, no social media, no more fourteen-hour days. He was losing focus on his hazy pilgrimage sites as well. No more Shiva or Chassors. No more human beings either. He hadn't spoken to anyone since leaving Ashland. People passed by in cars or passed by looking the other way. The lack of social intercourse made him realize physical intercourse had also disappeared from his life. No more sex. Not even the hope of it. He was dirty and undesirable. If the laws of karma decreed that every soul created its own destiny, what destiny was he now creating?

The following afternoon he arrived in Yreka, a former gold rush boomtown. He stood near the exit of a convenience store in the historic district and held out his cold cup. People walked by; a few stole glances at his unshaven face. Most of the paint had faded but the red *tilaka* still adorned his forehead.

Two dark-skinned, bejeweled women came out of the store bearing a few bags of groceries. The taller woman wore a sparkly t-shirt and jeans while her friend sported a classic Kanjeevaram sari. Tamils from southern India and likewise middle-aged American housewives out shopping. Their dark eyes lit as they approached him. The taller woman said she had never before seen a sadhu in northern California. Her friend nodded enthusiastically. They asked for his blessing.

"My blessing?" he mumbled.

"Please, holy sir."

For nearly a week his ridiculous appearance had shamed him. Now that it made sense to someone, he felt even more shame. He explained that he wasn't what they thought. He wasn't even Hindu. He was American.

"A sadhu is a sadhu," the tall woman said. "You have no race or nationality. You love and serve the world."

"What?"

"And expect nothing in return."

The second woman added: "You do not hope to live or long to die."

Their dark eyes radiated joy and awe and something near worship. He shook his head.

"This is wrong," he stammered, "I can't give a blessing. I don't even know how."

"It's easy," the woman in the sari said. "You just put your hand here and bless me."

She lifted his right arm and placed his palm against her forehead. A moment later the tall woman did the same. In astonishment he watched as, one after the other, their faces cleared, their personalities dissolved, their eyes emptied of all desire, even the desire for a blessing.

"Thank you, *Baba*," the tall woman said, and handed him a five-dollar bill.

They were the last words spoken to him for days. But they stuck, making him feel not only loony, but a con man on the wrong continent. As his clothes became increasingly shabby, passersby either steered clear or pretended not to hear his entreaties. Even the few who nodded a timid greeting, acknowledging him as a fellow life form, quickly scurried on. The two Indian women had seen a holy wanderer dead onto his own being, a "ghost self" and renunciant of earthly life. *You love and serve the world.* Everyone else saw a derelict who might be deranged, capable of some sudden bizarre act. No one asked for a blessing.

He lost more weight and his gaze roamed. The latter worried him. He remembered reading on some DMT ad campaign that the average human's attention span was about eight seconds, less than that of a goldfish. He tried to keep centered and mindful as his stomach rumbled and his legs and back ached. Dehydration forced him to increase his water intake. Lack of sleep shrouded him in fatigue. As he passed farther out of the fog and chill of the mountains, the northern California sun blazed in his eyes. He stopped to rest in small town parks where pensioners gathered on benches, yakking like old roosters on barnyard fences. He sat nearby, listening as they yammered about drugs, guns, violence, perversion. Sometimes they gave him a few coins;

other times they warned him not to get close. One day, eavesdropping on a conversation, he became so interested he mistakenly assumed he was part of it.

"From bad to worse to even worse yet," said one pensioner.

"What do you expect?" Eric suddenly chimed in. "There's a buffoon president spinning plates for a carnival nation. A dying empire hypnotized by glamour and the grotesque."

"Who the hell are you?" said the pensioner.

"It's the end of sweetness," Eric went on. "The death of tenderness. Wake up."

The pensioner brandished his cane. "Homeless idiot, get outa here!"

Two of the bigger men gave Eric a push and he stumbled out of the park, back onto the road heading south.

CHAPTER SIX

One Friday morning Eric catches an early flight to Oregon and attends a meeting at DMT Worldwide. Afterwards a taxi drops him on Barbara Street just as his son Billy arrives home from school.

"What's up?" Eric asks. "I thought classes didn't get out until four on Friday."

Billy scratches his crotch, mumbles evasively, smirks. At fifteen, he is already an inch taller than his father and looks down at him as if from atop a step ladder. Eric keeps grilling him and finally learns that a recent multiple shooting in Boise has caused the Oregon school system to enact new safety measures, including lockdown drills. Billy has just been sent home for refusing to participate in a drill.

"Bunch of crap," he says.

"Crap?" Eric stammers. "You stare at TV, cell phone and computer screens all day long. Don't you see what's happening there—multiple shootings, mass murders, drive-bys, slaughter in every corner of the damn country?"

"Chill out. I got a right to get shot if I want."

Cool and scornful, he adds that mass shootings are a conspiracy anyway. Professional actors play the parts of both victim and mourner. They are called "crisis actors" and the same ones perform at different "fake scenes." He says Eric wouldn't recognize a "false flag" if it waved in front of his nose.

"Some active shooter dude shows up at school," Billy says, "and I laugh in his puss, dare his trigger finger to twitch. False crap. All of it. Just like you."

Eric flies into a tantrum that is loud and futile. Kathy warns him that his once-a-week dose of paternal discipline won't accomplish a thing. She urges him to let it go. But he can't. He doesn't doubt that Billy might be brainless enough to provoke an active shooter. Secretly, he fears Billy might become the shooter himself. From then on, every Friday when he arrives from Austin, he rages and shouts; the noise only magnifies all other problems in the house. Billy stays out later each night. He pops pills, cracks up cars, shoplifts, vandalizes, rings up legal bills. "Absent father," Kathy says. "Wayward son."

Maybe, Eric thinks, or maybe just a bottom-line tax levied on success. He is 53 years old and still at the top of his game. There are clients at the door, money in the bank, new opportunities at every corner. And it all feels normal, like good health until the day you catch the flu. Or cancer.

When the housing bubble bursts in 2007, he is still a DMT hero and superstar, virtually invulnerable. He doesn't see the train wreck coming. The following year the unemployment rate jumps to over 6% and clients begin to delay payments, mostly because their own clients are doing the same. A chain reaction is under way, felt by every enterprise in a foundering nation. Especially felt, as always, by advertising and marketing companies. And by couples seeking divorce.

As the national economy bottoms out, Eric is plunged into a maelstrom of demotions, pay cuts, dismissals and a fight for survival amid corporate clamor. DMT Worldwide reels him home from Austin and kicks him year by year, rung by rung down the company ladder. His sessions with Walt now long over, he spends money on abuse instead. Maker's Mark,

Marlboro, Major League Baseball OD, prescription meds, porn, more Maker's Mark. At DMT he calls on past favors, invents new strategies and hides when the heat grows too hot, but his future is now written on a granite billboard. He will soon be offered a choice: a pink slip or a pink slip disguised as the rosy glow of early retirement.

He and Kathy hit rock bottom in their finances and love life in the same crash landing. Separate bedrooms, bathrooms and living areas, separate televisions, yet still husband and wife. Locked doors to a kitchen with individual cupboards, drawers and refrigerator shelves. Even separate silverware. Lips that had once pressed together in burning passion now refuse to graze the same spoon.

Then one day Billy disappears along with Eric's Lexus, $265 from a desk drawer, most of Kathy's jewelry and every prescription med in the house. He leaves behind no written note, no voice mail message. Five months later, while wading through bills in a downtown bar, Eric receives a call from a Vehicle Impound lot in Fairbanks, Alaska. His Lexus has turned up as a total wreck, the front end so mangled the engine now sits on the roof.

"Hard to win a fight with a tree," the lot manager tells him.

"Do you know anything about the driver?" Eric asks.

"They say he skipped off without a scratch. The rear wheels are still worth some if you're interested."

Every night Kathy's television drones on and the racket of canned laughter and gun shots drifts down the hall to Eric's room. He can imagine her drunk and drowsily caressing the remote control, an empty bottle of Chardonnay next to her

Valium on the nightstand. Some nights he wants to charge down the hall, storm through the locked doors, grab her wine bottle and hurl it straight at the relentless television. But he is usually too drunk and drowsy himself, about to drop the remote control from his own hand. Also, television blare is not his only source of rage. He knows that she is now at it with a new lover, a guy named Abe, a co-instructor at the Health Center, a personal trainer adept at weight and cardio-workout routines. Ten years her junior, Abe boasts two ex-wives and two kids from each marriage. After-hours, he and Kathy meet in the weight room. Part of the reason Eric drinks so much at night is to wash from his mind the image of their rock-hard bodies slamming together in wild sex.

At first, Jessica is sensitive and understanding of her parent's situation. She visits them one at a time and never plays favorites or carries salacious whispers between warring camps. Instead, she avoids the issue entirely by talking obsessively about her bruxism and damaged gums. She uses the term "occlusal overload," making it sound like an external disease visited upon her. She has found a Medford dental office offering a reasonable payment plan for prosthetic restorations. Reasonable if Eric guarantees the finances. He tells her what she already knows and doesn't want to hear. He and Kathy might not share kitchen utensils any more but they still share crippling debt. The house is underwater and they are behind on payments everywhere.

"There must be some way," Jessica insists. "This mouth is killing me."

One Sunday she invites Eric over for Spaghetti Primavera.

They talk about occlusal overload for a while and then about a friend of hers who wants to buy an apartment and is looking around Medford to avoid high-priced Ashland. The real estate talk leads to the house on Barbara Street, still underwater. Jessica says she has been surprised to hear that "Mom is going to sell the house." She says it casually, as if referring to some common buzz known to all the neighbors. As she goes on jabbering, Eric trembles in fury.

"If Mom sells it," she says, "some of the money can go to my prosthetics. That would be awesome."

Eric suddenly throws his fork down into his spaghetti.

"She can't sell it," he spits out. "Because it isn't her fucking house to sell."

Some cell cluster in his brain bursts. He shoves his plate across the table so violently half the spaghetti splashes out. He rails at Jessica for being in league with Kathy, for conspiring against him. He calls Kathy—her mother—a "fucking bitch" and accuses her of stealing money, sleeping around, being an alcoholic. "That's your Mom," he says, "a lush and a whore and a bitch who's fucking her personal cardio pervert while all you care about is your goddamn mouth."

Jessica's tiny teeth chatter together as she rises to her feet. Her look of disgust leaves no doubt Eric has just flung the remains of his family onto the table with the spaghetti. Son gone, wife gone, and now enraged daughter stumbling across the room. His family designed to fail him. Jessica yanks the front door open. "Leave my home, Dad. Never come back. Never."

CHAPTER SEVEN

He continued south on Old Highway 99, now baptized the Cascade Wonderland Highway. He passed through small towns, often no more than a motel, some pickups, a rural post office, a few scattered buildings. Grenada, Edgewood, Weed. In Mt. Shasta outside the Strawberry Valley Inn, a woman dropped a roll of pennies into his crumpled cold cup. Near Azalea on the Old Stage Road, a shadow passed over him. Looking up, he spotted an eagle. Farther south, he stopped at Mossbrae Falls near Shasta Springs. Beneath a lush, moss-draped cliff, he sank his tired feet into the icy waters of the Sacramento River. Amid the thunder of falling water came a whoosh and clatter from somewhere above him. A passing train. Then nothing but the breeze through the trees, the roar of the river: *Go home. Go home now.*

He pulled his feet out of the water and let them dry in the sun. He dozed off, sleeping like a puppy in the warm grass. When he awoke, he noted a burning sensation near the heel of his left foot. He located a small red spot. At least it was something to think about besides the hunger pang in his stomach.

A few hours later, hiking southward, he removed his shoe and sock and found the spot had turned white. Fluid now seeped into a cavity of chafed skin, forming a gelatinous bump. A king-sized blister. It slowed his progress and finally brought him to a stop in the small community of Mountain Gate just south of Lake Shasta. He managed to beg a needle, rubbing alcohol and a cotton swab from a kindly housewife. He punctured the blister at its edge, drained the fluid, wiped it clean, applied a band-aid. The same housewife brought out a turkey sandwich and bowl of pea soup and let him sleep on a foam pad in her garage. "I don't think we've ever had a homeless person in Mountain Gate before," she said. She added a quick goodnight and hurried inside, locking the door tight as a tomb.

Eric's stomach was full and his first night of good sleep followed. Never mind the stench of oil and mildew, or the nocturnal creaks and rasps, the garage put a roof over his head. In the morning he brushed his teeth at a tap at the side of the house and then washed his face, removing the last remains of paint as well as the grit stuck in his beard. The woman gave him a few extra band-aids and another turkey sandwich for the road. She seemed relieved to see him go.

Revitalized, he limped on southward beneath a stunning blue sky. The sky put him in mind of how he used to call Kathy's eyes her "baby blues." He had barely seen her eyes or any other part of her since they had split the house in half. Kathy, once his lover, his wife, his heart's desire. How did a sadhu die onto himself when he still possessed memory? He may no longer have race or nationality, no longer hope to live or long to die, but memories sustained and renewed. Could he live his life without his daughter, Jessica of the tiny teeth? He should have foreseen the ache of her absence. Stupidly he had thought the past would recede into nothingness. Now, barely two weeks into his journey, he felt the past growing immense. He had turned himself into a cliché, the American outcast roaming in search of self. What in holy hell was he doing? He had dreamed too much poetry, not written enough. Was he really a sadhu, a ghost self wandering between the gods and humankind? Or just another lost soul needing a bite to eat?

He devoured the turkey sandwich and enjoyed every bite except the last. Now hunger would start again, consume him again. He hobbled along, resting his foot every hour or so, covering what he judged to be five or six miles a day. In the whoosh of traffic, the highway whispered, *Keep going. Don't stop*

Early Thursday afternoon he arrived in Redding. Every restaurant he limped past displayed the same Helped Wanted sign. Foot aching, mind full of road roar, he saw the sign not as a simple advertisement, but as the cry of all mankind. He passed a Wal-Mart, the Cascade Theater and finally came to a stop at the Old City Hall Arts Center. In front of him stood the sculpture of dancing Shiva. His first pilgrimage visit was no longer hazy. The stylized, twelve-foot statue towered over him, gleaming in the harsh sunlight. Shiva, the transformer, the destroyer of evil. Shiva who protected sadhus.

Eric asked a woman passing by where the statue had come from, why it existed, what it meant to the town of Redding. She shrugged: "It's been here forever."

He had hoped for more. A drop of inspiration, a glimmer of understanding. He limped on and soon found a bench in front of a place called Donny's Diner. He felt dizzy and depressed. He took off his tennis shoe and changed the dressing on his wounded foot. Like the other restaurants he had passed, the diner also displayed a Help Wanted sign, but a second sign hung beneath it:

"We need you and you need us. We all need each other."

Eric lurched to his feet, walked closer, read the sign twice. Still dizzy but aware of his appearance, he stumbled past the front entrance and headed around back to a screen door. Hesitantly, he stepped into a kitchen redolent of fried onions. A short, fat man was flipping burgers at a grill. He turned and regarded Eric with large eyes.

"I saw the sign..." Eric said woozily. "Out front, I mean... and I... I need..."

The man slapped a burger onto a plate, snatched a Neoprene apron off a hook and looped it over Eric's head.

"I can offer you three squares," the man said breathlessly, "and the shack out back."

It was Donny himself, the proud owner of the diner. Two days ago his dishwasher had quit, he told Eric, leaving him and his waitresses—Mary and Glenda—to fend for themselves. "Never fire until day's end," he went on. "That's the rule. But you can't stop 'em from walking out on you."

He led Eric across the kitchen to a dishwashing machine buried beneath stacks of dirty plates and glasses. He leveled a sincere gaze on Eric.

"This is a good place," he said. "We treat people right."

Chapter Eight

Gone were the pebbles kicked up by passing cars, gone blistered feet, gone the wandering ghost self. In the kitchen at Donny's Diner cups clattered, onions sizzled, and Glenda and Mary flew by dropping off dirty dishes, snatching up loaded plates, scooting trays out to hungry diners. The sun no longer hammered Eric's skull but rock 'n' roll blared out of a radio perched on a shelf above the grill. Oldies but moldies. Donny flipped burgers and drained fries and belted out every tune. The Stones, Brenda Lee, Janis, Eurythmics, Pearl Jam, Credence, AC-DC. Old time rock 'n' roll and, every hour on the hour, the news Eric hadn't heard in a month. Murder, mayhem, madness. The song remained the same. A hamburger nation in turmoil, a French-fry culture swirling the drain.

Meanwhile, he showered cups and plates and loaded racks into the commercial warewasher. A whoosh came from inside the machine and jets fired 180-degree water and suds. When he pulled the rack out, steam billowed over his sweaty face and his sixty-year-old legs and back ached more than when he had tramped the road. Aside from a teenage summer job as a landscaper's assistant, he had never done physical labor. Now, day after day—muscles, bones, fingers, toes—everything ached.

Everything except his stomach. Canadian bacon, eggs and pancakes for breakfast. Burger and fry lunches. Fajita and pizza dinners. Within two weeks he had piled on his lost pounds and allayed his fears of dehydration. Once again, he was sheltered and warm, no longer a beggar tempted to steal stale bread. People didn't avert their gazes. He was back in worldly life, no longer dead onto himself.

Every day after the lunch rush, he joined Donny, Mary and Glenda at the corner table. They served up coffee, cake and more conversation in thirty minutes than in his last thirty days. Three pudgy, good-hearted souls. Mary a foot taller than the other two. Glenda the pudgiest of the three. They waved their cell phones in front of his cleanly shaven face and showcased their children, homes, cars, dogs, cats and Mary's pet gerbil. When he described his Sadhu journey, they stared glassy eyed, then asked if he suffered from a terminal illness or if he had made a wager with a friend. Glenda said, "It must be tough on your family."

"Not really," Eric replied. "I'm not even sure anyone knows I'm gone."

"Either way," Donny said, "we're glad to have you in the Diner family."

In their mid forties, they all had teenage kids. They asked for Eric's two cents as a "broken-in and been-around Dad."

"Just tell us how you got through it all," Mary said.

Where to start? He told them about Jessica, how she feared "pressure situations," which included sports, academics and boyfriends. She could have entered any university in Oregon but never even applied to a junior college. Now she worked far beneath her abilities as a lowly paid opthalmic lab tech. Her only life goal, as far as he knew, was to save her pennies, amass a fortune and one day purchase a dazzling smile.

"They're all nuts now," Mary said. "If it isn't their teeth, it's their lips, nose, tits, ass. It's like they drop out of the womb already neurotic."

"They don't just drop," Donny said.

"Donny's right," Glenda said. "The social media garbage makes them all nuts."

Then what about the damn radio news? Eric wanted to say. Why listen to that every hour on the hour? He already knew the answer. Psyches addicted to being shocked, exhilarated, saddened, depressed. He knew because he was no different. He had already fallen back into radio land.

"What about your boy?" Mary asked.

Eric shook his head. "Last I heard was a garbled message on the answering machine a couple of years ago. An urgent request for three thousand dollars. He said he was in Alaska and I should send it immediately. End of message."

Donny paid Eric in cash every Friday and Mary and Glenda gave him a percentage of their tips. He kept all the bills and coins in a jar beneath his cot in the shack behind the diner. Since he ate and slept for free, he had little to spend money on and the jar filled. So did his wardrobe. Glenda brought him two shirts and a pair of jeans her ex-husband had left behind when he fled to Los Angeles. Donny dug out sweaters and a jacket from the Lost & Found.

"Nobody's come to claim this stuff in years," he said. "It's public property now."

The diner closed every Sunday. Mary or Glenda always

invited Eric to lunch with their families but he spent half the week looking at their family photos anyway, so he passed. He also declined Donny's invitation to attend services at his charismatic church.

"We won't nail you to a cross," Donny told him. "And we don't preach. We sing."

Instead Eric strolled around town, caught a matinee, watched the river flow. Or visited Old City Hall where Shiva danced. The cosmic dance in which the universe was created and dissolved. Shiva jumped and jived to release all souls from illusion, jigged and jittered in the ballroom at the center of creation, the human heart. Eric felt like he was dancing too, not in Redding, California with Shiva, but at a witch's Sabbath in the fire-lit past. Ashland, Kathy, his kids. All of it kept coming back. Wistful yearning for a home that had never been that homey.

He knew that by now Kathy had re-opened the two central doors into the kitchen. Their house—her house— would no longer be a divided dwelling. She would have read the note he had left her and probably laughed derisively. He supposed she had given away his belongings to charitable causes. Now no shred of his former existence remained. He really had died onto himself. The funeral had taken place, his past officially buried. Come to think of it, what language did he speak? And what prayers did he pray? Years spent wringing his hands in angst yet he had never pressed his palms together. Agonize in existential despair and do nothing about it. How smart was that?

So he accepted Donny's invitation and joined a

congregation of a hundred people in a small church near Sundial Bridge. He took part in the heartfelt song and reverential bowing, but after a few weeks the clapping and shouting finally drove him out the door.

Every evening at six o'clock the oldies but moldies changed to an hour of classic blues. B.B. King, Lightning Hopkins, Aretha. They kept him drifting in sweet sentimentality. He thought of Mabel Shoemaker, his waitress at the Bright Day Cafe. Mabel had known him as a permanent, unchanging self: a coffee and roll guy. She used to say that if she had saved his daily tips over twenty-five years, she could have retired a millionaire. Sometimes when Mary or Glenda cleared away his breakfast dishes, he absently mumbled, "Thanks, Mabel." One morning Glenda said: "Who's this 'Mabel' you're always pining for?"

He had hoped to find meaning on his Sadhu journey. Now he had a new identity and he was back in society—a job, friends, food, drink and daily chitchat, even church on Sunday if he wanted—but it wasn't the same as redemption. Change not the same as transformation. He washed dishes. He didn't love and serve the world.

On Friday after the lunch rush he sat at the corner table with Donny, Mary and Glenda. They showed their latest photos and talked about their kids' latest hijinks. He listened, tempted to announce that their families were destined to fail them. Suddenly Mary pushed her cell phone across the table.

"Eric," she said, "call your daughter. You can hear her voice right now. She can hear yours."

"She must be worried sick," Glenda added. "Just like you are about her."

The urgency in their voices, the sincerity in their pudgy expressions, made his fingers tremble on the table an inch from the phone. He could almost hear Jessica's voice in his ear, the sound of her teeth grinding.

"If you can't bring yourself to do it," Donny said, "then use this..." He shoved his laptop forward. "Check Facebook or Instagram."

The slow-tempo, acoustic intro to *Stairway to Heaven* drifted out to them from the radio in the kitchen. Eric hesitated. Then he shook his head and rose from his chair. He marched through the kitchen as Robert Plant sang, "There's a lady who's sure..." and entered his room at the back. He shut the door and sat on his cot, shaven face buried in dishwasher hands. When was the last time he had cried? A decade ago? How could any sane human go years without tears? He felt raw and empty. He yearned for his ghost self, longed for the precious jewel of his Sadhu journey. It hadn't sparkled very long.

Chapter Nine

He gave his notice and by the end of the week Donny had hired a young Mexican freshly fired from a crosstown eaterie. Eric spent the morning training him at the warewasher. That afternoon marked the last gathering at the corner table, Eric's last look at photos of Donny's wife, Glenda's kids, Mary's pet gerbil. Then he surrendered shirts, jeans, a jacket and sweater to the Salvation Army Donation Center. He removed fifty dollars from his jar and donated the rest to the Youth Violence Prevention Council. The fifty dollars was his concession to common sense. The money would last until his beard grew and his clothes dirtied, enabling him once again to beg.

His leave-taking occurred the following morning. "Call us," Donny said, hugging him. "Let us know where you are and how you're doing." Mary mistakenly referred to his Sadhu journey as his "sad" journey. Glenda packed him a lunch. Tuna salad sandwich, chocolate fudge brownie and bottle of sparkling water. "There's a napkin in there," she said, "and a couple of baby wipes in case the fudge sticks."

Only a few days ago he had brooded over his failure to shed tears. Now they ran off his cheeks all the way to Old City Hall. There Shiva still danced in his ring of fire, the destroying fire which purified all. Sunlight gleamed on the statue from head to uplifted toe. Eric turned and set off southward.

It didn't take long to migrate out of society. Three days

and he was back on the other side of the fence beyond the pale of identity. His clothes wrinkled, his beard grew and he became invisible once again. Now his only contact with others came from eavesdropping. On his way through the small town of Anderson, he listened to two middle-aged women.

"Why didn't she divorce him from the start?" asked one.

"Why didn't we all do what we shoulda done at the start?" said the other.

"Cuz we didn't know then what we know now."

"What we think we know now."

Trudging south toward Cottonwood on Locust Road, he listened to oldies still resounding in his head. He missed Donny, Mary and Glenda, missed their sincerity and good will. He covered six or seven miles a day, stopping every hour or so to get out of the sun. His back muscles throbbed, his legs cramped and his old companions, loneliness and hunger, returned. He looked at his reflection in a shop window and felt revulsion. He didn't want to be that person anymore. Questions pounded behind his sweaty forehead. How far did he have to walk before he never returned?

One thing he knew for certain. Water. He had to carry water. At all times. No path was so pleasant that it couldn't turn dry and dusty beneath the murderous sun. Water. The day he forgot it would be the day he lost all. Drink, swallow, exult.

Sometimes he had no choice but to come out onto I-5 and hike alongside the blast and roar of traffic. South of Red Bluff, he finally got onto a quiet secondary lane and soon arrived in the town of Weston. He paused by the town library, where a small marble memorial stated the vow "Never Again" and listed the victims of a mass shooting.

He read the names, grimly recalling Billy and lockdown drills. For the first time on his Sadhu journey he wished he had a cell phone. Technology, a push-button path to redemption. He could talk to Billy and make everything right. Technology, the new aristocracy. Of course, even if he had possessed a phone, he had no number to dial. So he stood there as if in front of a memorial to his collapsed life.

An old man hobbling down the sidewalk came up to him.

"Thank you for stopping to pay your respects," he said.

Eric left Weston, still heading south, guided by the flow of the Sacramento River or I-5 traffic. The sun burned down on him. How long did it take to burn away the past? Maybe that was the purpose of prayer. To set the mind on one litany instead of a dozen detours. What prayer might he learn that would release him, that would let him drop from the world like a ripe plum from a tree?

In downtown Corning he begged for an hour and managed to acquire two dollars, some Manchego cheese and a plastic bag of olives. South of town, trudging along Kirkwood Road, he came upon an abandoned farmhouse in the middle of an olive grove. Half the roof had caved in and the windows were blown out or hanging in shards. Not a soul in sight. The front door tilted open on a single rusty hinge. Inside, there were a few stained mattresses, some blackened pots and pans, a mound of ashes and charred wood chips. Someone else had once passed a night there, or at least built a small fire. An upside-down stove had made its way along the hall into the bathroom while the kitchen contained two broken chairs and a door-less refrigerator. Not a drop of water fell from any tap. Gloomy place, but it beat sleeping in a clump of bushes.

He ate the olives one at a time, savoring each bite. Through a broken window he watched light fade from the silver bark of the trees. Finally, he pounded dust and grime out of one of the mattresses. He breathed a loud sigh as his sore body and tired bones eased into the lumps beneath him. Staring up through the missing roof, he observed the night sky. The stars. The meaninglessness of his tiny drama.

Falling asleep, he slipped into a dream. Camping with Kathy and the kids at Lake of the Woods, back when times were good. The four of them around a crackling fire beneath a starry heaven. A family bonded by nature, togetherness, firelight. Then the dream became troubled. He felt anxiety. A sense of foreboding. Some evil thing moved in the darkness beyond the fire, coming closer. He snapped awake and discovered flames leaping in front of him.

Chapter Ten

He sat up with a start. It was no dream. Two burly men half his age squatted on the other side of a fire. Sparks and shadows flitted around the gutted house. One man had a large mole near his downturned mouth. The other sported a tattoo on his left cheek: a tiny pitchfork and the words, "Born to be..." A scar near his earlobe obliterated the final word in the phrase. "Mole" was working a wooden spoon around a pot held near the fire. There was the smell of fried beans. "Tattoo" watched Eric's hands as they emerged from under his bed sheet.

"Well, looky here," he said.

Eric was still half asleep, still camping with Kathy and the kids. "Hey, guys..." His voice broke. "Wh—what's going on?"

"How 'bout you tell us," Tattoo said, scratching his forearm.

"Nothing. I was just sleeping..."

Tattoo inclined his large head toward Mole. "Says he was just sleeping."

"Yeah, I heard."

"Nothing wrong with that," Tattoo went on, "if you don't snore too loud and you're in the right place."

Tattoo was doing the talking but Eric had the impression Mole was in charge and just hanging back, waiting his moment. He made a point of not looking at Eric while he stirred the beans. Tattoo's eyes ran up and down Eric's body as if conducting a weapons search.

"Problem is," Tattoo said, still scratching his arm, "you're sleeping in my bed."

Eric sat up straighter yet, shook his head at his own foolishness, started rambling on the edge of incoherence. "Sorry for that. I didn't know. I mean, I came in dead beat and looked around and all and didn't see anyone, and you know, I figured it'd be okay, just for one night anyway. I didn't mean to... to trespass and I didn't know it was your place so if I've bothered you guys, there's no problem. I don't want to cause any trouble. I apologize and I'll just pack up my stuff and push on."

He reached for his shoes but Mole shook his head, still stirring the beans.

"You stay put," he said. The beans sizzled in the pot. "We let you go, maybe you come back in the night when we're asleep. We don't know you. Maybe you come back with a blade."

"A blade? What? You—you got the wrong guy. I don't even own a butter knife."

He tried a quick, friendly chuckle but neither of the two took the bait. Plain and simple, they were an ugly pair. Dull and mean and looking for trouble. If they couldn't find it, they'd invent it. He guessed they were both strung out on meth but didn't know how to tell for sure or what to do about it. Physically, he was no match for either of them, let alone both. Even without youth on their side, they were each taller than him, thirty pounds heavier. He felt small, endangered, effeminate.

"If you guys are trying to scare me," he went on quickly,

"you're doing a great job. I just—you know, what I told you—I just needed to bed down for the night, that's all. I saw this place from out there—out on the road, I mean—and it looked abandoned and no one was around so I came in and looked around and then I figured—"

"Fast-talking fuck, ain't he?" Tattoo asked Mole.

Mole grunted, lifted the wooden spoon and sniffed at some beans. "Trying to sell us a line," he said, and turned and looked at Eric directly for the first time. His pupils were dilated. "You a salesman, mister?"

"No, I'm no salesman." It was exactly what he was. A marketing man, a developer of strategies and plans, spots and promotions. He did brand audits and cost structures and SWOT analysis. Strengths, Weaknesses, Opportunities, Threats. All of it to sell sell sell. He couldn't recall how much money he still had on him. Six dollars. Maybe seven counting change. Not enough to buy many crystals. Or to buy his way out of a beating.

The sound of an approaching car came through the broken windows. Mole and Tattoo stiffened as if a magnetic charge has just passed through their large bodies. The vehicle seemed to slow down, brake. The two men traded a glance. Mole motioned Tattoo toward a window. Tattoo rose quickly but unsteadily to his feet, took a few steps toward a broken window, peered out. Mole set the pot of beans aside and pulled a nearby duffel bag closer to his leg. He reached inside and took hold of something. Eric couldn't distinguish the shape.

"You expecting company?" Mole asked.

Eric shook his head. "No, I'm alone but, you know, the other night a state cop rousted me out of a place like this. Sometimes they run checks. He might have seen the fire."

The strain of maintaining a calm expression began to exhaust him. Mole's hand moved inside the duffel bag. Tattoo remained standing, peering out into the darkness. "Nothin'," he said.

He came back and sat down and stared at Mole, awaiting his next command. Eric chewed his tongue, felt the heat of the fire on his cheeks. Mole still had his hand inside the duffel bag. Eric had tried to issue a subtle warning, let them know the state police might stop by at any time. Remind them the police arrested criminals, arrested meth heads who tried to harm innocent citizens. But if Mole and Tattoo were tweaking, he had just reminded them he was on the side of the police, which meant not on their side. His ploy had only made them more paranoid.

"What's your name?" Tattoo demanded.

"Eric. My name's Eric."

Tattoo laughed. "Eric. Dick. Hick. Prick."

"You here for the olives?" Mole asked.

"The olives?"

He picked up the pot and went back to stirring beans. "That's what I said. The olives."

"No. I mean, I ate some. A guy in town gave me some."

"What kind were they?"

"Kind?"

"You repeat what I say one more time and you get a face full o' hot beans. The olives. The fucking olives. What kind were they?"

"I don't know. They were in a plastic bag. That bag there. I—I just ate them. I mean, I was hungry."

"If you ain't a salesman and you ain't an olive picker, what the fuck are you?"

"I'm a monk."

It just came out. Came out before he had any chance to gauge where it might go. He should have said *poet,* at least he might have faked it. Sadhu was meaningless and holy man comical, so his panicked mind had taken a frantic leap and latched onto Jessica telling him he wasn't a monk or Jesus crossing the desert. But it was out now, hanging in the air above the crackling fire.

Tattoo gave an ugly laugh. "And what the fuck is that—a short monkey?"

"Shut up," Mole said suddenly. He stopped stirring the beans. "It's like a chaplain." He leaned forward so far it seemed he would stick his grizzly chin into the flames. "Was you over there?" he asked.

Eric looked into the fire as if thinking deeply. His mind raced. Over where? They were too young for Viet Nam. What then? Iran, Iraq, Somalia, Syria, Afghanistan? He had no idea. It didn't matter anyway. Getting the country right would only help for a moment. Then he'd get painted into a corner of place names, battalions, incomprehensible military jargon.

He shook his head. "No, but I had friends who went. You guys were there?"

"Damn straight on that," said Tattoo, still smarting because Mole had shut him down.

"Then what the fuck you doing here?" Mole demanded.

"Nothing. Just walking."

"Walking?"

Now he was repeating Eric's words. Eric nodded, tried to put an amiable look on his face minus a smile. "Like our Lord Jesus did in the wilderness. He walked for forty days. He had little food, no friends—"

"I know about Him," Mole snapped back. "But why *you* doing it?"

Both of them stared at Eric. In the flickering firelight they looked like twin gargoyles inflamed by meth and some shared sadism. Pagan blood, Eric thought.

"Jesus our Lord walked in the desert trying to clean out," he said in a monotone. "I follow his inspiration. I'm trying to get rid of dark times. I'm trying to clean out too."

Neither of their expressions changed even slightly. He held their gazes with his fake spirituality and then looked into the fire again, no longer feigning contemplation. He had wanted prayer and now he prayed ferociously, terrified he had painted himself into a different corner. What if one of them asked him to quote a scripture? *Though I walk into the valley of what?*

"So if I've trespassed on your turf," he went on quietly, humbly, "I apologize again and I'll try to make it right by pushing on before—"

"You stay put," Mole said. "Just don't try to pull anything. One of us—him or me—is always awake."

Eric nodded as if it had been a logical conversation that had arrived at a lucid conclusion. Shut up, he told himself.

Not another word. No sudden movements. He yawned contentedly, lay back down, rolled onto his side, watched the fire for a moment, fluttered his eyelids, closed his eyes. He put a peaceful, sleepy expression on his face while his stomach heaved, partly from fear, partly from the aroma of the beans.

Mole and Tattoo whispered something to each other he couldn't catch. Something about the beans. Then came the clatter of forks scraping plates. The fire went on snapping. Some truce had been declared but it had stopped short of friendship. They hadn't offered him a single bean and he could feel their eyes on him, inspecting between bites. He was sure he wouldn't sleep a wink. He was still in Tattoo's bed. How many other mattresses had he seen? He couldn't remember.

Just then a car engine sounded out on the road. Once again it seemed to slow down near the house. The forks stopped scraping. Eric kept his eyes shut, tried to quiet his pounding heart. Fearful prayer still consumed him.

"What if it's the cop again?" Tattoo murmured.

"We don't know it was a cop."

"He said it was."

"He don't know shit."

"But maybe he's right."

"He ain't right. He's an asshole."

"You said he was a chaplain."

"He's an asshole chaplain. Now shut up and look."

Eric's heart went on thumping. He considered jumping up and racing for the door, racing out of the ruins into the night. If it was the state police or a Sheriff patrol or anyone at all, he could throw himself into the car, tell them to drive off, get away as fast as possible. Instead he lay there trembling, thoughts crackling like the fire. Where had his life gone? Not the years but the direction, that he should come to ground in this gutted-out shell of a house, near this fire, these two pagan savages.

"Nothin'," Tattoo hissed from across the room.

An hour passed, maybe two. Any cough or burp, one of them spitting or grunting, a sizzle in the fire, tempted Eric to open his eyes. Then the fire crackled less. Tattoo mumbled sleepily. Eric lay still. Even if he heard both of them snoring, he dared not chance a look. He felt certain that, as Mole had said, one of them would be watching him, a hard gaze fixed on his eyelids. He was even more certain that sudden eye contact would fuse crossed wires, kindle danger, ignite his doom. He had no doubt they were armed, at least with knives. Mole had something in his duffel bag and his remark about a "blade" hadn't come out of nowhere. So Eric lay there face red hot, hands icy cold, brain beset by lunatic prayer. He was on the edge of the continent. Let the lights go out in towns and villages at dusk. His day was done; he was leaving America. The ocean air would burn his lungs. Maybe angels would come to save him.

The night fell away in the orchard, drained of all sound except a periodic hoot or chirp. Did owls inhabit olive groves? He remembered that the olive tree was a symbol of peace and friendship. Some olive oil campaign he had once done at DMT. God, what madness. Peace and friendship with Mole and Tattoo. *Get up. Run. Get out.*

Exhausted by hyper vigilance, by hellish prayer, he fell asleep sometime before dawn. He awoke all at once, but managed to keep his eyes shut. His right eye fluttered into a slit admitting a few rays of light, a blurred, ground level view of ashes. Then a wider, larger view of the room.

Mole and Tattoo were gone. Eric rolled onto his side. No sign of anyone anywhere, no remnant of anything, no cooking pot or wooden spoon, not even a fried bean on the floor. Maybe he had dreamed the whole thing. He stretched out his hand palm flat and held it above the ashes. A slight sensation of heat. Dream or not, he had to get out before they returned.

CHAPTER ELEVEN

Within ten minutes he was half a mile down the road, walking fast despite stiffness in his hips and legs. His breath came in short gasps, his heart thumped near his brain. On another day he might have admired the morning, cool and clear and exalted by birdsong, but an hour later, two miles onward, and he still glanced back over his shoulder. He hadn't heard Mole and Tattoo arrive in the night and he hadn't heard them leave in the morning. Proof, if he needed it, that anyone could sneak up on him at any time. Anyone with a club or pistol or *blade* might steal into whatever darkness he slept in. Jessica had been right: pathetic and crazy. What had he thought—that he was going for a stroll in exotic Rajasthan? Not one of the thousand million souls in India would ever think of doing harm to a sadhu. Wrong country, wrong obsession.

In a kind of ironic panic, he thought of quiet, peaceful Ashland, home to Mr. Shakespeare, who had written, "Hell is empty and all the devils are here." But he should calm down. Nothing could happen now. His fast pace, his runaway mind and fear were out of proportion to the threat. He was miles down the road, free of danger. Mole and Tattoo had forgotten about him and were seeking new victims in their noxious lives. Trouble was, he hadn't forgotten them. His soul was bleeding and he couldn't staunch the flow. He had asked for the courage to meet his destiny but what place did destiny have in a world bereft of vision? How fast or far he walked didn't matter. He could cast looks back over his shoulder every thirty seconds but the devils waited in front of him. Who was he praying to now? Jesus again? Shiva? He was desperate for any god in the pantheon of divine beings and he prayed to any of them on duty that day. But he prayed out of fear, prayed not to save the world but to save his own skin.

Please guide me so that Your will and my desire forge the same path. That would be closer to true prayer. It might also bring him closer to destiny. Instead, he was praying for his comfy armchair. Nothing in mind except run-on thoughts and nothing in earshot except heat buzz, breeze, birdsong. He needed to stop and rest, catch his breath, drink some water. But he walked faster, a terrified savage beseeching a pagan god. *Please return my bleeding soul and sunburned flesh to my armchair.* Not so long ago he had forsaken his second pilgrimage site and now he was racing to it.

He was southeast of Corning on an isolated stretch of asphalt called Hoag Road. The blacktop turned due east and became Rhode Island Avenue. Just before the Sacramento River he came upon the Woodson Bridge Mini Mart and Deli. A half dozen beat-up cars and pickups were parked in front. He still had money in his pocket, enough to buy a power bar, some fruit, some juice. Maybe refill his water bottle. He started for the building entrance but then stopped, arrested by the thought that one of the pickups was the type of vehicle Mole and Tattoo might have owned. Broken wing mirror hanging down over the door panel. Dented front fender decorated with a vinyl flame decal, not so different from a tattooed cheek.

He told himself not to invent wild scenarios. He must have covered five or six miles by now. He was far from the farmhouse. On the other hand, he was far only for someone traveling on foot. A car could cover the distance from the farmhouse to the Mini mart in a few minutes flat. Mole and Tattoo knew he was on foot. He had no idea what might be going through their thuggish skulls. If he had run into them in some Ashland bar and had managed to escape, he would have headed home, poured a few fingers of Makers Mark, chalked the incident up to bad luck and a close call, and forgotten about it. But he wasn't safe in the comfort of his home. That's why he was praying like a maniac. He was out in the open, slow as a turtle yet lacking a shell, easy to spot, easy to catch. If for whatever demented or sadistic reason they decided to hunt him down, they could and he had better not assume they wouldn't because it didn't make sense. Much better to assume he didn't know what made sense in their screwy heads. If they got the notion to chat some more about olives or to pound him flat like they should have last night, they only had to jump behind a wheel and get some kicks cruising country lanes while chugging down a bottle of hooch. First north, then east, then south. They could cover all directions in less than an hour, long before they became bored by the game or too drunk to play.

What was instinct and what was fear? He didn't know, but he could still hear Tattoo's laugh—"Eric. Dick. Hick. Prick."—and it was better and smarter and safer and sounder to steer clear of that pickup. He could flog himself for cowardice later.

He turned toward Woodson Bridge. A small white sign preceded it. "No Jumping or Diving." The river was flat and quiet, reflecting the trees along its far bank. As he hurried across the narrow bridge shoulder, he felt trapped between the iron railing and the cars blasting past. But he would soon arrive at a hallowed place where Mole and Tattoo and goons like them couldn't enter. He let out a crazed shout of victory. He had won. He had been smarter. Mole and Tattoo were fools. He laughed out loud, gave another shout, shook his fist at the sky. What idiots they were. They had bought the sales pitch. A monk, a chaplain. He had escaped. He was free.

The road shoulder widened. The trees and orchards to either side of his path thinned as he came to a set of railroad tracks. Across the tracks lay a cracked stretch of asphalt called Rogers Road, running southward. In the distance he could distinguish his goal, the small town of Dunding. He turned onto Rogers Road and soon arrived at the Tehama County Farm Authority—Department 7, all closed up. Five minutes later he came to First Street. A few houses, a few cars, an RV, an overturned canoe and not a soul in sight. The area was too isolated for a knock on a door. He walked on to the center of town, quiet except for a faint whine of electrical machinery. Population of about a hundred, he guessed. A tiny post office flew a ragged American flag. Dunding Farm Supplies displayed a spillover scrap heap of used tires, punctured radiators and rusted engine parts.

In the intense afternoon heat, a sleepy relief came over him. He felt sudden tenderness for the sky, so blue, so detached from his frantic prayers and plodding steps. A string of maroon clouds like sacred cows grazing on the horizon. He wanted to collapse onto the grass and take a glorious nap. Instead he entered the Dunding Market and Deli. A woman greeted him. She was about ten years older than him, slim and gray, alert green eyes. Dressed in a flowered gingham apron, she had the air of a granny who spent most days alone, humming to herself. She seemed unconcerned by his sweaty, disheveled appearance.

"Retreating for a little walk today, are you?" she asked.

He had no idea what she was talking about, so he responded with a vague smile. He was just glad she hadn't wrinkled her nose and told him to leave. He asked her the price of some walnuts and then bought a candy bar and two bananas. She offered to fill his water bottle.

"Anything else?" she asked.

"Yes, I've been looking for a sign for Chassors Monastery. I know it's near here."

She squinted at him and then reached into her apron pocket and brought out two pairs of glasses. She set one pair on her nose and squinted again.

"Aren't you one of the retreatants?" she asked.

"I don't know what that is."

"At the monastery. It's the only reason anybody comes here. For the tasting or the retreating."

"It's what I'm trying to say. I'm looking for the monastery. I don't understand what you mean by—"

"Sure you do. The Abbey of Chassors. It's famous all over the world. Stone by stone from France in Europe. Just a minute down Silver Street there." She lifted a thin hand and pointed. "People come from everywhere for the wine tasting and retreating. Turn left and you'll find your sign and then the monastery."

He thanked her and left, prayers half answered.

Chapter Twelve

A minute later he arrived at a small sign announcing Chassors Monastery. Farther on, he passed a six-foot metal crucifix casting a shadow across the asphalt. Then came the photograph on the wall of Walt's office, the wrought-iron entrance gate in real life. He had intended to pause there as he had in front of Shiva, pause for a quiet moment and then walk on. But the game had changed and he needed refuge.

A guide to the monastery grounds stood on the other side of the gate. A map showed vineyards and walnut and prune orchards as well as a church, a chapel, a guesthouse, retreat cabins, a bodega and a wine tasting room. There was a dining hall, a library and a cloistered area on the edge of a forest. A hand-printed note read: "All visitors kindly report to the Welcome Center."

Inside the Welcome Center and Bookstore, a white-haired man sat behind an Information desk. He could have been a lay assistant or a monk dressed in street clothing. Two visitors wandered the aisles, perusing books and retreat pamphlets. Eric stopped in front of a display labeled "Volunteer Program." An applicant was required to fill out a form which listed current or recent occupation, hobbies and skills, educational background and volunteer service offered.

When the two visitors left, Eric approached the white-haired man, addressed him as "Brother" and gave a complicated explanation intended to cover all bases. He described himself as a visitor but also a friend of a former monk and a person interested in volunteer work and perhaps a retreat and also "shelter from the storm." He succeeded in confusing the man, who gestured toward two wooden chairs near the door and asked Eric to wait.

Five minutes later the man returned with a younger man dressed in the white robe of a Trappist monk. The young monk sat in the chair beside Eric. He explained the monastery's policy toward volunteers and retreatants. First, he said, the applicant filled out a petition or made a formal request and then the request went through a review process before a final decision.

"Yes, I understand," Eric replied too quickly, "but I'm asking if an exception can be made."

"An exception?"

"Maybe you knew Walt Cummings? No? Well, he was a monk at Chassors who became a spiritual counselor and he counselled me for many years and I feel... I feel a need..." He didn't know what to say next—a need to get away from Mole and Tattoo? A need to pray frantically to an unknown God? "I feel a need to be here..."

The monk blinked twice. "I see," he said, though clearly he did not. "I'll have to make a consultation."

He instructed the white-haired man to offer Eric some herbal tea and a piece of fruit cake. When he left, Eric drank the tea and ate the fruitcake; both were delicious. He browsed a few books and then went next door to the chapel, which was empty. The silence seemed to mock him, accuse him of fraudulence. All the same, he felt out of harm's way, at least for the moment. But how should he explain himself? Did he dare describe his ghost self, the grind, the road, his rancor and betrayals?

Back in the bookstore, he looked over a section devoted to Thomas Merton and found his Collected Poems. A thousand pages. When was the last time he had even read a poem? A decade ago? He picked up "Thoughts in Solitude" and read random lines until one struck home: "My Lord God, I have no idea where I am going." He shut the book and set it back down. Finally, a fifty-year-old man appeared. Tall, slender, robust, he wore a gray goatee and monk's robe. He introduced himself as Abbot Paul and guided Eric into an adjoining room, a type of office. They sat facing each other on two wooden chairs.

Eric had expected the abbot of Chassors to be an ancient and serene fellow, an older version of Walt. Except for the robe, Abbot Paul looked more like a corporate lawyer in a downtown Seattle firm: sharp, discerning, potent.

"First and foremost," Abbot Paul said, "let me welcome you to Chassors Monastery. For centuries our order has greeted all who knock on our door—visitors as well as aspirants to monkhood—with a traditional question: 'What do you seek?'"

Caught off guard, Eric sat mute and motionless. He had planned to begin by talking about Walt, establishing a common ground. "That's... a difficult question," he murmured.

"And an important one." Abbot Paul paused for a moment, then said: "Tell me about yourself."

Eric nodded. It was what he had thought. Describe his ghost self. Let it all out. So he talked about Kathy, his career at DMT, his life in Ashland, Oregon, about Barbara Street. Rambling on, he even described Jessica grinding her teeth, the ache of Billy's absence. He felt ridiculous explaining his Sadhu journey but discerned no judgment from Abbot Paul, no criticism, no opinions running off onto another track. He's empty, Eric thought, like the chapel. And like the chapel, his emptiness made Eric uneasy. Even if he wasn't out-and-out lying, he was telling his tale to get what he wanted, to manipulate Abbot Paul into sympathy and acquiescence. "A fast-talking fuck," that's what Tattoo had called him. Mole had accused him of trying to sell a line. *You a salesman, mister?*

And now he was selling a line to convince Abbot Paul that he wasn't some homeless guy. He was a real person. A good friend of Brother Walt. But, of course, all homeless guys came from somewhere and had some tale to tell. Abbot Paul wouldn't judge their stories either, just listen and nod and absorb it all into his empty self.

Eric refrained from mentioning Mole and Tattoo but he repeated what he had said to the young monk—that he wondered if an exception could be made in the monastery's policy. He hadn't known about the retreats or the wine tasting; his close friend Walt had never mentioned them. Finally, he fell silent. Abbot Paul seemed to be contemplating his story but he suddenly let out a loud belly laugh. "Well," he said. "I sure didn't expect you to come knocking at the door today!"

Eric went mute again.

"Let me explain..." Abbot Paul reached forward and touched him affectionately on the knee. "You see, our monastic order has a thousand-year-old tradition of hospitality. That's our real 'policy.' Providing warm welcome to a guest is fundamental to our practice. We believe you are a gift sent to us by God and we welcome you as we would welcome Jesus Himself."

"I... didn't know that," Eric murmured.

So it hadn't mattered if he was a vagabond, a billionaire or Walt's friend. He felt demeaned by his attempts to finesse his way into the monastery, to pull Abbot Paul's strings if he had any to pull. But he also felt a surge of relief. Refuge was at hand.

"Please come with me," Abbot Paul said.

He led the way outside and down a path toward a cluster of retreat cabins. The same young monk Eric had spoken to earlier emerged from one of the cabins carrying a bucket of cleaning supplies. Eric swallowed. Abbot Paul had given the order to prepare the cabin even before meeting him. The vile sales pitch had been unnecessary. When you were a gift from God, you didn't need to name drop and put on a dog and pony show.

They entered a small cell. There was a single bed, a desk, a chest of drawers and a tiny bathroom at the rear. Everything spotless. Abbot Paul explained the daily routine at the monastery: Mass and Divine Office, vigils, meal times, Grand Silence at night. He said there were presently six other retreatants on the premises. Four had taken vows of silence, so Eric should refrain from engaging them in conversation. Eric was welcome to join the monks at morning choir or meals, but Abbot Paul hoped he understood that their cloistered area was off limits.

"Let's see, what else?" he added. "It seems you haven't brought along many personal belongings so we'll try to scout up a few necessities for you. I'm afraid there's no swimming pool or TV..."

Still smarting with shame, Eric missed the good-natured humor. "Yes, I realize that," he said gravely.

"... but there's a library," Abbot Paul went on, "and if you have any questions, we'll try to answer them as best we can. Please spend your time here as you wish. We can offer you silence, stillness and solitude. Perhaps they may help you find the sanctuary you seek."

He left and Eric sat down heavily on the bed. Safe at last but to remain so, what other lies would he have to tell? He didn't know, but the most difficult question of all—*What do you seek?*—had just been answered for him.

CHAPTER THIRTEEN

The sheets were clean and crisp, the pillow soft, the mattress firm, the crickets quiet in the night. Silence, stillness and solitude, but Eric churned and wheeled and couldn't sleep. He kept flashing on Mole and Tattoo. Finally, his mind exhausted itself and he dropped into deep slumber.

He awoke late in the morning, groggy, still unsettled. Outside his door he found a cardboard box containing clothes. A handwritten note explained that they had been left behind by "other retreatants." Not so different from his inherited threads at Donny's Diner. The box also held a razor and shaving cream, toothpaste, a comb, a mystery novel, a pen, a blank notebook, and a Chassors information pamphlet.

Alone in the cafeteria, eating a late lunch of vegetarian fare, he read the pamphlet. Chassors monks began their day at 3:15 AM when they rose for Vigils to "keep watch" in darkness and silence, and pray for all to be brought into "the light of a never-ending day." Lauds came at 6:30 AM, followed through the day by five other designated hours of prayer, the last of which, Compline, petitioned God's protection for the onset of darkness.

Over the following week Eric ate well, slept deeply and attended mass every morning. Afterwards, he walked the monastery grounds, where monks and Mexican farmhands labored in vineyards and orchards. A heavy silence seemed to suffocate all sound, even footsteps on the packed earth.

Every now and then, a wisp of breeze or a bird cry passed through the leaves and branches.

Down one of the forest paths, he met the two retreatants who had not taken a vow of silence. A thirty-year-old couple, friendly, attractive, there for two weeks. He learned they were Silicon Valley software engineers, who came to Chassors on retreat as often as possible. They made regular donations to the monastery on a "pledge payment program" and, like the other retreatants, paid a hundred dollars a night as a suggested donation. The woman worked in the fields with the monks and the man helped in the laundry room.

"Do the other retreatants also work?" Eric asked uneasily.

"It's not obligatory," the woman replied. "There aren't any rules. You could even say it's just part of the 'program.'"

"Work focuses the mind," the man added, "and prayer protects it. Turns off the tap on all that chatter."

"There's just so much to do," the woman said, "and every little bit helps."

Eric nodded. So the only freeloader on the premises was the person who had been welcomed as a gift from God. For a week he had been lounging around while everyone else paid a hundred dollars a night and toiled. The others must have noticed his abuse of divine hospitality yet no one had said a word. He slept badly that night. The silence plucked at his nerves. The wooden ceiling beams never creaked, the adobe walls, the night itself never emitted a sigh. Even the oldies but moldies had left his head.

He rolled off the mattress and stepped outside. The waxing gibbous moon shed silver light down onto the vineyards. Two monks and two Mexican farmhands appeared, walking single file, slowly as always to keep dust from rising onto the grapes, exchanging not a word. Silence, always silence. They carried wicker baskets, extension rakes and hoes, pruning shears and picking pans. Vigils and Grand Silence must have ended. Eric guessed it was around 4 AM. The four figures disappeared down one of the paths and he returned inside to shower.

He was torn between leaving and staying. He wasn't crazy enough to think that Mole and Tattoo lurked outside the monastery gate, but he also wasn't ready to return to shadowland. If he had operated a warewasher at Donny's Diner, he could scrub a few plates at Chassors Monastery.

He found Abbot Paul in his office. Eric told him that he wanted to volunteer for work.

"Did you have something specific in mind?" Abbot Paul asked.

Eric mouthed the words of the software engineers. "I know there's a lot to do and every little bit helps."

Abbot Paul rose from his desk. "Then let's see what we can find you."

Eric sensed that his request hadn't come as a surprise. Abbot Paul led the way down a winding path to a cabin just beyond the retreat facilities. He rapped his knuckles twice against the door jamb and entered. Eric followed him into a space similar to his own cell. There was a wooden crucifix, two straight-backed chairs, a dresser and a small table containing medical supplies. A shelf on the far wall held a dozen hardbound books. In the center of the room there was a hospital bed with bright chrome safety railings. A wheelchair stood nearby. In the bed lay a skeleton of a man. In his mid eighties, Eric guessed.

"Father Glenn," Abbot Paul said, "I'd like to introduce you to Eric Tyler. Eric, this is Father Glenn."

Father Glenn's eyes shifted in his skull-like head. His liver-stained lips fluttered in a kind of Parkinson's tremble. He not only looked frail and cadaverous, but like he might pass away in the next minute.

"Eric is staying with us for a while," Abbot Paul told Father Glenn.

Yes, Eric thought, I'm a gift from God. Just like Jesus Himself.

Abbot Paul turned to him.

"You will now be responsible for Father Glenn's care," he said. "It will be a great help to us, not to mention to Father Glenn. It will also free one of our brothers for other duties."

"I see..." Eric said. *What?* "It's just that I thought I might work in... the kitchen." He couldn't keep his mouth shut. "I have experience washing dishes... at Donny's Diner in Redding."

"Do you have any experience feeding the elderly?" Abbot Paul asked.

Eric shook his head. Elderly? Didn't he mean *the dying?* "No, no experience at all."

"But you must have spoon-fed Billy and Jessica as babies."

The names of his children suddenly spoken out loud rattled Eric. He had mentioned them last week when describing himself but he couldn't believe Abbot Paul had remembered. The man wasn't like a Seattle lawyer after all. More like the top dog in a corporate firm. A polite suggestion equaled an imperial command.

"It's basically the same," Abbot Paul went on. "Swallowing takes time. That's all. Switch places with him. Imagine how you might feel, how you would want to be treated. Have patience and all will go well. Isn't that right, Father Glenn?"

Father Glenn spoke but Eric couldn't distinguish his garbled words. Abbot Paul chuckled and touched the dying man on the arm. Just then a middle-aged Vietnamese monk entered the cell. He carried a tray with a bib, a rubber-edged spoon and a bowl of cauliflower purée. Abbot Paul introduced him as Brother Huy, then bid everyone farewell and left. Eric had to stop himself from racing out the door behind him. Brother Huy asked Eric to help raise Father Glenn on his pillows. Eric placed his palms under Father Glenn's shoulder blades. It felt like dragging a pile of loose bones across the mattress. Brother Huy tilted the old priest's head to the left and angled his chin downward.

"It minimizes the risk of choking," he said. He affixed the bib around Father Glenn's thin, wrinkled neck. "Now you can feed his good side."

He meant the un-paralyzed side of Father Glenn's mouth. Eric wanted to say, "I can't do this." Instead, he reached for the spoon and bowl of purée. Brother Huy watched him feed Father Glenn three spoonfuls.

"Exactly like that," he said, and left.

The door to the cell closed. The spoon in Eric's hand quivered above the purée. Was this sanctuary? It felt more like incarceration with a cadaver. I asked for this, he told himself. Now he had to man up and accept it. Father Glenn's limpid gray eyes were on him. The old priest was terminal but still breathing, still aware.

"More, please," Father Glenn croaked.

"Sorry, here..."

Father Glenn's lips stopped trembling as he took in the food. Eric feared the soupy substance might somehow make him choke. He wished Father Glenn would stop observing him. His tongue was swollen and got in the way of his words, made them sound like an alien language.

"Everything okay?" he croaked.

"Fine," Eric replied. "I'm just trying to get the hang of this..."

He checked the purée. Soon the bowl would be empty. Then he could get out of there. If Father Glenn didn't die in the next moment. His lips went on trembling between bites. Eric didn't know if it was Parkinson's or just a struggle to voice a phrase.

"Forgive me," Father Glenn said.

Imploring Jesus in a haze of senility, Eric guessed, decades of catechism expressed via dementia. *Forgive me, Lord, these are my sins.* Something like that. Eric wished the man would die for his own sake. But not now. Not while he was there.

"Forgive me," Father Glenn repeated.

His eyes were still on Eric. Eric stayed the spoon above the bowl.

"Forgive you for what?" he said.

"I distress you."

"What? No, it's just that..."

"My condition distresses you."

"No, I..."

"More, please."

Eric guided the rubber-edged spoon toward the left side of his mouth. Father Glenn swallowed and his lips began fluttering again. Eric examined the bowl. Only two spoonfuls left, thank Jesus. One after the other. He scraped up the last of the purée and fed it to him. Father Glenn's stomach rumbled. Air traveled up through his skeletal frame and exited as a loud, uncontrolled burp. His broken body lay motionless. No flicker of movement. He's dead, Eric thought, killed by a burp. Then the thin chamber of Father Glenn's torso expanded and he slowly drew in another breath.

CHAPTER FOURTEEN

As soon as Eric mastered one chore in Father Glenn's care, Brother Huy taught another. Eric shaved Father Glenn, washed his face and arms, sponge-bathed his body. The man was already a corpse, yet somehow still breathing. His flesh was liver-spotted and wrinkled, falling off his bones like overcooked meat. Rolling him onto his side, Eric was afraid the spine would break. Lifting his head off the pillow, he feared the sound of his neck snapping. "I can't do this," he thought. Then Brother Huy taught the next lesson. Eric pulled on plastic surgical gloves and changed Father Glenn's diapers, cleaned up his urine and excrement, all the while thinking, "I've got to get out of here."

Twice he was on the verge of slipping out of the monastery under cover of darkness. But the following morning found him guiding a spoonful of purée into Father Glenn's half-paralyzed mouth. As days passed, as Eric witnessed and engaged in monastery life, he began to suspect that Abbot Paul purposely assigned people to tasks for which they were unsuited. While Eric clumsily fed a dying man, the monk in charge of marketing the monastery's wine was gentle and warmhearted, an ideal caregiver. Abbot Paul knew of Eric's years at DMT Worldwide, knew that he had directed ads, promotions, branding and sponsoring for every product imaginable, including northern California wines. Why not make use of his talents?

As Eric lifted Father Glenn out of bed, he could hear the arthritic bones cracking, feel the ancient heart pounding against his own. Father Glenn's grizzly chin rested on his shoulder, his mouth near Eric's ear.

"Dancing," Father Glenn whispered.

"A light fandango," Eric mumbled, swinging him off the mattress.

He strapped Father Glenn into a wheelchair and pushed him around the grounds. When he pushed too fast, Father Glenn let out a muffled groan. "Sorry," Eric whispered, slowing to a crawl. Father Glenn pointed this way and that, his manner grouchy, imperious. Eric guessed he had once been a handful, a surly character who had ruffled monastery feathers, but now his surliness came from inner struggle. With the end so near, perhaps the old priest was engaged in a final battle of faith. Age, illness and diminishing resources were battering the ill-humor out of him, thumping and kneading him like bread dough.

Eric let Father Glenn bask in the sun for an hour, inhale the fresh air. Sometimes he read aloud from the Book of Psalms or Thomas Merton. ("He's like a rock star for us," Brother Huy had said.)

"Father Glenn mumbles a lot," Eric told Brother Huy one afternoon. "He repeats the same sounds. His lips flutter but nothing clear comes out."

"He's praying," Brother Huy said. "For all of us, for the world and our suffering, so that we may each bear our cross."

At times Father Glenn's lips stopped moving and he fell silent. Eric thought he had died but Brother Huy said Father Glen's heart had stretched out and he was now in prayer "too deep for words." Eric imagined the old priest's mind like a pool in a forest—cool and clear—but underwater currents still turbulent, churning.

Each day Eric rose to attend Vigils at 3:30 AM with the monks and retreatants. At dawn he returned for Lauds, which celebrated the gift of light appearing to dispel the darkness of the previous night. When Father Glenn seemed strong enough, Eric wheeled him into morning mass at 7 AM. Eric liked the soaring architecture of the French church, the sprinkling of Mexican farmhands, heads bowed, praying before their work day began. One morning he nodded off during the service. The rattle of his own snoring woke him. Afterwards, as he fed Father Glenn his breakfast purée, the old priest said, "You had a good nap."

Eric tried to adhere to the Liturgy of the Hours. Over decades the gears of Father Glenn's internal clock had run from Holy Mass to the pause at Terce to the prayers at Sext to the sun declining at None to Vespers and finally Compline, when the monks sang the Salve Regina and it resounded in the church like an ancient lullaby.

After the last notes vanished into the stone walls, Grand Silence began. Abbot Paul sprinkled holy water onto all of their heads, a type of nocturnal baptism as they prepared to enter darkness and sleep. In his cell Eric undressed and lay on his back. Throughout the day, he was actively concentrated on some task at hand. Now all activity had ceased. The monks and retreatants were in their own cells meditating and praying while he lay awake in disquiet. No prayer to pray, no tap to turn off the inner chatter. Only more silence, stillness, solitude. Where was the whoosh of traffic, the highway urging him onward?

Days passed. The husband and wife software engineers left Chassors. Other retreatants arrived. Eric wondered why Abbot Paul let him continue to stay. His cell could have been bringing in a hundred dollars a day. Instead, he took up space, ate the monastery's food. Yes, he provided a small service by caring for Father Glenn, but any retreatant could have done it better, adding prayers and blessings and rites of worship.

One day he read Psalm 39:3 to Father Glenn: "I was silent and still; I held my peace to no avail; my distress grew worse, my heart became hot within me..."

Another day he read Thomas Merton: "Anxiety is the mark of spiritual insecurity."

He had expected the monks to be an even-tempered, God-fearing bunch but many were troubled and insecure. The strains of living together showed. One monk was openly bitter, another overly cheerful. In the evenings Eric sat outside the chapel with Brother Huy and two others who cared for AIDS victims and drug addicts in nearby communities during the day. Although conversation was minimized at Chassors and the monks usually spoke only when necessary, the foursome talked quietly for twenty minutes before Grand Silence began. Eric guessed Abbot Paul had arranged the sessions for his benefit. The few times Eric spoke, the others listened so attentively they made him think he was saying something important. Then he talked too much trying to discover what it might be.

"I served in a mission in southern India for two years," one of the monks told Eric. "It was near a pilgrimage route so sadhus used to pass by every day. The abbot usually let them spend the night in the mission."

"What did you think of them?" Eric asked.

"They scared me. They seemed wild. Their war paint reminded me of North American Indians—Apaches or Navajos going into battle. I suppose they were just like the rest of us—at war with themselves."

"The paint sounds like a mask," Brother Huy said, "a way to send a message to the outer and hide the inner. Or change the inner through the outer."

"I thought it turned me invisible," Eric said. "But rain washed my face clean in a week."

"Paint or not," one monk asked, "is it really possible to change? Aren't we always who we are?"

"Memory is who we are," Brother Huy said. "Everything else is who we're becoming."

Eric said, "I feel like memory stops me from being who I am. From being who I should become."

The following morning, he requested a private audience with Abbot Paul. The two men met that afternoon in Abbot Paul's office. The window was open but not a wisp of breeze entered the quiet room.

"My first day at Chassors," Eric began, "you offered to answer any questions I might have."

Abbot Paul smiled. "I offered to try."

"You've assigned me to be a caregiver but I could be of greater service to the monastery by helping to market the wine."

"You indicated that you wanted to leave behind that

part of your life," Abbot Paul said, "but if you wish, we can consider a change. Are you prepared to relinquish your duties with Father Glenn?"

The question surprised Eric.

"I'll have to think about that," he said. They sat quietly for a moment, and then he added: "Brother Huy says that Father Glenn is praying for all of us so that we can each bear our cross."

Abbot Paul nodded.

"I've never prayed," Eric said. "Or prayed only to save my own skin. I don't even know any prayers."

He sensed Abbot Paul absorb the words into his empty self.

"It's not difficult," Abbot Paul said. "It's something we learn by doing."

"Then what kind of prayer should I pray?"

He had expected a specific recommendation—the Our Father or Hail Mary—but Abbot Paul answered: "There are prayers of adoration, contrition, intercession and gratitude. Does one ring a bell for you?"

"Not adoration," Eric said slowly." "Maybe contrition..."

"Then begin there and see how it goes."

"But how do I begin?"

"Humble yourself. Be contrite. Bare your heart."

"You mean make a confession?"

"If you want. It's always here available for you. But I meant to express sorrow for your sins and wrongdoings. Ask forgiveness."

"And if asking doesn't do it?"

"Then beg."

CHAPTER FIFTEEN

As Eric swung Father Glenn around toward his wheelchair, he again felt the man's heart thumping against his chest. He lowered the fragile bones into place and set his spine firmly onto the backrest. Father Glenn let out a grunt and a puff of air grazed Eric's cheek. Eric adjusted his forearms on the armrests, tucked his elbows in, wheeled him out of his cell into sharp daylight.

"Do you want a hat for the sun?" Eric asked.

"No... no hat..."

The vineyards were quiet. No sign of monks or Mexican farmhands. Eric pushed the wheelchair toward the southern edge of the woods, but Father Glenn raised a forefinger and pointed to a lane they had never gone down. "What do you seek?" Eric said, thinking he had made a clever joke. Father Glenn gave no answer, only looked eagerly ahead. Eric wheeled him forward, scanning the path for bumps. Father Glenn's forefinger continued to jiggle and point. Eric glanced back over his shoulder as the distance to the main complex increased. He didn't like getting beyond earshot. In an emergency he had no cell phone.

Father Glenn finally gestured for Eric to stop at a small clearing bordered by bushes and trees. A few crucifixes stood near a rectangular hole in the ground. At the sight of the crucifixes, Eric assumed Father Glenn wanted to pray so he waited quietly behind the wheelchair. Something about the clearing reminded him of his garden in Ashland.

The size and shape, the fringe shrubbery. No barbecue though. He watched four crows peck at the dry earth thirty yards to the right. He looked behind him. Two church spires rose above the treetops. A breeze played through the shadows and light. All was quiet. Then the caw of a crow. He turned back. Father Glenn's lips weren't fluttering, so he wasn't praying, just staring. A minute passed before Eric realized the obvious. It was Father Glenn's future home. He reached down and set the brakes on the back wheels, stepped around in front of the wheelchair and motioned toward the rectangular hole.

"Is this yours?" he asked.

The old priest's eyes sparkled. "Yes, yes... all mine... waiting..." He wiggled his fingers, waving Eric ahead. "Go look..."

Eric walked forward onto the grass and peered down into the grave. A small tripod orchard ladder stood upright in the hole, leaning against the packed soil. The monks who had dug the grave must have left it behind. Very unusual. Everywhere in the monastery the monks devoted extreme care to tools and appliances. Eric had once seen a monk wipe down a hammer after pounding a single nail.

"There's a ladder here," he said.

Father Glenn again wiggled his forefinger above the armrest.

"What?" Eric said. "You want me to look closer?"

Hesitant, he got onto his hands and knees and swung a leg over the edge of the grave, guiding his right foot down onto the ladder's top rung. He tested the purchase and moved the rest of his body off the grass. Now the crucifixes were at eye level. A dozen other monks and priests must have been buried there. He looked at the church spires behind Father Glenn and realized that the grave sites afforded the departed brotherhood a view of where they had worshiped.

Urged on by Father Glenn's forefinger, he descended two more rungs. His body broke into a sweat. He didn't want to go any deeper into the grave. The possibility of an emergency, he reminded himself. What if he fell or the ladder broke or Father Glenn suddenly needed him? But it wasn't fear of an emergency. It was plain fear. He was sunk into a grave up to his armpits, staring at the spectacle of the dying priest in his wheelchair, the church spires crowning his white head. Eric had never been in a grave. It wasn't just morbid, but macabre. He could feel—or thought he could—the tingle of the tomb. The sensation penetrated his body, coursed through him like a January chill. He felt color draining out of his face. He swayed on the ladder.

"Well, everything seems fine," he said.

Hurriedly, he climbed back up and crawled out onto the grass. He started forward but Father Glenn again wiggled his finger.

"...ladder..." he said.

Eric reached back down and pulled the ladder up and out. He shook off the dirt and hung it horizontally onto the rear handles of the wheelchair, leaving enough space for his hands. After releasing the brakes, he headed back down the lane. He still had goose bumps. Had Father Glenn wanted to gaze upon his final resting place or had he wanted Eric to feel the glacial chill?

That night after Grand Silence had begun, Eric sat in his cabin with a catechism text he had checked out of the library. He opened to a section on Contrition. There were two types, perfect and imperfect contrition. Perfect contrition was sorrow for sin arising from perfect love. The sinner detested sin because it offended God, who was "supremely worthy of all human love." Imperfect contrition was less pure. It rose from fear of divine retribution and the fires of Hell. Eric didn't know if he could make either act of contrition but he knew which was more likely. He discovered himself mumbling a prayer.

Hail Mary, full of grace, the Lord is with thee, blessed art thou among women, and blessed is...

...the fruit of thy tomb? He couldn't remember. But he could still feel the winter chill in Father Glenn's grave. What would he feel plunged into the shadows of his own grave? A sadhu died onto himself, attended his own funeral before leaving the world. I'm still Eric Tyler, he thought, but now I feel cold.

CHAPTER SIXTEEN

Two days later Father Glenn began to blabber nonsense. At first Eric thought it was another mumbled prayer but then Father Glenn described a recent visitor to his cell.

"Your grandfather?" Eric said. "That's impossible."

"We talked. He told me about Grandma..."

Eric threw a light blanket over Father Glenn's thin frame and went to Abbot Paul's office. Two members of the Dunding town council were visiting and he had to wait until their meeting ended. Afterwards he sat at the desk across from Abbot Paul.

"Yes," Abbot Paul said. "Father Glenn began to show pre-Alzheimer's symptoms some time ago. Every so often he 'leaves' us for a while."

"Leaves?" Eric said. "Has he seen a doctor?"

"When the first symptoms appeared, Father Glenn specifically requested us not to do anything. He wants his dementia to serve as a parting gift."

"You think Alzheimer's is a gift?"

"We are taught that everything we believe we possess is in the process of leaving. Our clothing and jewelry, our homes, our loved ones. None of it is ours. It is all leaving and that includes our thoughts, our memories, our very mind. St. Benedict instructed us to 'keep death daily before our eyes.' Father Glenn feels his illness helps serve that purpose for the monks at Chassors."

"He should be visited by a physician," Eric said. "He could be taking some kind of medication..."

He watched Abbot Paul quietly absorb the conversation into his empty self. The Seattle CEO again. Eric could talk all day and nothing would change. The CEO ran the show whether marketing plan or monastery policy.

"I will consider your words, Eric. I know they are heartfelt and sincere. However, if caring for Father Glenn begins to weigh on you, you must say so. Caregiving is not easy work. As I'm sure you realize, many emotions are associated with it—anxiety, fatigue, guilt, fear, feelings of being overwhelmed—so if you need a break, please let me know."

Eric left the office, thinking that the phrase "begins to weigh on you" was the same as, "If the cross becomes too heavy to bear." He had suspected it all along: Abbot Paul hadn't assigned him to care for Father Glenn by chance. Abbot Paul had seen something that suited him to the task or, more likely, a lack of something. Patience, compassion, courage. Eric didn't know which, but Abbot Paul had decided that Eric needed to receive Father Glenn's parting gift as much as the monks. Of course, the cross could be tossed aside at any time, just like Abbot Paul had said.

But the following day Eric returned to Father Glenn's cell and he returned the following week and the week after that. He fed and washed Father Glenn, listened to his increasing babble of nonsense. More visits from his grandfather. More mumbling. Before long Eric couldn't distinguish between dementia and prayers on automatic pilot. Father Glenn had been at it for so many decades, not even Alzheimer's could stop his lips from mumbling prayers. His death dance had become a whirl of prayer, a worn body opening a shriveled heart, spinning like Shiva for all who suffered. And Eric knew—felt deeply—that Father Glenn wanted him to be there as part of the dance, no matter how poorly he tangoed.

Father Glenn slept more often and it gave Eric more time to clean, to prepare his clothing, organize the bedding, make sure the supply of adult diapers was well stocked. One afternoon Brother Huy gave Eric a haircut. Eric sat on a chair outside his cell and watched the farm workers in the vineyards, watched wisps of his hair fall to the ground and skitter off in the breeze.

"I don't remember my hair being so gray," he said.

"At least you still have some," Brother Huy said.

"But it's all going away, isn't it?"

"Every strand."

The "talk group" went on meeting before Grand Silence. One evening they started talking about music. They spoke of acid house, heavy metal, chill out, easy listening. They named names across genres: Van Morrison, The Melvins, B.B. King, Nas, Aerosmith, Ravel, Bam Bam. The sudden presence of the external world surprised Eric, as did the discovery that Brother Huy had once played bass guitar in a grunge band.

"Arvo Part makes gospel music," one of the other monks said. "Toned-down gospel, fine spun gospel, but gospel all the same."

Eric attended Vigils, Lauds and Mass. He wheeled Father Glenn along on walks. Every evening he joined Vespers, followed by Eucharistic Adoration and Benediction, and then Compline. By that hour, he was stifling yawns and, as Grand Silence began, he sometimes nodded off. The only rituals he didn't take part in were confession and communion but when the Mexican field workers exited the confessional, their leathery faces aglow, he felt the urge to enter the dark booth himself. He could humble himself, as Abbot Paul had said, and confess the mess he had made of his marriage, the broken relationships with his children, his affairs and years of abuse.

Most evenings he read to Father Glenn, even when the man babbled about his grandfather. Usually Eric couldn't tell if he was babbling, praying or snoring lightly. What good were silence, stillness and solitude when they led to dementia like everything else? Yet every so often Father Glenn's eyes popped open and in a clear voice he said, "Everything okay?"

Eric still read from Thomas Merton or the Book of Psalms. He couldn't deny that a great deal of Thomas Merton made sense. ("Solitude is a way to defend the spirit against the murderous din of our materialism.") But he found the individual laments of the Psalms tiresome and the thanksgiving laments worse yet. The repetition annoyed him, even though Brother Huy insisted that the litany was "poetic." The word itself made Eric grimace, as if in cutting his hair, Brother Huy had somehow sensed his severed relationship with poetry. Brother Huy offered Psalm 27:1 as an example of poetic litany: "The Lord is my light and my salvation; whom shall I fear? The Lord is the stronghold of my life; of whom shall I be afraid?"

Dull and monotonous, Eric thought, but better than the psalms full of rage and turmoil, curses, violence, enemies, bloodbaths and hyperbolic war. He hadn't seen the television news in months now and the dark verses like the talk of grunge music reminded him of what dwelled beyond monastery walls. Yet inside, he felt little in the way of monastic peace and tranquility. He slept badly and awoke only to witness more of Father Glenn's dying. Another day to watch him wither away. Another day to wipe his tender, rotting flesh with no sign of divine mercy in sight.

CHAPTER SEVENTEEN

Late one night Eric sat by Father Glenn's bedside, a bowl of broccoli purée on his lap. As he stirred the rubber-edged spoon into the purée, watching the swirl, it struck him that he didn't have to make an act of contrition in the church. He could do it right where he sat. Father Glenn might be demented and dying but he was still a priest who had listened to hundreds—thousands—of tormented souls coming clean. All Eric had to do was follow Abbot Paul's instructions and bare his heart, express sorrow for his wrongdoings. Ask forgiveness. Only that.

He spoke as if to the purée. "I'm going to make a confession, Father Glenn."

The old priest's silver head lay unmoving on the pillow. The paralyzed side of his face stared back at Eric more intensely than the other half.

"I don't know the exact words for the rite," Eric went on. "I mean, the sacrament." He pulled his chair closer to the bed. "...so I'm just going to tell you... everything."

Their faces were inches apart, Eric's head on one side of the chrome safety railing, Father Glenn's on the other.

"I was married," Eric began, still holding the purée, "but I lost my wife. I blamed it on her but really I lost her all on my own, lost her because of what you would probably call the sin of Pride. I committed other sins too. Poetry came to me as a gift when I was young and I... I betrayed it. I took it for granted just like my wife—that old story. No devotion or fidelity to either one. My vows became marketing slogans. And, believe me, I know all about that."

Even to his own ear, let alone the Creator's, his words rang hollow. Father Glenn's good eye seemed to roll in its socket. It was the dead of night. No other utterance sounded across monastery grounds. In making his confession, Eric was breaking Grand Silence.

"I have two children, Father Glenn. Their names are Billy and Jessica. Neither of them speak to me any longer. Can you imagine that, Father Glenn—two children of your own flesh and blood who won't even say hello to you? That's Grand Silence, let me tell you. Billy vanished into ice and snow somewhere up in Alaska and Jessica turned to ice around me ever since I... since I froze her out of my life. Another sin of Pride. Or ignorance, I'm not sure which. Is there a difference, Father Glenn?" Eric was gaining steam, on a roll, but veering off into prattle. "The other day in the library I read that 'ignorance' is a translation of a word that means 'wandering' or 'going astray.' Then I read in another book that it comes from a Latin word meaning 'to disregard' or 'not know.' Which is it, Father Glenn? Does 'ignorance' mean I sinned unintentionally or due to lack of knowledge? Or does it mean that my children were never really mine to begin with and that I should have been more careful and less ignorant turning desire into flesh and blood?"

Now he was the one babbling, the one talking to his grandfather. The Thomas Merton quote he had read in the bookstore his first day at Chassors sprang to mind like a cry in the night. "My Lord God, I have no idea where I am going. I do not see the road ahead of me."

"Father Glenn, I confess I had an underwater marriage in an underwater house and I was drowning. It was half my house and half my marriage—always my half—that was underwater and drowning. I was sinking back then and I keep on sinking because I lack whatever it takes to stay afloat. Maybe I lack death. Dead bodies float; only live bodies sink. But why do dead bodies always float face down? Is it because they can no longer bear to look at the sun and moon, eagles and galaxies? Father Glenn, I confess that I don't know and I make this confession so that I can stop sinking, stop drowning..."

Father Glenn's lips seemed to be fluttering but whether from babble or prayer Eric couldn't say. He was too busy expressing his own dementia, the moment when the savages came ashore and pitched him into emptiness. Hunger, thirst, hooting and... dance, dance, dance.

"My career also sank, Father Glenn. I tried to keep my marital melodrama out of DMT, but the scuttlebutt of Kathy's infidelities ran through executive suites like a hot marketing campaign. Behind my back, DMT jackals and wolves snickered and joked. My boss, the vice-president, the same people kicking me down the corporate ladder made sure I heard their cackles. I hated every one of them, and I fantasized about charging in there with a machine gun and just blasting away, mowing them all down into little pieces of blood and gut. I lived on that fantasy, ate it for breakfast, chewed it for lunch. Then I bit into a reality sandwich called early retirement. I became a sadhu in reverse—a kind of beggar and ghost self—or that's what

I said, what I thought. People—Jessica—my golf buddies Earl, Pete and Tony—other people too—said I was going nuts but I just couldn't live any longer without dying." He swallowed hard. "So... so I've been searching in cheap diners and gutted farmhouses and even this monastery but I can't find my funeral anywhere so I can't die onto myself. Do—do you understand what I'm saying?"

How could Father Glenn understand a word when Eric didn't himself? Badly shaken, he fell silent, the rubber-edged spoon still in his hand. He stirred the purée. He had made his confession and not a thing had changed. No sense of relief or deliverance. He felt no different than ten minutes ago. The same long road stretched in front of him. Same bumps and cracked asphalt, same stones and potholes. He remembered Walt saying that children, friend, lover, religion were all designed to fail. Now confession had failed as well.

CHAPTER EIGHTEEN

A moment passed before Eric realized he was feeding creamed broccoli to a dead man. The bowl fell from his hands, hit the floor and cracked into pieces. He lurched to his feet, knocking back his chair. Father Glenn lay lifeless in front of him, his wizened, drooping features now a veil shrouding his face. Like a mask, Eric thought.

He stepped in the purée, kicking the spoon and bowl shards under the bed. He stared in horror. Perhaps Father Glenn had just fallen asleep, or suffered another stroke. His mouth hung ajar as it sometimes did when he uttered invocations, beseeching Jesus to have mercy on the world. Eric touched his palm to the paralyzed cheek. The sensation of warmth momentarily convinced him that life still surged beneath the parchment flesh.

But, no, he was dead. His suffering had ended. Wasn't that what people said? Give thanks that he was no longer suffering. "My time here is over," Eric thought, but his feet wouldn't move. A presence filled the cell, nothingness swelled the air. No reason to be afraid but he was afraid all the same. How had it happened so suddenly? For weeks he had known that Father Glenn might die at any minute. Many times he had asked himself, "Is he going to take his last breath now right in front of my eyes?" He had watched the old man's nostrils, the imperceptible rise and fall of his fragile chest, and now, sitting in front of him, he hadn't seen a thing. Father Glenn's last breath had left him, a wisp on a fugitive breeze. Gone from this world into the next in front of Eric's blind eyes.

Or was his spirit still in the room? Something was there, but Eric couldn't name it. Wraith, specter, shadow, all failed to describe the thing he sensed. Whatever it was, it made him recall Abbot Paul's advice. Switch places. Imagine what Father Glenn might want. Eric didn't have to imagine. He knew, he knew. Father Glenn would want him to wash his body. Eric had bathed his body daily and the process had struck him as repulsive. Now he could do it one last time as Father Glenn would have done for him: without the least repulsion. But there was some ritual for washing and dressing the deceased. The monks would do it better. They could enact a ceremony with prayers.

Finally, he reached forward. He didn't know how long rigor mortis took to set in so he quickly removed the bedding and Father Glenn's white dressing gown. He closed Father Glenn's eyes with his fingertips. They popped back open, startling Eric so much he let out a small cry. But it was only a reflex action. He pressed down gently on the lids, holding them closed. They stayed closed. Father Glenn's mouth shut easily, stayed shut.

Eric cleaned up the purée and bowl shards. He took a sponge and ran water into a plastic container. Now it made no difference if the water was warm, but he still tested it. He sponged the forehead and cheeks, the lips and chin. He didn't remove the dentures. He was afraid he wouldn't be able to put them back in once the body stiffened. He opened Father Glenn's mouth again, cleaned with a toothbrush.

Months attending mass, lauds, vespers, and the Liturgy of the Hours, and not a single prayer came to mind. Why was he still unable to pray? Then he remembered the start of the Lord's Prayer. *Our Father who art in heaven, hallowed be Thy...* He became confused and couldn't go on. He had to master emotions, struggle against tears. He reminded himself he was no longer washing Father Glenn, just his corpse. He had difficulty rolling the body onto its side. Had rigor mortis already set in or was it the usual arthritis? He sponged down the chest and stomach, penis and thighs. The Hail Mary would be better, he thought. Calling upon the Virgin Mother to cradle the body of her no-longer suffering child. But he couldn't remember it either. He washed the wilted feet, taking care to cleanse the space between the toes. How crooked they were.

He covered Father Glenn in a clean sheet, put away the soap, water and towels and checked the time. Five minutes to three. The monks would awaken in twenty minutes for Vigils. They would "keep watch" in darkness and silence, pray for all to be brought into "the light of a never-ending day." Eric winced. Pitiful how he could remember all that but not a single prayer.

He didn't want to see anyone. His stay had ended, that he knew. One monk would be on night duty. Eric hurried to his own cabin, packed his bag, scooped up the coins and dollars that had sat on the dresser since the day of his arrival. He left the cabin and found Brother Huy on night duty, immersed in a book.

"This is an emergency," Eric said, "so I have to break

Grand Silence. Father Glenn has died. You have to tell Abbot Paul. But first you have to open the main gate."

Brother Huy stood up slowly, uncertainly. As they walked toward the entrance, lights began to flick on in the retreat cabins. Eric looked at Brother Huy. A long while might pass before he again looked into such kind and trusting eyes. Brother Huy opened the gate. Eric stepped outside monastery grounds.

"Father Glenn's body is washed," he said, his lower lip trembling, "but it... needs prayers."

He turned on his heel and set off across the parking lot. A moment later he passed the metal crucifix and then the battered sign announcing Chassors Monastery. He continued on through the town of Dunding. The streets were empty, the sky still dark. He couldn't calm his thoughts.

Hours passed and he kept on walking. Months gone by and he traveled the same aimless direction. Sun rising on his left, setting on his right. The void straight ahead. Cars and trucks blasted past. The driver of a van shouted an incomprehensible curse. No more silence, stillness, solitude. He felt like a patient pre-maturely released from a hospital, thrust out into sickness and pandemonium. He already missed the Liturgy of the Hours, the rhythm and structure, the serenity. He still felt his hands on Father Glenn's skeletal body, washing the rice paper skin, cleaning his toes.

Later he came to a busy gas station. There was a small convenience store crammed with food and drink machines. He bought a bottle of water and a bacon, scrambled egg and cheese sandwich. Outside at a picnic table he chewed on the sandwich. No more vegetarian fare blessed by monk chefs. He watched a steady line of cars pull up to the pumps. Credit card, gas, squeegee windshields, kids to the restroom, junk food, hit the road. Humans coming and going. A woman let out a shriek of laughter. For a second Eric's mind roiled in panic. The clock, he thought, the clock had yet to strike the hour of despair. Would he be transported like a child? To revel in paradise, oblivious of all suffering? Hurry! Were there other lives to live?

He commanded himself to calm down. A pay phone stood at the side of the station. Circled by graffiti, it looked like a relic from another century. People on the way to the restrooms passed it without a sideways glance. Then a black woman in a green dress lifted the receiver and dropped some change into the coin slot. She talked for several minutes. After she hung up, Eric went into the station, exchanged some dollar bills for coins and looked through an old phone book.

Abbot Paul's voice betrayed no surprise. It was as if he had been in his office waiting for the call. He said arrangements were still being made but that Father Glenn's funeral mass and burial would take place in three days. Until then, his body would lie in repose in the chapel. Father Glenn's relatives—a younger brother, two nephews and a niece—would arrive the day before the funeral. Strange, Eric thought, but he had never considered that Father Glenn or any of the monks might have families.

"We will say the *Officium Defunctorum*, the Office of the

Dead," Abbot Paul explained. "We will say it on the day of the burial and on the third and seventh day after his funeral. We will pray that he—and all departed souls—be released from Purgatory and behold the Beatific Vision. We will ask that they share in the Resurrection."

There was a tradition at Chassors Monastery, he went on. Monks who wished to pay their respects to a deceased brother were invited to say a few words at the memorial service. "Eric, you would also be welcome to speak."

Eric replied without hesitation.

"I won't be returning."

His throat clogged up as he expressed thanks for the "tradition of hospitality." Behind him people walked back and forth to the restroom. A child whined to a parent. "But I don't have to tinkle." The same loud peal of female laughter came from near the pumps.

"Eric," Abbot Paul said, "why have you called? What is it?"

In other words, *what do you seek?*

Eric's voice lowered. "Right before Father Glenn died, I made a confession."

"Yes?"

"But he didn't give me any penance. I thought there was always penance after confession."

"I'm not sure how to answer you, but if you feel you didn't make a complete confession, you can confess to any of the other priests. Tell me where you are and I'll send a car."

Eric caught his breath. "My confession was complete. I don't want to make it again."

"Then I can't say. Perhaps there was no penance for your sins or Father Glenn thought you already knew your penance, or that it would come to you in time. Or perhaps his Alzheimer's prevented him from understanding you."

"Goodbye, Abbot Paul," Eric said. "Thank you for everything."

He didn't ask for the man's blessing because he knew at that very moment Abbot Paul's hand was cutting the air above his desk, making the sign of the cross in short bold strokes. Eric hung up before Abbot Paul could say anything else. He stood by the phone, head bowed as if beneath a sprinkle of holy water at bedtime. Then he set off past the gas pumps toward the road.

CHAPTER NINETEEN

The first week brought back all the leg cramps and foot pain he had suffered upon leaving Ashland six months ago. In the middle of the night, spasms coursed through his calves and thighs. Once again sleeping on hard ground, he was back to point zero. Same doubts, same fears. And still no prayer to pray, no tap to turn off the chatter.

He tramped through Chico, Oroville, Palermo, Gridley and Live Oak. He passed a night sleeping near a mosque, the Islamic Center of Yuba City. A young Pakistani man gave him fifty cents. The man said the mosque had been destroyed by arson just after completion, and later rebuilt. "It was a hate-crime," he said. "The first mosque destroyed in America."

Eric spent the next three nights in a rundown park near a Taco Bell. He ate leftover nachos, quesadillas, tacos and listened to hip hop music blaring out of cars. From a clump of bushes, he watched the drive-thru window where a teenage girl in a Taco Bell hat greeted customers. Her smile dazzled so brightly she might have been handing out gold bars instead of burritos.

To love and serve the world, Eric thought. And what service did he now render? Hard to render anything when people avoided him, cast their eyes aside, seldom sent a word his way. What could he say to them anyway? Hello. What a lovely day. My feet are sore, my legs ache, I can't pray.

He could only think of one service he rendered. He saw it in the expressions of people who stole a glance his way. Momentarily, he stopped their stream of envy, malice, resentment, lust. "I want this, now I want that." Stopped dead. For a single moment they felt gratitude. "Things are awful but thank God I'm not that guy."

Maybe that was the real function of a sadhu. In India the saffron-clad holy man covered in sacred ash served the community by the example of his renunciation, by the wealth of his patience, wisdom, kindness. Eric recalled the two Tamil women in Yreka. Who in America would ask him for a blessing now?

South of Yuba City he paused near the fence of the Feather Lake Golf & Country Club, arrested by the thwack of a driver smacking a dimpled white ball into the blue yonder. He thought of Earl, Pete and Tony, his golf buddies, and their Saturday morning sessions. The last time he had seen Tony was at the Irish Pub in Ashland. He had been surprised to find Tony sitting alone in a dark corner. Tony had spluttered drunkenly, saying he hated his life, hated his wife, especially hated Eric. "Go on and leave, you son-of-a-bitch," he had said. "You lucky fucking son-of-a-bitch."

Another thwack sounded and Eric pushed on. Two weeks later, he was still heading south. He had passed through Lincoln, Rocklin and Roseville, then Sutter Creek, Jackson and San Andreas. He scratched at the layers of sweat and dirt on his flesh. He listened to the traffic roar. *Don't stop. Keep on. Keep on.* In Angels Camp, a woman gave him two dollars and said, "Jesus loves you and He always will." At another time, in another life, he would have brushed off her words like dandruff, but they stuck with him for days. Contrition, gratitude, adoration. Why couldn't he pray? At night he looked up at the black sky. Cold stars across the Milky Way. Across heaven. Why were they described as cold? What kind of false poetry was that? They were super-heated bodies, enflamed demigods in empty space.

More traffic roar, heat, exhaustion. He walked in a trance. He saw his garden in Ashland, sunlight dappling the bushes. Did he need Alzheimer's to make memory vanish? He saw Jessica's tiny teeth. He pictured Billy lost in Alaskan wilderness, hunted by wolves and Kodiak bears. He heard a voice. *Go home. Go home now.* Was this his penance—to tramp the world for the crime of a disenchanted existence?

Or maybe he was just thinking crazy thoughts. The sun pounding his skull didn't make him more levelheaded, that was for sure. One afternoon a homeless guy with an amputated hand plopped down next to him on a park bench.

"Are you some kind of movie person?" the guy asked

Eric shook his head, emerged from his trance. "Not that I know of..."

"You wouldn't know, would you?" the guy pressed. "Movie people never do. They're in the movie."

"I don't understand you."

"You understand. You're only pretending you don't. Just like a typical movie person."

It was the last conversation Eric would have with another human soul for a solid month. If he had known it at the time, he would have dragged the talk out, milked it for a drop of humor or wisdom or prattle or hot air. He could have analyzed the different kinds of movie people. Instead, he walked off wondering if he would end up like the guy, spewing out nonsense to strangers who hurried away from him.

The Liturgy of Hours had not only governed his days, but kept him sane. Now he missed the sense of order, missed the chanting and singing at Mass, Abbot Paul's comments on the psalms. "Keep death daily before your eyes." Where was death now without Father Glenn? Death and lunacy and disorder, and movie people never understood any of it.

Weeks later, passing through Ceres just south of Modesto, his trance stopped in front of a store called Pete's Appliances. The display window showed coffee makers and fans, a vacuum cleaner, hair dryer and steam iron, all guaranteed for two years or your money back. The shiny gadgets of a former life. Then he fixed on the haggard figure reflected in the plate glass. He reached for his glasses but couldn't find them. How could he lose anything when he barely owned six items? Now he understood why the world had been such a blur. He peered at his reflection. He had shed ten pounds since leaving Chassors, the same ten pounds he had shed in departing Ashland. Back to point zero all right, except he had aged more than seemed possible. People used to compliment him on what a trim figure he cut at age sixty. Now he looked seventy-five. Every day he ate undesirable food and slept in an undesirable place. Where was that leading? Down and farther down.

More time passed—he wasn't sure how much—days, weeks—before he found the courage to pause in front of another shop window. In Fresno this time and a menswear store: the type of clothing he had once worn. Dress shirts and slacks, a fancy sport coat. No longer haggard, he had become skin and bones, dirty white hair and filthy white beard, enlarged eyes, skeletal face. He was still running away from the monastery, but Father Glenn had caught up to him. Daily death before his eyes. In a display window.

He lost track of the days of the week. No newspaper, cell phone or radio to tell him it was Tuesday. He couldn't even remember the month. It felt like mid summer but it might have been October. What had happened to Memorial Day, 4th of July, his own birthday? California's central oven cooked his flesh. Walking through Bakersfield, he became obsessed with shop windows. Obsessed with avoiding them. But there he was in the blur of discount objects. A reduced-cost derelict. Marked down, cut-rate, closeout sale.

A palpitating sign on a bank building. Thirteen minutes after one and 103 degrees. He stepped off Highway 99 near Buck Owens' Crystal Palace. Live Music and Dancing. Entertainment provided by the World Famous Buckaroos. America, America. How you entertain your denizens. He crossed the Kern River and rested in the shade of Saunders Park. His knees had begun to shake. He needed help but the murderous heat had driven all sensible humans into air conditioning.

He turned east on Brundage Lane. He passed a medical center—should he check in?—and then a McDonald's. Then a flat, featureless expanse of desert road. Ugly houses and a Seven Eleven. Chevron, Motel 6, Travel Plaza, another McDonald's. He was dizzy, faint, knees still shaking. He longed for a grave to fall into. *Go home, go home.* Another dusty road shoulder. As dry as his throat. Cars and trucks blasting past on his left. Heat haze on his right. Nothingness. *Keep on, keep on.* No cross too great to bear. Skeleton steps, rattling bones. Then he distinguished a mirage-like figure tramping toward him, also in a trance, also skeletal and haggard. The figure had stepped out of a display window. Finally, he would meet him face to face. His ghost self, the sadhu in reverse. I'm going to die, he thought.

He had reached the impasse Abbot Paul had foreseen. Nothing to do but beg. Facing traffic, he fell to his knees. He clasped his hands together. The chatter in his skull became a chant like Father Glenn's mumbled prayers. But no longer contrition. Now he implored an onrushing stream of vehicles. To no avail. Cars and trucks roared past in the blur of his lost vision.

The sudden blare of an air horn startled him. Bits of gravel struck his arms. He stumbled back onto his feet, tripped but caught himself before falling. A pearl-white limousine had skidded to a stop on the road shoulder. The tinted passenger window whirred down. Eric peered into the front seat, where a giant of a man sat at the steering wheel. He wore a handlebar mustache and ducktail beard. He was dressed in a white tuxedo and white silk Stetson. Impossible hallucination. Some kind of gleaming cowboy archangel.

"Hey, old timer!" he called. "It's your lucky day. Hop in!"

CHAPTER TWENTY

An arctic blast from the air-con vents threw Eric back against the ostrich-skin seat. He was on the verge of passing out. The limo picked up speed, merged into traffic. He struggled to stay conscious.

"So how's the family?" the man asked.

"The—?" Eric shivered in the icy air. "I... I'm not sure what you mean..."

"Your family. How are they? How're they doing?"

"My family? I—I don't know. I'm separated and..."

"Busted like a bad hand of Hold'em."

"I guess... you could say that."

What was the man talking about? He didn't look crazy but he wasn't making any sense. He swiveled his gaze from the road to Eric and back to the road. White pants and white buck shoes complemented his white tux and Stetson outfit. He must have been six foot eight. Large arms, thick chest. Eric blacked out for a moment, shook himself awake. The man was talking again. Booming voice.

"...and so I took in the whole scene in a flash, which I can do because I drive LA to Vegas once a week, every week, every month of the year except March, every Monday there, every Wednesday back, so I see it all and take it all in and figure it all quick-like, so I see you on your knees and I figure this poor skunk either doesn't know he's heading straight into the Mojave or doesn't care and either way he's a goner, so I say to myself, I say, Jamie John, do the right thing and answer his prayers. Save him from himself. Don't think twice just save him and so I tap the brakes, reel you in, and off we go from high to low. That's right, the City of the Angels to Sin City limo express, five hours counting lunch in Barstow, five hours of rolling wasteland, and all you have to do is sit back, kick up your heels and enjoy the scenery, one long view of desert scrub brought to you free of charge by your new best friend, Jamie John Smith, born and raised in…"

The shift from oven burn to arctic chill would have been enough to stun Eric mute anyway, but this—what was this? It was the most anyone had said to him since Chassors and the monks had never raised their voices above a library-level whisper. Jamie John's thunderous blare along with the polar jet stream still gusting out of the ivory dashboard pressed Eric back against his plush seat.

"Thanks, Jamie John," he managed to say. "My name's Eric."

Jamie John removed a large right hand from the steering wheel, a catcher's mitt that swallowed Eric's dirty fist. His grip was strong but his shake was warm and gentle. He kept the limo on a beeline heading due east. His six-inch long forefinger pointed at a stainless steel champagne bucket affixed to the dash. Eric hadn't noticed it. A water bottle peaked over the brim and an attached silver tray held four glasses.

Water, Eric thought. What was he doing without it? He had vowed to carry water at all times. Always. Sweet delicious water. Drink, swallow, rejoice. He had warned himself that the day he forgot it would be the day he lost all.

"Help yourself," Jamie John said.

Eric poured and drank greedily, choking as the icy liquid spilled down his parched gullet. Still woozy, he glanced around. The back of the limo held a semicircle of ostrich skin seats facing a counsel with a built-in television, sound system and marble bar. He had dropped into an orbital spacecraft, rocket boosters throttling a thousand pounds of thrust. In a few minutes the limo covered the distance he would have walked in a day. Looking at the empty expanse flashing past, he saw Jamie John was right. He had been about to become a dead skunk on the side of the road.

He tried to get hold of himself. Glancing downward, he fixed on his tennis shoes. What was left of them. Synthetic leather in shreds, soles worn to a slant, covered in filth. He looked back up. Jamie John smiled. Gentle blue eyes and a friendly grin. The limo still cruising along at high speed. Eric noticed a silver plaque mounted on the center of the dashboard near the champagne bucket. Embossed letters read: "Little White Chapel." He read it twice, suddenly anxious. Who was this guy and what did he want? Why was he asking strange questions about family? Eric quashed his anxiety, blamed it on the desolate terrain and surreal limo. He still had the mumbled prayer running through his skull, asking, begging. The world was good. He should bless life. There were no more childhood dreams. No escape from old age and death.

"Risk is the baby brother of greed," Jamie John said, "and the big daddy of down and out. The whole scene keeps coming back like a bad penny, bad not because it's counterfeit but because it's real, bad because we don't want it in our life but it's a fun ride on a big roller coaster, and it gets so we don't know if the ride is the thing itself or just wanting the thing the next time around, even when we blackballed it out of our head long ago, years ago, and so that's the thing, you know what I mean?"

"I think so..." Eric said.

Though maybe not. He wondered how far into the desert he would have gotten before keeling over. They had probably passed that point five miles back. Jamie John lifted his eyes off the road, looked at Eric again. He might have picked him up out of a kind and caring heart but he was on some mission. Eric felt it oozing off him like lava off a white volcano. But Jamie John had just saved him from dead skunk land and if Eric wanted to stay saved, he had better play the big man's game.

"If I understand you right," Eric said, "this is connected to what you said before about family..."

Jamie John tipped the Stetson back an inch on his large forehead. He ruminated quietly, gaze on the road. They passed a few cars, a delivery van. The driver of the van turned and looked at Eric. Their eyes met but then Eric realized he was invisible behind tinted glass.

"The word *separation* is like a dagger in my side," Jamie John said. "Everything I work for, everything I believe in exists in opposition to that word. It hurts me even more than the word *divorce*."

"I see..." Eric said. He took another drink of water, forced himself to swallow slowly. He still felt ice plunging down his throat. "And... are you separated yourself?"

"Never been married."

Then what were they talking about? Eric cautioned

himself. He didn't want to court trouble. Fits of mood, depravity, madness: the soaring toward catastrophe. He wanted to cast off his burdens. His cross.

"Does... your feeling have something to do with your work?" he asked.

"Everything to do with it. I'm a solemnizer."

"I... I don't know what that is."

"A wedding officiant. A marriage celebrant. I believe in the power of ceremony and ritual to create lasting and joyful union and I perform my duty accordingly. I've been on the job for twenty years now."

His cell phone rang. He engulfed it in his paw and began talking. Eric gave his head a shake, tried to joggle his thoughts back into working order but the freakish scene rattled him beyond reason. He had hit bottom. He could have died and now a tuxedoed archangel was transporting him in cold storage across the flaming desert of hell itself. As Jamie John talked, Eric heard the word *family* again or imagined he did. Feared he did. He looked back out his window. How many other lost souls did he see plodding across the barren land? Not one. He had been acting out a fantasy. Not Sadhu in reverse, but American dream dissolving down Route 66. An outdated matinee with Kid Kerouac in a has-been role. Have cool adventures, be different from normal people. Fuck it all. Find yourself. The road, the road. Once a surefire classic, now a box office bomb. That's what happened when you hit bottom. The film in your head stopped rolling. You stopped being a movie person.

CHAPTER TWENTY-ONE

Eric was on the brink of nausea. Jamie John had just hung up and was now talking about weddings in Vegas. "But many people ask me to come to LA," he said, "and I endeavor to please." He worked seven days a week, ten hours a day and was booked solid for the next five months. Straight wedlock, that was it. He didn't do Elvis, Star Wars or any religious hokum but The Little White Chapel on the Strip radiated more joy than a maternity ward. Hundreds of couples had "kicked off their honeymoon" in his famous limo. Shining faces, the birth of sacred union, a shower of nuptial bliss.

In his plush seat Eric felt like he was sliding off an iceberg. He looked out through the tinted glass. Dry land sharply outlined in piercing light. Heat waves shimmering above rock and sand. Flat nothingness dotted by an occasional trailer. He had thought he was alone. No mantra to murmur, no prayer to pray. Just destiny, whatever that was. But now he had a prayer of petition reverberating in his skull and it scolded him, reminded him he wasn't alone at all. The housewife in Mountain Gate, Donny, Mary and Glenda, Abbot Paul, Brother Huy and now Jamie John. Everyone helping him, keeping him alive while he pretended to be the great lone pilgrim. Heat and hunger had twisted his mind. What had he done for anyone? What service rendered? Nothing except complain every day about his duties with Father Glenn. Then fake contrition to soothe his sorrows. A sadhu asleep in an oven, baked until done.

He read road signs—"Safety Corridor Drive Safely" "Call Box"—and listened to the purr of tires, the whirr of the air con. He watched desert ravens pecking at the scrub. A battered sign appeared, announcing Barstow as the "Crossroads of Opportunity."

"Lunch time," Jamie John said. Before Eric could say a word, he added: "This one's on me. You can get the next one."

He pulled into a McDonald's parking lot full of homeless characters. The sight of them put Eric at ease about entering a restaurant the way he looked. Jamie John had trouble maneuvering the limo around the lot but then swung it into a spot not far from the drive-thru. They got out and everyone in sight—a few families, a couple of truck drivers, a half dozen homeless guys—turned to look. Scruffy derelict and tuxedoed archangel emerging from a pearl white limo.

The McDonald's was housed in a few converted train cars with classic McDonald's benches retrofitted into the seating areas. Jamie John ordered a variety of burgers and fries. As he and Eric headed to the rear of a passenger car, other diners looked up, at Jamie John with awe and curiosity, at Eric with disapproval. They sat in a booth and Jamie John removed his Stetson, revealing shiny black hair combed straight back. He took a call on his cell phone. It seemed to be an assistant. "Just got in with a friend," he said. "Right on schedule." He listened intently, then said, "Okay, don't worry. I'll call her now." He hung up, told Eric to "dig in" and he would join him in a minute. Then he speed-dialed a number.

"Hi Kathy," Jamie John said.

Eric went rigid. There had to be ten million other American women named Kathy, so it was hardly a stunning coincidence or divine message, but in his perturbed state, he suddenly feared Jamie John was talking to Kathy, his ex-wife. It was crazy and impossible but he waited in horror, expecting Jamie John to shout into the mouthpiece, *He did what?* Instead, he spoke in a reassuring tone.

"Doubt is part of the journey," he said. "It helps you figure out if you really want to travel on, but it's not a stop sign, just a detour. Renewing vows isn't a one-off thrill event. It's a long-lasting commitment, a testament to your union. Didn't you have similar doubts when you married? Let them serve as part of the ceremony. You can customize your package to include them if you want. Reflect on it for a while. We're not going anywhere and you shouldn't rush a decision. We can always reschedule."

He hung up and began tucking napkins into his collar and tux pockets. He made sure every inch of white material was covered and then reached for his French fries. Still stiff with apprehension, Eric tried to chew on his Big Mac. He was ravenous but could barely swallow a bite. He set it back down onto its paper packaging.

"Nothing does it like a vow renewal ceremony," Jamie John said reflectively, munching on fries. "It takes you back to the beginning and reminds you that your vow hasn't changed. It was made sacred by a power greater than you, whether civil, godlike, or your own higher self. A part of you knows that, the same part that will be forever haunted by separation."

Eric sat motionless, the half-eaten Big Mac spilling out sauce in front of him. He couldn't shake the feeling that Jamie John really had been talking to Kathy. His Kathy. He forced himself to chew on the Big Mac. He might not eat again for a week.

"Anyway," Jamie John went on, "it's a chance for good people to wake up and renew their commitment." He reached for more French fries. "Did you try it before separating?"

There was nothing imperious or aggressive in his manner. He spoke sincerely, even kindly, but it seemed he knew exactly how to poke his long forefinger into Eric's wound.

"Jamie John," Eric said, "I need to ask a favor."

"Sure," Jamie John said, wiping a dot of ketchup off the side of his mouth. "Hope I can accommodate."

"I need to make a call."

Without hesitation Jamie John pushed his cell phone across the table. Eric used to make and receive ten calls an hour at DMT, roughly one-hundred a day, almost all business related and on his cell menu. The only number he had memorized was DMT itself, the marketing department. A hard one to forget. 541-770-7700. The receptionist answered. He couldn't recall her name but she instantly recognized his voice.

"Hey, Mr. Tyler, we haven't heard from you in forever. How's retirement going?"

"Great. It's going great. Listen, I need—"

"We heard you went on some cool hiking trip, a yoga program for seniors."

"Well, something like that..."

Jamie John rose from the table, checked his pocket for keys, put on his Stetson. "Time to go," he mouthed.

Eric walked alongside him back through the car. At every booth they passed, heads turned. The Receptionist still chattered in Eric's ear.

"Listen," he told her. "I lost my cell and need to call my wife. You've got her number there in the data bank. The name is Kathy Tyler." He couldn't remember if it broke some DMT regulation but he sensed the receptionist hesitating, so he quickly added: "I wouldn't ask if it wasn't serious. You know me. I'm not some nut calling." Her name suddenly popped into his mind. "Come on, Cindy, this isn't a joke. It's an emergency."

He felt like he was lying to Brother Huy again. Jamie John turned his large head. Obviously it wasn't an emergency but Eric nodded at him as if they both understood the situation. They pushed through the glass door out into the sweltering parking lot. Cindy mumbled something he couldn't distinguish but she seemed to be searching her computer. Once again in contact with DMT, he recalled an old truth: life ripened through the fruit of labor. Now his life lacked weight. He was adrift, floating far beneath the roar of the world's applause. Two of the homeless guys stood next to the limo, peering through the tinted glass. At the sight of Jamie John, they backpedaled. He thanked them for "guarding" his car and handed them each a dollar.

Cindy came back on line and rattled off Kathy's number. Eric made her repeat it twice. "I just better not get in trouble over this," she said.

Before he could forget the number, he dialed Kathy. She would have arrived home from her afternoon Pilates classes an hour ago. She would have dressed in sweat pants and running shoes, gone for a half hour jog along the bike path, and then returned to the house and showered. After checking every inch of her sculpted body in her floor-length mirror, she would have uncorked a bottle of Chardonnay. He steeled himself for the sound of her voice, wondering what words were going to come out of his own mouth. By now she would be on her second or third glass of wine. Whatever he had to say, he had to say it before she got any farther down into the bottle. The phone rang twice. A tired voice answered. It was Jessica.

"Hi," she said. "You've called Kathy Tyler. I'm her daughter Jessica. Can I help you?"

The murderous heat in the parking lot had turned the asphalt to black magma, throwing up fumes. Eric looked at Jamie John as if searching for an explanation for Jessica's voice. The two homeless guys were trying to cajole more money out of him. Jamie John shooed them aside with a wave of his giant paw. The familiar sound of Jessica grinding her teeth formed a hard lump in the center of Eric's chest. He slid into the passenger seat of the limo. Jamie John started the engine. The homeless guys backed off, grinning stupidly, waving bye-bye.

"Hello," Jessica said. "Is anyone there?"

"Jessica, this is Dad," Eric said.

Stunned silence.

"Hon, it's Dad," he repeated. "What's going on?"

"What's going on?" she snapped back. "Why don't you tell me?"

He had never before heard sarcastic anger in her voice. She retreated from even mild conversation, disappearing behind a shy murmur. Jamie John drove through Barstow, glancing sideways. Eric made his own voice calm and natural, as if he and Jessica had chatted earlier that day, as if they chatted every day, a model father-daughter relationship.

"Hon, I just mean I don't get it. I dialed your Mom's number. Did you and your Mom switch cells or something?"

"Yeah, something like that," she said, spitting. "We switched cells when she went into the fucking hospital."

She hung up and refused to answer three more calls.

Chapter Twenty-two

Eric shivered as cold air once again streamed out of the dashboard vents. Jessica spewing out the word *fuck?* Something was wrong, very wrong. Jamie John cruised through Barstow on Main. They passed innumerable signs. Car Wash, Desert Inn, O'Reilly Auto Parts. The Mojave Freeway. Eric recalled they were still Vegas bound. Barstow Dental, State Farm Insurance, Stardust Inn. They rolled through the eastern limits of the dusty town. The Big Mac sat in the pit of his stomach like a lead hockey puck. What had happened to Kathy? The landscape flashed past in a series of jump cuts between vehicles: brown wasteland, red Toyota pick-up, barren emptiness, black SUV. As they overtook a semi-truck, the driver smiled and raised a thumb, saluting the limo. Jamie John looked sideways at Eric.

"Can I have my phone back?" he said.

"Wha—?" Eric was squeezing his hands together hard enough to pulverize a brick. "Sure, of course, sorry." He held the phone forth. Jamie John stowed it in a niche beneath the dashboard before it occurred to Eric to add: "Thanks. Thanks very much."

They passed two more semis and then the road cleared. Not another car in sight. Empty road, empty desert. Eric looked down at his lap. He was still squeezing his hands together.

"You all right?" Jamie John asked.

"What? No... no, I'm not. I've got a problem." His voice sounded like it was coming into the limo from across the Mojave, as if a hot breeze forced it in a whoosh through the air con vents. "A serious problem. My wife—my ex-wife, it seems she isn't well. I'm not sure exactly what's going on but... I'm sorry to lay this on you, Jamie John."

Jamie John regarded him. "Lay what on me?"

"I mean..." Eric looked out his window. What had he imagined—that he would leave Ashland and life would continue frozen in time, no changes, no one ever sick or in trouble? He had wanted freedom through redemption and now a prayer of petition ran through his head but was he truly healed or still wounded and weak?

"I mean I haven't got anything...," he went on desperately. "I'm in a bad way and I need to... to ask you for a loan... beg you for a loan. I'll pay it back as soon as I get to Ashland. Ashland, Oregon That's my home and I've got.... got...."

His words faded into the airstream. He became aware of how pitiful he sounded. What was he talking about anyway? His hands throbbed with pain. He was squeezing the bones out through flesh.

"I like to do a favor," Jamie John began slowly, "and I try to practice kindness to all souls. It's part... of who I am." He rubbed his chin with his right hand, returned the hand to the wheel. "But I'm not a charity, Eric, and I don't go where my instinct tells me not to. If you're open, I can suggest help. If not, then I won't be much use to you."

Open? Eric had no idea what he was talking about, but it wasn't like a dozen other options resided in his shirt pocket.

Jamie John was all he had going. If Eric started acting crazy, he would end up back on the side of the road, not at the start of the Mojave but in the middle. He tried to put himself in Jamie John's large shoes. Practicing kindness, he had picked up a down-and-out guy, fed the guy a Big Mac, let the guy make a call on his phone. Now the down-and-out guy was turning into trouble. How much more trouble was the guy going to cause?

"I appreciate all you've done already," Eric said quickly. "I can't thank you enough so... so I'm definitely open to help. I mean, that's what I need, that's what I'm asking for." Once again asking, begging, depending on others. He stopped short of uttering the word *money*.

"Okay," Jamie John said. "As soon as we get into Vegas, you can talk to Stevie, a friend of mine. Stevie's in recovery himself, been in recovery for a dozen years so he understands the game inside and out."

Eric turned in his seat. "The game?"

"When Stevie bottomed out, he had a tough time but he stuck through treatment and ended up becoming one of the top counselors on the Strip. Now he's state certified in a private practice but one morning a week he treats people on the street free of charge."

"I'm not following you. Treats them for what?"

Jamie John looked at him. His gaze had turned suspicious.

"Gambling addiction."

Eric let out a short, incredulous laugh. "What?"

"You heard me."

"I've never bet a penny on anything in my life."

"Come on, Eric. You think I haven't heard the sick wife story before?"

Eric's mouth opened but nothing came out.

"Well, it just so happens that I have," Jamie John went on, "me and everyone else on the Strip. Your brother had a car accident, you need a kidney operation, you have to get back to LA because you've got a big part in a movie, your friend is in trouble, your baby was kidnapped, your wife is sick... you name it and we've heard it on a looping tape."

"Jamie John," Eric said, sounding as serious and reasonable as possible. "You've got it wrong. Look at me. How in hell can I gamble? I haven't got a dime to my name."

Jamie John nodded. "That's right. Not a dime, but you're on your way back because this time it'll be different. This time you'll really hit it." He shook his head and reached for his cell phone. "You decide, Eric. Do I call Stevie or not?"

Eric looked out at the expanse of Mojave. Cloud banks covered the sky. Best case scenario: he ended up destitute walking at night beneath the bright lights of the Vegas strip. Worst case: he ended up destitute walking across sand and rocks beneath the blazing sun.

"Please call Stevie," he answered. "I'm open to help. And thanks again. Thanks very much."

CHAPTER TWENTY-THREE

As they drove into the flash and trash of Vegas, Eric wondered if guilt and heartache were making him run scared. Jessica usually resided in a bubble of false calm but every now and then she burst into flames. She had once ignited in rage when a passing cyclist had kicked Cookie, the dog across the street. It could be nothing more than that. A flare-up. No doubt Kathy had been in the hospital, but it might have been for a broken finger, a few stitches, a minor operation.

"The darkest day in the history of this town," Jamie John said. "Fifty-eight dead—59 including the perp—and 851 injured."

Eric glanced up at the facade of the Mandalay Bay Hotel. He murmured a response but his thoughts were on Kathy's cell phone. It contained her private dealings, intimate secrets, messages from Abe, her ripped lover. She never let anyone near it, let alone her delicate-minded daughter. Likewise, Jessica had never attacked Eric so vehemently. Foul language in her prudish mouth? Even her teeth grinding had sounded off key. In the icebox limo he began to sweat. He felt trapped, frozen, compelled to act. If he was wrong, what could he lose that wasn't already gone?

"Sad and tragic day," Jamie John went on. "There was a unity prayer walk the following week but it didn't make it any less sad."

Five minutes later he slotted the limo into a private

parking spot across the street from a few motels and in front of a tiny church. A neon sign twinkled on a white facade. "The Little White Chapel. Serious and delightful ceremonies conducted by Reverend Jamie John Smith and his team of certified wedding officiants."

"'Serious' means what I told you before," Jamie John said, as they walked toward the chapel entrance. "I don't do Elvis, Santa or Michael Jackson. And I sure don't do goth, Trekkie or surf themes."

"So what does 'delightful' mean?" Eric asked.

"It means I'm not stupid and we do Hawaii, Cuba and Grand Canyon helicopter affairs, courtesy limos, boutonnières and bouquets, DVDs, live streaming, custom napkins, koozies, t-shirts and garters. We also offer a whole range of commitment ceremonies and renewals." He removed his Stetson. "Don't get me wrong. Nothing in this life does it for me like saying, 'I now pronounce you man and wife.'"

The small chapel consisted of a carpeted central aisle with five traditional wooden pews to either side. Shimmering rose wallpaper ran around the room and a crystal chandelier hung above a carved oak altar. Jamie John led Eric through a door marked "Sacristy" into an office where a middle-aged woman named Ophelia tapped at a keyboard. She made a point of not looking at Eric. He guessed that Jamie John brought home a lot of lost puppies.

"Stevie jogged in a minute ago," she told Jamie John, nodding toward a door at the rear.

Jamie John ushered Eric over the threshold into a second

office identical to the first. A thin, balding man dressed in a blue parka, sweat pants and running shoes stood up from a straight back chair, pocketed his cell, motioned Eric into a second chair and said:

"So what's your story, friend? The full story, I mean."

Jamie John shut the door, leaving them alone. Eric still had no idea how he was going to explain his "gambling addiction," but he had crossed the Mojave and arrived in Vegas in one piece. So, good enough. Now full steam ahead.

"I'm not sure what you want to know," he said.

"Just begin at the beginning," Stevie encouraged.

You asked for it, Eric thought, and launched into an account of his honeymoon with Kathy in India. Stevie had never before heard of sadhus, so Eric described them in detail. Then he skipped through the first few years of married life up to Billy's birth. Stevie chewed at the corner of his thin lower lip and listened without blinking a pair of dark brown eyes. After a few minutes he began throwing out questions, interrupting Eric in the middle of his stories. Eric jerked to a stop, thought for a second and answered as best he could, but then had difficulty getting back to his narrative. Twice he had to ask: "Where was I?"

He talked about poetry, about Billy and Jessica's childhood and the good days at DMT, including his celebrated year in Austin. He described his sessions with Walt and growing financial and marital strain, financial and marital disaster, and finally forced retirement and his inglorious exit from Ashland. He covered details of his Sadhu journey, including Donny's Diner and Abbot Paul offering him "silence, stillness and solitude." He choked up describing his duties with Father Glenn. Stevie went on chewing at his lower lip, now the opposite corner. Then his questions started jumping back to things Eric had already said. "What were the names of the two women at Donny's Diner?"

Eric suddenly felt tired. His forehead throbbed and darkness spun in the room despite the sunlight streaming through the windows. Where were the questions about gambling?

"So tell me why you think like that," Stevie said.

"Why?" Eric replied, growing hot. "I think like that because that's how I think."

Stevie changed tack and asked about booze, grass and coke. Eric told him he had snorted coke a few times but hadn't even caught a buzz. Grass made him lethargic and thick-headed, so conventional alcohol had always been his drug of choice, usually Maker's Mark, sometimes amped up by Ibuprofen. He described his withdrawal symptoms upon leaving Ashland.

"Tell me why you think your confession with Father Glenn wasn't real."

"This jumping back and forth is making me dizzy," Eric said. "I already explained that. I'm not going to explain it again."

"Okay," Stevie said, standing up. "Then we're finished."

"No, wait." Eric feared he had just thrown himself out onto the street. "It was real. I think my penance is here now. I've got to get back to Ashland."

Stevie's dark brown eyes blinked for the first time in thirty minutes. He opened the door and Eric followed him back into the outer office. Ophelia still tapped at her keyboard, still ignored him. Jamie John stood nearby, dressed in a different model tux, now powder blue with a classic butterfly black tie.

"This dude isn't hooked on anything," Stevie told him, "except some looney ideas. He's all yours."

Jamie John looked at Eric in surprise, then stepped toward Stevie. They hugged with genuine affection and Stevie threw a goodbye kiss to Ophelia. As soon as he was out the door, Jamie John turned to Eric. "Sorry if he twisted your toes, but I didn't know. Tell me what I can do for you."

"I have to get to Ashland, Oregon," Eric said, and felt he might burst into tears.

"Does it have an airport?"

"In Medford. Next town over."

He spoke in spurts to keep his emotions in check. If one tear fell, the floodgates would open. Ophelia tapped quickly, watching her screen.

"Delta," she told Jamie John. "McCarran to Rogue Valley International. Departs at four sharp. One hour fifty-seven-minute flight time."

"That do it?" Jamie John asked.

Eric nodded. He wanted to say he would get the money back to Jamie John as soon as possible but he couldn't bring the words out.

"What else?" Jamie John asked.

"A shave. Maybe a shirt. Some pants. Goodwill will be fine."

"We can do better than Goodwill."

"I don't want better. Please, just Goodwill."

He shuffled his feet. How had he fallen so far? What had he become? He had swallowed poison. His insides were on fire.

"Do it," Jamie John told Ophelia.

She spoke to Eric without removing her gaze from the screen. "Driver's license."

"I— I haven't got one..."

"Passport? Birth Certificate? Anything?"

Her orange nails hovered two inches above the keyboard while her orange lips betrayed the trace of a smirk. She spoke to Jamie John. "Then it's no way on a flight. But there's always Greyhound. We could do a walk-up. Marco still works in Tickets. If there's a hitch, he can unhitch it... smooth him through, get him on his way."

Get rid of him, Eric thought.

Ophelia studied the screen. "Bus leaves at 3:45 PM, it says."

"Then make it work," Jamie John told her, "and put him into the Twin Palm for the night."

Ten minutes later Ophelia drove Eric in an old Volkswagen Beetle to the Boulevard Mall and a Goodwill store, whose facade advertised "Fashion. Housewares. Décor. Career Opportunities." He selected a shirt and trousers based on what fit. Ophelia paid with cash and made sure to get the receipt. She still hadn't spoken a word directly to him. As they headed back to the car, he became determined to make her say something. Casually, he remarked that the surrounding area was less sleazy than he would have thought.

"Worse at night," she said. "Lots of soiled doves and freelance pharmacists. Lots of *homeless*."

Yes, okay, he got the point, and in case he had missed it, she turned on the radio as soon as they were in the car. No more talking. Just noise. The hourly news. War, death, mayhem. He was on his way back home.

The Little White Chapel had an arrangement with the Twin Palm Motel across the street and Eric was soon showered, shaved and dressed in his new clothes. A delivery man brought him a salad and lasagna dinner. He ate, slept nine hours straight and awoke with a start the following morning. When he arrived at the Little White Chapel office, he insisted on using the computer on the desk next to Ophelia's.

"Just stay the hell out of our files," she warned. "I'll be watching."

He tried to revive his email account but had no luck, so he opened a new one. He couldn't decide if he should write to Kathy or Jessica first, then couldn't think of what to say anyway. Feeling Ophelia's eyes on him, he clicked onto the Little White Chapel webpage.

He stared at the screen, thinking he had lost it all: identity, status, character, integrity. No existence except in his own troubled psyche. His identity had become the story he told. If no one listened, he became no one. Anxiously, out of the long ago and faraway, he summoned his lionized and immortal DMT self. He scrolled through the website's menu, ran through the offer of Traditional Ceremony, Vow Renewals, Licensing, Commitment Certificate, Gown & Tux Rentals, Eloping Couples, non US Citizens. Then he reached across the desk for a legal pad and pen, and scribbled notes on competition, trends, targeted exposure, strategy, conversion optimization and profitability.

"What're you doing?" Ophelia demanded.

"I'll show you in a minute."

He opened a Word document and typed three pages. Once again in the world of Research and Analysis, Advertising and Inspired Hype, he felt drugged and punch-drunk, like he was going back to where he shouldn't be. He kept at it until he had drawn up a four-month work plan, which included suggested changes to the Little White Chapel webpage.

He printed the document and closed the webpage. Ten minutes later Jamie John entered the office, dressed in his white tux. When Eric handed him the three pages, he said, "What's this?"

"A thank-you present," Eric said. "See if you can use it."

Ophelia rose from her desk and leaned her head over the crook of Jamie John's elbow. They read the document together. After a minute she looked at Eric for the first time.

Chapter Twenty-four

Jamie John insisted on driving Eric to the Greyhound station on Main in the limo, saying that "everyone should leave Vegas in style." Marco turned out to be a Mexican guy missing his front teeth. He issued Eric's ticket: fourteen and a half hours to San Francisco followed by a three-hour layover and then a fifteen-hour trip to Ashland. "Why not just fly?" he asked.

The boarding line featured battered suitcases dragged along by scruffy-looking passengers, which included Eric in his Goodwill clothing. The others stole glances at Jamie John, huge and aglow in his white tux and Stetson. Eric's nerves were on edge. He kept rubbing his freshly shaven face, thinking that his Sadhu journey ended here.

Jamie John handed him five crisp twenty dollar bills. Eric felt shamed by the cash and glad to have it. He withstood Jamie John's suffocating hug, exchanged a handshake with Marco and climbed onboard. He had an aisle seat in the middle of the vehicle. A well dressed Asian woman in the window seat nodded imperceptibly, urbanely. As the bus rolled out of the station, Eric eased back and tried to relax. Five minutes later they hit a road block. The police had cordoned off the area. They directed the driver to detour from the main road.

"Maybe it's terrorists," someone behind Eric said.

"Or just some local nut," another voice added.

"That's terrorism too," said a third.

Everyone leaned forward, clutched the seatback in front of them, craned their necks. The bus circled a block and came to a second checkpoint. The driver spoke out his window:

"What's up, officer?"

Eric caught a few words of the reply: "Just keep on... next corner... left..."

"They never tell you nothing," said a voice farther up front.

Finally, the bus cleared the cordoned area. The High Roller appeared in the large front windshield.

"I don't even like normal Ferris wheels," the man in the seat behind Eric said. "I wouldn't go up in that thing if you paid me."

"It costs more if you go at night," a woman remarked.

The Asian woman had fallen asleep and the gentle sound of her breathing seemed to emit an all-clear signal. They were safe. No terrorists. No local nut. Only a giant Ferris wheel and miles of desert to come. Eric spotted two men scavenging a trash container behind a supermarket. His Sadhu journey had hit some lows, he thought, but he hadn't rummaged in pestiferous alleys. He had come close more than once, but a stink-hole stench and noxious fumes had driven him off. Did that mean he would arrive back in Ashland still possessing a shred of dignity?

He found it hard to imagine Kathy in a hospital. Her rock-hard body had always been impervious to injury and illness. She coughed and blew her nose one week a year and quickly returned to running ten miles a day. He couldn't remember her ever complaining of a headache. Maybe a car had slammed into her while she was out on a run. He winced, imagining screeching tires, broken bones, her blood on the road. He had always warned her to be careful. Years ago when they still spoke. But she was alive, that much he knew, alive and covered by insurance, probably on the mend right then, maybe completely mended. Meanwhile, he was rushing pell-mell toward a home he had abandoned and a wife who had abandoned him. Rushing in a slow-motion bus. A man who wanted to wake out of slumber was doubly damned. You think you're in hell; therefore, you are.

He let out an audible sigh, which seemed to penetrate the Asian woman's sleep. Her head rolled, landing her nose an inch from his shoulder. He experienced a moment of intimacy and wondered who she was, what she was dreaming, what language she was dreaming in. Funny how they hadn't exchanged a word yet shared some elemental closeness. If she awoke, would she jerk her head away in embarrassment or offer a timid, friendly smile and slip back into dreams?

He shifted positions, gave her more room, gave himself more space for thought. It didn't matter if he walked or rode Greyhound. The same question dogged at his heels, at his wheels. *What do you seek?* He was no longer who he had been. Yet he was returning to square one. Except now with a prayer to pray. Maybe the question had changed. *What do you ask?* He would have to get a cell phone, credit cards, a driver's license.

He fell asleep and woke up to find the bus parked in a

station. It could have been anywhere. He yawned, rubbed his eyes, rubbed his chin, and discovered the seat next to him vacant. He had really conked out. The Asian woman had somehow climbed over him and he hadn't noticed. Most of the bus was empty, only dozing passengers remained. Then the others came back, squeezing down the aisle bearing food and drink, wreaking of hastily smoked cigarettes. He stood up and let the Asian woman back in. She offered him half of a plastic-wrapped tuna sandwich and he accepted, promising to get the next one.

"Do you live in The City too?" she asked. She pointed at his ticket stub peeking out of the net bag on the seat back in front of him, revealing the name San Francisco.

"I'm catching an onward bus to Oregon," he answered. "To Ashland."

She had offered him a sandwich and some conversation, filling his old needs: hunger and loneliness. He felt like he had re-entered civilization. He asked if she had been in Vegas on a holiday. She perked up and answered that she had been there to apply for a job. She had passed two previous interviews by Zoom and the company had required her to appear in person for a third. They had offered to fly her down but she was frightened of planes and hadn't wanted to drive all the way either. The interview had gone well, she said, but now she didn't know if she wanted to live in Vegas. "I knew it was weird, but I didn't know it was that weird."

She went on talking, spilling out every thought that crossed her mind—her last job, her current job, her ex-boss, her ex-husband—until she eventually put them both to sleep. Eric blinked his eyes open every now and then, took in barren land flashing past, bits of passenger conversation, the smell of bodies now thick in the stale air. Sometimes he opened his eyes and found the Asian woman checking her cell phone, texting messages. Other times she blinked her eyes open as well, their faces only inches apart. "I used to be the regional product manager," she told him in a whisper. "Used to think I was someone important. Then I learned I was just a person like everyone else."

"I used to be a person too," he said. "Then all that changed."

"I know what you mean."

In the San Francisco Greyhound terminal, he helped her get a large green suitcase with a purple bow out of the luggage hold. He walked her through the station and out the street door onto Folsom. They stood in the shade beneath towering glass edifices. Pedestrians passed by on either side of them.

"Watch your step in there," she warned, nodding back at the station.

"I will," he promised, raising his battered day pack off his shoulder, "but I don't have much worth watching."

"Thanks for listening," she said. "People never do any more."

He reached out to shake her hand but she suddenly threw herself forward. Her body pressed against his, and he felt flesh and curves, not sexual, just feminine warmth, tenderness.

A cabbie loaded her suitcase into his trunk and they

drove off. Eric couldn't recall the last time a woman had hugged him. His body still trembled. He wanted to shout after the taxi, but didn't know what to shout. Three hours later he boarded the bus to Ashland. The vehicle was half empty. He had two seats to himself so he stretched out his legs, kicked off his shoes, watched small towns pass by: Hersey, Arbuckle, Williams. He scratched an itch on his jaw, felt stubble. I need a shave, he thought.

Then the bus rolled into Redding and he sat up. Now he remembered the last time a woman had embraced him. It had happened right there where dancing Shiva lived. His leave-taking from Donny's Diner. Mary and Glenda had hugged him so strongly the Mexican dishwasher's eyes had filled with tears, as had his own. "You always got a home here," Donny had told him.

The bus had a forty-minute layover, enough time for Eric to rush over to the diner and surprise the crew. But he couldn't bring himself to do it. Nor could he summon the grit to visit Shiva in front of the Old City Hall Arts Center. Shiva, the transformer, the destroyer of evil, Shiva the Supreme, who created and protected the universe.

At the start of his Sadhu journey, he had taken over three weeks to arrive in Redding. He had suffered an aching back and injured foot. Now Ashland was only three hours away and he was terrified. Was he rushing to get there out of genuine care and concern, or outright guilt and madness? He only knew he had to get there, had to see Kathy, had to play a part in an unknown drama. The hour of penance and homecoming had arrived.

So he walked around the corner and entered a place called the Déjà Vu Restaurant & Espresso Café. He told the waitress he wanted the fastest thing she could serve. She said they had a Déjà Vu Veggie Benedict just sent back to the kitchen as a mistaken order.

"That's for me," he said.

A moment later a spinach, tomato and avocado Eggs Benedict concoction landed in front of him. It was delicious but twice the size of any meal he had eaten in months. He asked for a doggy bag and returned to the bus where he found a new seat partner, an eighteen-year-old kid in torn t-shirt and rent jeans. The kid threw a smug glance at his Goodwill clothes, stuffed a pair of earbuds into his ears and began to play a mobile game Eric thought he recognized. As a teen, Billy had played it or something similar for hours on end, driving him into fits. Eventually Eric had realized that Billy had no real interest in the game; he had been playing it only to enrage him. Jessica had never played video games or tried to irritate him. She had been a withdrawn child, who had read Harry Potter in her room. She had never been the least bit aggressive. Not until that last phone call.

The bus pulled out of the station and drove through Redding. Neither Donny's Diner nor dancing Shiva appeared in the window.

Chapter Twenty-five

Three hours later the bus dropped Eric and two other passengers at the Safeway on Siskiyou Boulevard in Ashland. Thirty yards across the parking lot a man was loading groceries into the trunk of a blue Mercury. Eric quickly turned aside. It was the neighbor who owned Cookie, the cocker spaniel. He was obviously heading home after shopping and would offer Eric a ride to Barbara Street, a ride full of questions. Why hadn't he seen him around lately? Where was his own car? Why was he dressed like the bums who frequented the Goodwill Retail Store on Tolman Creek Road?

Eric waited until the man had driven off and then started walking. The Rogue Valley Transportation District provided a public transit bus that ran from one end of Ashland to the other, covering the two-mile run in a couple of minutes, but he wanted to arrive home as he had left: on foot.

Halfway on, he grew conscious of his weather-beaten face, disheveled hair, stubbly chin. Not exactly the conquering hero arriving home. He should have planned it better. He had no key. He would have to ring the doorbell of his own house. If Kathy wasn't home, what would he do—take a nap in the garden and wait until she arrived? Then what?

Fifteen minutes later familiar street signs sent a charge through him. Blackberry Lane, Diane Street. Then Barbara Street. He didn't know if he should turn tail and run or drop to his knees and kiss the pavement. A short way down the block, he came upon one of the neighborhood kids, a fifteen-year-old boy mowing a lawn.

"Hey, Mr. Tyler. How you doing?"

"Fine," Eric lied. "Looks like you're hard at it."

"Yeah, almost done."

A minute later Eric arrived at his house. He had expected some change. A painted mailbox or new curtains in the bay window, but everything looked the same. He approached the front entrance. Kathy's entrance. Then he noticed that the lawn was overgrown and weedy. The bushes near the bay window needed trimming and the window itself needed some Windex and a squeegee. The place had a dusty look, almost haunted. He felt pressure in his head, his silent prayer turning into a steady roar. He pressed the doorbell, listened to the vintage *ding-dong*. No answer. Maybe he really would have to nap in the garden. Or turn tail. He looked at the houses across the street. No one around. He had made a mistake. He never should have returned.

Just then the inner door opened. A tall woman appeared on the other side of the screen door. She had a bush of silver-gray hair with long white streaks. In her mid forties, she wore a black sweater and black ankle-length skirt. A witch, he thought. All she needed was a broomstick and a wart on her nose, but her creamy complexion was smooth, her nose classical Greek: straight bridge, slightly pointed tip, narrow nostrils. He was already tense and the sight of an unknown woman answering his front door rattled him more.

"Who are you?" he said.

He had spoken too quickly, too aggressively. Her eyes became dark stones. She looked behind him, scanned the sidewalk, the street.

"Tell me what you want," she said.

His nervousness gave way to irritation. "I want to come in. This is my house and I want to know what you're doing in it. Where's Kathy? Where's Jessica?"

Her gaze swept over his clothes. She took a small step back. "If you know someone who lives here," she said evenly, "you should call and arrange an appointment."

"An appointment?" He laughed out loud. "Listen, just open the door."

"I'm not going to open anything," she said. "Now please leave."

She was his height and their eyes met on a level plane. He sensed the shadowed recesses of a powerful psyche but despite her composed bearing, something about her was off balance, disturbed. On impulse he reached forward, grabbed the screen door handle and pulled. It was locked. Fear and anger filled her dark gaze.

"Go away!" she commanded.

"Listen, damn it. I'm Eric Tyler. This is my house. My home. I don't know who you are. Open the door."

The woman raised her voice. "If you don't leave right now, I'm going to call the police."

"Call whoever you want," he said. "I'm not going anywhere except into my own damn house."

She slammed the door shut. He heard the lock turn, then the security chain slide into its track.

"Open the damn door," he shouted.

He stepped across the lawn toward the bay window. She was already there pulling the drapes closed. He shouted again but she ignored him so he started around the side of the house. When he arrived at the rear, he found the back door locked, just as he had left it a year ago. All the curtains were drawn. Had he left them like that when he departed on his Sadhu journey? He couldn't remember. He trotted around the far side to the kitchen window. She was already shuttering the blinds. He raised his voice against the glass. "Whoever you are, could you listen to me for a minute?"

Again no answer. He spun on his heel and marched back to the rear door, breathing heavily. Then he noticed the garden. Overrun with weeds, even more unkempt than the front yard. The barbecue grill had tipped over and lay half-buried in a pile of dirt. One of the warming racks had rusted and a gas valve looked broken. Nearby, a plastic bag had become entangled in a cranberry bush. He had never been a fanatic horticulturist but he had kept the yard clean, the plants watered and trim. He felt like he was standing in someone else's garden. The clock had stopped ticking. He was no longer in the world. Rapture, illusion, a cave of flames. He recalled his blowup with Jessica and wondered if Kathy had somehow managed to sell the house after all. Maybe this witch woman was the new owner and didn't care if everything went to seed.

He headed back to the front of the property, dead set on ringing the bell as long as it took to get her to answer the door again. As he came around the side, two patrol cars pulled up at the curb. Instantly he knew he had been right. He should have planned it better, shouldn't have been in such a rush. A female officer stepped out of the first car, a male out of the second. Eric headed toward them.

"Thanks for getting here so fast," he said, bathing them in a friendly grin. "I appreciate it, but I'm afraid I might be wasting your time."

Behind him, he heard the front door of the house open. The female officer walked up the path while the male told Eric to step toward his patrol car. Eric could sense eyes peering out of living room windows across the street.

"Wait," he said. "This is my house and I don't know that woman. I want to hear what she says."

The cop blocked his path. "Sir, I have just told you to step toward my patrol car. I am a police officer and that was a direct order. Did you understand it?"

Eric realized the cop was about to do the obvious: ask for his ID.

"Yes, of course, thank you," he said, "and before you ask, I just want to say that I lost my driver's license... lost all my ID." He began to stammer. "I mean it might be somewhere in the house. I've been gone a long time and I'm just arriving home. I'll have to renew all my ID. I know that. I should have done it before but... I haven't yet." His nerves were so hot-wired he couldn't tell if he was still grinning or not. "But you can ask the neighbors. Ask them and they'll verify—"

The cop's look was half smirk, half withering stare. "You're telling me I should pay a visit to all the neighbors and ask if they know you?"

"Not all of them. The guy over there just arrived home from Safeway a minute ago. You can ask him. I'm... just suggesting it as a way of establishing my identity. It won't take long and—"

"Thank you for the suggestion, sir. Now step toward my car. I don't want to issue the order again."

Eric turned, nails digging into palms. "Come on, officer," he spoke over his shoulder. "It'll only take a minute. Ask the guy. Even his dog knows me."

When they had come up next to the patrol car, the cop said: "Remain standing there. Right on that spot. Do not move from that position."

He walked up the path and met the female officer halfway. They spoke out of earshot, both their bodies turned in Eric's direction. Twice they looked at him. The woman in the doorway was also looking, her gaze still dark and wary. Then both officers went to the front door and spoke to the woman. The male officer stood at an angle, his eye still on Eric.

Waiting in upheaval, Eric suddenly recalled a middle-of-the-night incident from a dozen years ago. Kathy had shaken him awake, saying she had heard a prowler outside the house. In the moonlit darkness he had assured her that it was probably a stray cat or fallen branch but then he heard noises as well. He scrambled out of bed, told her to call the police. Once he had roused Jessica, he grabbed her aluminum softball bat and hurried both her and Billy down the hall. He stood with his family, sweaty hands gripping the bat, Jessica whimpering at his side. Twice they heard strange noises and twice more Kathy called the police. They finally showed up an hour later and found nothing suspicious. They said it was a windy night and they had received dozens of calls. "We could have been killed twenty times over," Eric snapped at them. "Two hours to get here!" Now he was the prowler outside his own house and the police had arrived in two minutes flat.

The tall woman continued speaking and the female officer jotted a few notes into a pad. Finally, their conversation ended. The male officer approached Eric, opened the back door of his patrol car and told him to get in.

"What did that woman say?" Eric asked. "Who is she?"

"Get in the car, sir."

Eric slid onto the seat and the cop shut the door. The tall woman had gone back inside and the corner of the bay window curtain had parted a crack. In the shadows Eric could just make out the side of her face, her bushy silver hair. The cop got in behind the wheel and started the engine. On the way down Barbara Street, Eric remained quiet as long as he could. When they reached the corner, he leaned forward.

"Officer, could you please tell me if that woman is a friend of my wife's or a renter or the new owner or what?" When the cop made no reply, Eric couldn't stop his voice from raising. "You have to tell me what she's doing in my house."

The cop's eyes stayed on the road.

"I'll tell you something else instead," he said. "Do yourself a favor and shut up."

CHAPTER TWENTY-SIX

Three days of paperwork and shame followed. Eric had no choice but to submit to cavalier questions and snooty looks, to be chewed up and swallowed by the system he had cast aside a year ago. Once digested, the powers that be spit him out as an officially stamped resident of the picturesque town of Ashland in the great state of Oregon. (State Motto: *Alis Volat Propriis.* "She flies with her own wings.") Governmental, legislative and banking authorities proclaimed him a member in good standing of the community: a taxpayer, retired businessman, registered voter, homeowner and married father of two as well as a season ticket holder at the Shakespeare Festival (last few years excepted). In short, no longer dead onto himself.

So he was grateful for the hard-won approval—grateful to have the process over and done with—but his deepest, heartfelt thanks went to Mabel Shoemaker, chubby and stalwart waitress at the Bright Day Café. Not Earl, Pete and Tony, his best friends and great golf buddies, but Mabel, whom he had tipped fifty cents every workday morning for a dozen years. What did that amount to—a thousand dollars? A tiny price to pay for her generosity of spirit. When he entered the Bright Day, she served him even before he could speak and he saw his reflection in her cheerful gaze. He saw his unchanging essence, his undying self: he was a coffee-and-roll guy.

"You look super," Mabel said. "What kind of diet have you been on?"

She had always been his morning pal and well-wisher. Now she became the great friend who welcomed him home. Exhausted by the grilling the police had put him through, barred by an unknown woman from entering his own house, anxious yet fearful of seeing Kathy, he opened his wounded heart to Mabel. When he had finished, she said: "Eric, you're coming home with me. No arguing. I've got a spare room and you're going to use it until you're back on your feet."

So three days wasted punching through red tape, but he wasn't going to make the same blunder twice. When next he rang his own doorbell, he would be a citizen with an identity, not a homeless vagrant. The last bit of paperwork he put in order was at the bank, which gave him access to his monthly pension. It also gave him a view into his joint account with Kathy, now thirty thousand dollars less than when he had left. "My god," he thought. "We're broke again." But the Assistant Branch Manager also had some good news: in Eric's absence, housing prices had risen. Technically, he no longer had an underwater mortgage.

He had resisted calling Jessica until he had everything else in order. He guessed that the witch woman wasn't a renter because he had overheard one of the cops refer to his case as a "domestic matter." If Kathy had been in the hospital as Jessica had said, then the woman had to be some kind of assisted-living person. When he finally called Jessica, the sound of her *hello* made him clutch.

"Hi, angel. This is Dad. I'm just calling to say I'm back. Also to say *hi* and share a few... thoughts."

He was speaking directly into her ear but felt and sounded like he was leaving a message on her answering machine. He had always been able to sense her freezing up, even over the phone. She had just congealed into ice.

"I wanted to talk to you about Mom and the house," he went on. "I know you said Mom was in the hospital. But there's a woman at the house and—"

"Anna." Her tone was hesitant, guarded. "That's Anna."

"Oh, okay, and what's Anna doing there?"

A sharply indrawn breath. Then the sound of teeth grinding. Eric took in a gulp of air himself. Many years before he and Kathy had started shouting, they had simmered. As a little girl, Jessica had gotten it into her head that she was to blame for that unspoken rage. Guilt and confusion froze her into silence.

"Okay listen, honey," he said. "I don't know what's going on but I know that's my house and I'm moving back in. So call Anna and tell her I'm coming. That way she won't be surprised or frightened. I'll talk to her when I get there and she and I can work everything out." He let a moment pass. "And I want to ask you how—"

"Dad, I can't talk right now. I—I think someone's at the door. I better go."

The line clicked dead before he could blurt out: *How's Mom? What the hell's wrong with her? What the hell's going on? Have you heard from Billy?*

The hollowness in the pit of his stomach confirmed that he was no longer anywhere else, nor anyone else. He had come home. He was himself again. His daughter was grinding her teeth in his ear. Yet he knew that no matter how much she froze up, she remained efficient. At that moment she would be calling Anna and dutifully repeating everything he had just said. He also knew he couldn't endure any more delay. He had to get over to Barbara Street. He opened a glass cabinet in Mabel's living room and pulled out a bottle of Passport Scotch. He splashed some into a glass and drank. The first drop of hard liquor in a year. It made him grit his own teeth.

An hour later he arrived at his house. The prayer in his head droned louder. He rang the bell. Anna opened the door, once again dressed darkly, this time a black cardigan and jeans. It made for a striking contrast with her bush of white-streaked, silver hair. Street-level elegance cloaked in a kind of uniform: prison garb, a nun's habit, a witch's cape. He stood straight and tall, trying to gain a half inch over her height. Then he unfurled a rehearsed apology like a personalized welcome mat. He felt like he was about to enter her house, not his.

"I think we got off on the wrong foot the other day," he said.

"Mr. Tyler, you—"

"Please call me Eric."

"Eric... you've arrived at a difficult moment. I need an hour with Kathy."

Once again he had the feeling she had a screw loose, maybe two. She was off balance, that was for sure, but also alert, clever, tough. A one-track mind, maybe some axe to grind.

"Please be patient and wait," she said.

She stood aside, swinging her long arm across the living room toward the hallway. A simple gesture, but powerful enough to compel him to follow its bidding. Or perhaps he just felt powerfully compelled to follow the hallway down to what had been his half of the house.

Stepping over the threshold, he took a quick look around. It was the first time he had been in the living room since he and Kathy had split the house in half. He recognized the television, the fireplace, a macramé wall hanging, Kathy's favorite serving bowl, but the sofa and two end tables had been pushed against the side wall. The marble coffee table held medical supplies.

"Please," Anna said, again gesturing toward the hallway.

He sensed that Kathy was in the room to his left, Billy's old bedroom. He had long since squashed the notion that she might have a broken arm. Something was dreadfully wrong and once again he was unprepared for whatever it was. So he kept his mouth shut and did as he was told. He headed for the hallway and continued down to the kitchen. The fridge greeted him like an old friend humming a once shared song. But strange jars and containers of dried herbs lined the countertop along with oils and tinctures, a muslin bag, a sack of green clay, a pestle and mortar. He peered at the labels aligned in alphabetical order. Aloe Vera, Chamomile, Comfrey, Echinacea, Golden Seal Mullein, Plantain, St. Johns Wort. It looked like discount day at a natural health shop.

The door to his end of the house was locked. He opened

the nearest cabinet, reached into a corner and came back with a key. He sensed it hadn't been touched since he had left on his Sadhu journey. He unlocked the door. Pushing it open, he was struck by a musty odor. Like entering a tomb.

The note he had left Kathy was on his desk pinned beneath his Seattle Mariners mug. His house and car keys were there as well. Nothing had been moved even an inch. All the bureaucracy he had just painstakingly reacquired. Bank book, credit cards, driver's license, cell phone. He ran his forefinger across the desktop and came back with dust. Dead flies like peas escaped from a pod lay along the window ledge. He had buried himself and no one in his family had ventured into his crypt.

He unlocked the rear door and propped it open, letting in a gust of fresh air. Outside, he took a closer look at the garden. Tree branches drooped above the undernourished soil. Lichen had grown over the brick walls. The fallen barbecue grill emitted defeat.

Back inside, he opened his closet. Shirts, pants, sport coats hung as if patiently awaiting his return. Five pair of spotless track shoes on the floor. A pair of glasses in the top dresser drawer. He selected a shirt and jeans, underwear and socks. He had showered every day at Mabel's but now he scrubbed his flesh until it turned red and raw, kneaded shampoo into his hair until his scalp burned. After toweling down, he shaved and splashed a handful of aftershave onto his face. Dressing, he had to tighten his belt two notches. The mirror revealed his weathered complexion, his inflamed gaze. It's me, he thought. I'm home. Thank all that's holy, I'm home. And now, finally, the reason he had come. He marched down to the other end of the house and met Anna just as she emerged from Kathy's room. She noticed his change of clothes. She noticed everything, he thought.

"I want to see my wife," he said forcefully.

"Your ex-wife," she replied in a lowered voice. She motioned him away from the door. "I won't wake her out of schedule. It breaks her rhythm. Let's have a cup of tea."

"No, thank you."

He was in his own house. A stranger didn't offer him anything. Besides, he had seen the herbal dispensary in the kitchen and guessed she would concoct some witch's brew to calm his nerves. He didn't want tranquility. He wanted answers.

"Well, I'm going to have a cup," she said, turning down the hall.

He was tempted to walk straight into Kathy's room, but then thought better of it. He trailed behind Anna down to the kitchen.

"Tell me what's going on," he said. "How sick is Kathy? Are you a nurse?"

A glint of surprise lit her dark eyes and he saw tiredness there as well. She sat on one of the wooden counter stools and motioned him toward the other. Again her gesture was imperious, a motion made by someone used to being obeyed. He remained standing.

"I'm a caregiver," she said. "I thought you had spoken with your daughter."

"Only briefly."

"So you don't know anything about Kathy's condition?"

"Not a damn thing and I want you to start telling me."

She reached for a tea bag, appraising him under her forceful gaze. Now he was sorry he had remained standing. She looked like a queen on her throne. He felt like a vassal petitioning her.

"First of all," she said, her tone still low, "please don't raise your voice to me. I don't like it. I have a patient to care for and I already have enough on my hands. It's not my job to deal with family problems or to pass information between family members. Your daughter should have explained the situation to you."

"She was... busy."

"Your daughter is a child."

"What?"

"Your daughter is emotionally stunted. She's a 23-year-old child. She makes my work more difficult and if you do the same, I'll leave this disturbed house." She spoke without blinking, without moving her hands or even her fingers on the teabag. "Now I'm going to make some tea. Join me if you want."

He manufactured a pleasant smile and sat on the stool. She was probably a good person, he told himself, just doing her job. A lowly paid and difficult job. And, yes, she looked exhausted from a bad night. And, yes, he should be grateful for the help she provided. But he couldn't shake the feeling that he didn't like her. Haughtily waiting on him in his own kitchen, she made not the slightest acknowledgment that they now sat in his home, not hers. He held himself in check and accepted her calming tea, but as soon as he got matters under control, he would remind her who owned the roof above her silver head, the walls around her regal person.

CHAPTER TWENTY-SEVEN

Anna moved her tea mug on the counter, set her gaze level on his. Her dark eyes revealed little, at least to him, but besides tiredness he sensed some blade of pain in their depths, perhaps only the pain she witnessed daily as a caregiver.

"I'm very sorry," she said, "sorry to say that Kathy has Stage IV pancreatic cancer. I'm sorry for you and sorry that I have to be the one to pass on this terrible news. Kathy is dying."

His hand tightened around his own tea mug. He could feel the heat across his palm; for an instant he wondered if his fingers were burning. Ever since talking to Jessica on Jamie John's cell, he had prepared himself for this moment. Now the moment had arrived and once again he was nakedly unprepared.

"How much longer does she have?"

"You should speak to your daughter. And to Kathy's oncologist and radiation therapist. I'm not a medical professional."

"But you must know what the oncologist said."

"I only know what Jessica told me. According to her, the oncologist said Kathy doesn't have long. The case manager nurse from the Hospice agrees."

"What about you? As her caregiver, would you say the same?"

She shifted on her stool, displeased by the question. Her

long hand rose and she brushed a streak of silver hair off the side of her face, momentarily revealing an ugly white scar beneath her jawline. A facelift, Eric thought, and a clumsy one at that. He wouldn't have pegged her as a candidate for plastic surgery but he could imagine her trying to save a few dollars on the job. You get what you pay for and she had a scar to prove it.

"A week ago Kathy could still speak clearly," she said. "Now she struggles to say two words. She has stopped eating and she's on morphine."

"I'm asking how long you think she has."

"Her light is fading. That's all I can tell you."

"Okay, that's it." He shoved the tea mug aside, lurched up onto his feet. "I want to see her now."

Anna made no move to leave her own stool. "You might want to take a minute before going in."

"I've waited long enough."

"I mean take a minute to center yourself."

That stopped him. They were in his house but on her terrain, whether he liked her or not. He slid back onto his stool.

"Drink your tea," she said.

It was a command and he obeyed. The liquid flooded down his throat, releasing warmth into his chest, his stomach. Caught in a swirl of emotion, he realized she was right. He should center himself. Find some faith, a balm, his prayer. She was also right when she said she shouldn't have been the one telling him the news. No matter how grand she acted, she was a modestly paid employee hired to bathe and dress, to cook a meal, prepare a mug of tea.

"What do you suggest?" he said.

"Watch your words. Don't say anything that will hold her back."

"Back?"

"From where she's going."

Now in a cold sweat, he had to admit he hadn't even considered that he would speak to Kathy, let alone what he might say. He experienced a surge of guilt, as if he had been the cause of everything, as if his Sadhu journey had been nothing but a selfish act from the start. His life was such sweet idiocy. Of course, he had no way of knowing Kathy would become ill, but that was exactly why families stuck together—because accidents, emergencies, unexpected horrors occurred.

He followed Anna down the hall. Months tramping dust-blown roads and his legs had never trembled so violently. She pushed open the door to what used to be Billy's room and his thoughts leapt to his wayward son. Did he know his mother was dying? Did he care?

The chrome guardrail of a hospital bed threw him back to Father Glenn's cell. Even covered by a sheet, Kathy looked cadaverous. Her once robust complexion had turned as pallid as spent candle wax. Somehow he had expected to see her ill but in her same buff body. Anna took Kathy's hand and the bony fingers curved around Anna's grip.

"...na?" Kathy murmured. "... notha dream."

"You'll tell me later," Anna said, and Eric realized she meant later when he wasn't there. "You have a visitor. It's Eric. Eric is here. Remember, I told you he would come?"

She released her grip and Eric replaced her hand with

his. Kathy's fingers didn't curl over his hand as they had over Anna's. He couldn't tell if she lacked the strength or the will, but it was the first time he had touched his ex-wife in four years and it wrenched a sob out of him.

"I'm here now," he croaked futilely. "Everything's okay."

First time they had talked as well and there he was babbling stupidities. He searched for something else to say, something that wouldn't "hold her back." A great deal of time seemed to pass. He was aware of her withered hand, brittle bones in delicate flesh. Still warm. He sensed the morphine like a cloud around her.

"I've been away," he went on in a whisper. "But now I'm back. I'm home."

He could feel Anna stiffen behind him. Kathy's eyes had closed or perhaps they hadn't been open. He couldn't remember. Her baby blues. No longer so blue.

As soon as he and Anna were out of the room, he said: "I need some more tea."

What he really needed was a double shot of Maker's Mark. He used to keep a bottle stashed in his bedroom closet. First tea, then the Maker's. Back in the kitchen he sat on the same stool. Anna prepared more tea.

"What did Kathy mean," he asked, "when she said she'd had another dream?"

"She's had recurring dreams."

"What are they about?"

She studied her tea mug. "I'm not comfortable sharing that."

"Under the circumstances, I don't think it matters very much."

She went on examining her mug, let him figure out for himself that no answer was going to come his way. She was like a tour guide exasperated by day-tripper questions. He sensed her about to tell him, "I've got work to do and you're keeping me from it."

She was running things around here, he thought, running the course of his ex-wife's death. She wouldn't answer his question but thin lines had formed across her alabaster forehead. A question of her own.

"You just told Kathy that you were back," she said. "Did you mean that you have come to stay?"

So Jessica had only given her half the news, the easy half.

"This is my house," he answered. "I come and go as I please."

"Yes, of course. I'm asking if you have come to stay."

"You don't need to worry about that."

"I'm afraid I do," she said, "and I would appreciate an answer. Before I took over Kathy's care, Jessica and I agreed to certain terms. These aren't them."

"What do you mean?"

"Jessica should have told you all this."

"Yes, I agree. She should have. But she didn't. So why don't you tell me now?"

She smiled faintly. She didn't like him any more than he liked her.

"I only accept patients who have no one else to care for them. I take them on with the understanding that I will be their sole caregiver. Of course, I allow visits from family and friends, but I do not accept family or friends or anyone else living on the premises."

He blinked, narrowed his gaze. "What agency do you work for?"

"I don't work for an agency. I'm freelance."

"But... how do you manage everything on your own?"

"Jessica drops off food and supplies twice a week. The case manager nurse from the Hospice stops by every few days. That's all the help I require."

She poured the rest of her tea into the sink and rinsed her cup. Her movements were controlled but beneath the surface of her smooth facial skin she was seething.

"You can't ask me to move out of my own house," Eric said.

"I'm not asking that."

He caught the implication. She was asking herself if she would be the one to leave. She twisted her long fingers through a dish towel, then spoke in a kind of repressed royal rage.

"Kathy is my patient. I have to know what's going on around her so I can decide what's best for her. And what's best for me, because I come and go as I please also. If the situation in this sick house is changing, I want to know about it."

Eric stirred sugar into his tea, fighting to hold his tongue. He was still badly shaken over the sight of Kathy and the phrase "sick house" riled him. It echoed other nonsense phrases—wrong Feng Shui, strange vibes, no nourishment, bad juju—but this woman's tone and manner also struck a warning. She had just reminded him of his best days at DMT. At the time he wasn't freelance but he was as close to it as you could get in a topflight international ad agency. He was hot and he was in demand. King of the Planet. He had single-handedly won the Pierce-Gladding account in Austin, Texas. If he got fired or walked out of DMT in the morning, he could stroll into ten other ad agencies that afternoon. He didn't put up with guff from his superiors because his phone was ringing. Blue-chip headhunters were on the line. Anna had the same self-assured air. She was unlike any executive or program manager in the DMT marketing universe, and therefore out of his trajectory, beyond his orbit, but she knew her value, or thought she did. She knew her phone was ringing.

So he backed off. "I've been gone a long time," he said. "I've just arrived to a terrible situation. I still need to digest it all. Please try to understand."

She stared at him expressionless. He nodded as if they had reached a temporary understanding. He slipped off his stool and walked through the doorway into his end of the house, heading straight for the corner of the bedroom closet. The nook where he used to stash the Maker's was empty. He walked out the rear door. Not a good idea, he warned himself, but he still headed along Barbara Street, around the corner and down Tolman Creek Road. The same path he had taken at the start of his Sadhu journey, now with an unpainted face, now backsliding toward a liquor store.

He returned a half hour later with a pint of Maker's Mark, some corn chips and Anna's single phrase still in his head. *Kathy is dying.* He paused in the yard. A garden gone to seed, a home gone to a stranger, an ex-wife all but gone. In the end what good was prayer, whether contrition or petition, mumbled or not?

Inside, he sat at his desk, ate a corn chip, poured a measure of the Maker's. His laptop started instantly. It surprised him. Didn't an unused computer wilt like an untended garden? He did a Google search on caregiver agencies in the greater Ashland-Medford area and came up with twenty. Why had Jessica ever hired a freelance caregiver when the agencies offered every possible service: laundry, bathing, errands, diabetes, Parkinson's, heart conditions, terminal care? Dozens of photos of the caregivers themselves. Mostly women, ranging from eager young ladies to perky grannies. He read the "Who We Are" section of a Medford agency called National Home Service. He dialed their number and a friendly female voice came on the line. Then he hung up without saying a word. He took a sip of Maker's. He had just recalled Donny's dictum for his diner. *Never fire until day's end.*

CHAPTER TWENTY-EIGHT

Eric took another sip of Maker's and called Jessica. He avoided upbraiding her for failing to tell Anna he had come to stay but he still went straight to the point.

"Where'd you find this Anna?"

Haltingly, Jessica gave a rundown of her hunt for a caregiver. She had visited many of the agencies he had just viewed online and had also called most of the registries. The first two caregivers she had hired were useless. The third even worse. "You can't imagine what we went through." Her tone was accusatory. "What Mom went through." She emphasized that caregivers were generally qualified to help the elderly or disabled but wanted no part of a live-in situation with a Stage 4 terminal cancer patient. Then a work colleague had recommended Anna.

"We were lucky," Jessica said. "She was between jobs. I called her and she came to visit. Mom could still talk then and we all interviewed each other and it went great. Anna started that day and she's better than the other three put together."

"What do you mean 'interviewed each other'?"

"We got to know each other. Anna's careful about the patients she accepts."

"Maybe we should have been more careful too. She isn't connected to any agency or registry. She told me she's freelance."

"And flooded with job offers. Like I said, we were lucky."

"That's what I'm trying to tell you. I'm not sure how lucky we've been."

"What?"

She was biting down, grinding her molars.

"Let's just say I'm not Anna's biggest fan. How do you pay her?"

"I take it out of your and Mom's old joint account."

"You pay her in cash?"

"That's the way she wants it. Who cares?"

Eric wondered if she could hear him sipping the Maker's the same way he could hear her teeth grinding.

"I do, honey. I care a lot. I'm not happy about this person being in our house and what you're saying makes me even less happy."

"Dad, nobody cares if you're happy. Where were you when Mom and I were in the middle of hell? You were off being happy somewhere else. No way to even get hold of you. Now you drop back into our lives and act like you're in charge. Are you even listening to what I'm saying? Mom was in pain and dying and the whole scene was hell."

"She's still in pain and dying," Eric countered, "and I'm trying to prevent more hell. What happens if Anna hurts herself moving Mom... trips and breaks an arm?"

"Does she look like the type who trips and breaks bones? My god, Dad, you play make believe and expect—"

"But what if she does? Think about it for a second. Accidents happen. Who's responsible? Who pays for it? We do. She's on our property, working illegally for us. If she gets it into her silver head, she can even sue us. I don't trust her. She thinks she's queen of the hill and she's..." He couldn't find the word. "...weird."

"Weird?"

"All her herbs and potions and nose-in-the-air act. Only working with terminally ill patients—doesn't that sound a little weird to you?"

Jessica ground her teeth harder. "It didn't take long, did it? A week back and you're at it again. Thanks, Dad. I forgot how great things were without you around. Even with Mom dying they were great."

No doubt about it, Eric thought, he had left the world. She had never talked to him like that. Her Mom's illness had changed her, fused backbone onto her spine or extracted bitterness from her spleen.

"Honey, that's not fair. Calm down."

"I *was* calm and then you called. Stop thinking about yourself for two minutes and think about Mom? What does she want? Ask yourself that. Does Mom want Anna to be there or not?"

She hung up. He swished the Maker's around the glass and drank, recalling the scene of intimacy he had witnessed. Kathy's frail hand curled over Anna's, a whispered invitation into a dying woman's dreams. Damn it, he thought. He downed the glass. Jessica's rebuke had left him inflamed and careless and he should have cooled down before choosing a course of action but he reasoned that whatever he did would be better than doing nothing. So he stowed the glass and bottle of Maker's in the closet and took off in search of Anna.

He found her in the laundry room pulling clothes out of the dryer. She folded a towel and held it against her breast, regarding him incuriously. Again he caught himself stretching upward, trying to gain half an inch on her height.

"I think we got off on the wrong foot again," he began benignly.

She stared at him, showing scant interest in whatever he was about to say.

"I'd like to ask you to consider something," he went on. "This is my home and I'm going to stay..." It felt important to get that out. "...but I'd also like you to stay. I'm sure it's what Kathy wants as well. She needs you and I wouldn't get in the way."

Anna shook her head, pressing the towel to her breast. "I told you that's not possible."

"I can help."

"Help?" Clearly, the idea had never occurred to her. She saw him only as a hindrance. "Help doing what?"

"Everything," he answered. "I mean, who relieves you? You can't possibly handle all of this on your own. Laundry, meals, cleaning, bathing."

"I told you. I manage."

He regarded her closely. At one time she must have been an attractive middle-aged woman but exhaustion had sucked the color out of her face. She stood tall but she was drained, wobbling on her feet. Not weird, he thought, but damaged. Some tragedy in her past.

"I can help you manage better," he insisted. She shook her head again and was about to turn back to the dryer when he added: "I have experience."

She raised an unplucked eyebrow. "What experience?"

He told her about Chassors. He didn't mention his Sadhu journey but he described caring for Father Glenn. She looked at him doubtfully.

"Why would a monastery take you in for that?"

"They didn't. They took me in as an act of hospitality. They have a tradition. I was in a bad way and they offered me food and shelter. Later I wanted to repay their generosity. Then..." He didn't know how to go on. "Then it became a service. A chance to... to love and serve the world. You must know what I'm talking about. I can't imagine that you're here doing this work just to earn some money."

In opening himself, he thought he might establish some gentle line of communication, but she wanted no part of it. She spoke harshly:

"I'm here because I saw a terminally ill woman unable to die in peace. Incompetent caregivers, your daughter out of her depth, a dysfunctional family, a home in disarray."

She wasn't just putting him in his place, he thought, or even snapping back out of spite. She was testing him. Throwing the wreckage of his family into his face, judging how he would handle whatever she now had in mind.

"I saw disease," she went on, "and dire need and I knew that nobody else would do it. Or they would do it badly. That's why I'm here."

He kept his mouth shut but noted her tone. She didn't talk like a lowly paid caregiver. Angry yes, and crazy too, but she sounded like a qualified specialist with years of training under her belt. He wondered what she had been before becoming a caregiver. She must have studied something. Despite her temper, she had a solitary bookworm air. Sociology or current affairs or world history, and then she might have slid sideways into some form of therapy and then farther sideways into alternative remedies. Or maybe she hadn't slid. Maybe she had fallen out of a marriage or a profession and landed hard on her regal head.

"I'll do whatever you want," he said spontaneously. "Tell me what and I'll do it."

The sincerity in his voice surprised both of them. She stepped backwards, bumped into the washing machine. He was sorry he hadn't taken longer—hadn't centered himself—before speaking with her. Also sorry he hadn't rinsed the whiskey off his breath. She set the towel aside.

"Tell me about Kathy's obsessions," she said.

"I don't know what you mean."

"Obsessions surface at critical moments like divorce, like death. Especially death. Compulsions and passions seeking release."

"What obsessions are you talking about?"

"You tell me. You know her better. When I touch her—bathe her, massage her—I get the feeling she's been obsessed with her body—her curves and muscles, her breasts and hips, her being defined by flesh and bone, especially flesh. As her body withers, becomes shapeless, decomposes, that obsession is surfacing like a demon."

Eric stared at her. What kind of caregiver talk was this? "You mean she can't let go?"

She weighed the question, then said, "Show me your end of the house."

Uneasily, he led her down the hall. As soon as they passed out of the kitchen into his end, she became wary, like a huntress stalking prey. She examined windows, walls, spaces where there was nothing but space. When she turned, he caught another glimpse of the white scar beneath her jawline. She was torn, he thought. It wasn't just that Kathy needed her; she needed Kathy as well. If she refused his suggestion, she would have to leave the house and she couldn't bring herself to desert Kathy. She had her own obsession. He felt sure of it. All the same, he was glad he had stored the Maker's in the closet.

She looked at his bed, at his laptop still on, a screen saver now hiding the list of caregiver agencies.

"Before anything else," she said, "you have to bring this end of the house back to life. Opening the door to air it out isn't enough. I'll tell you the necessary steps but you have to take them. Do you understand?"

He had no idea what she was talking about but he was getting what he had said he wanted. Also, years of negotiations at DMT had alerted him to the moment a client hit a final position. He knew when someone would budge no further. From this point on, either he went along or she went away.

"Do you agree?" she said.

"Only if you tell me what I'm agreeing to."

"You're agreeing to purify a diseased house." She observed his reaction. "We can't adapt to you," she went on. "So you have to adapt to us. That means adapting to Kathy. Her rhythms, her needs, her demons. I do what she says and you have to do the same."

"I understand." Actually he doubted she did what anybody said, but he took her point. If she had a boss, it wasn't him. Not for the moment anyway.

CHAPTER TWENTY-NINE

The following afternoon at five-thirty Eric showed up at Jessica's apartment unannounced. He knew she would have just arrived home from work and he figured that once he stood in front of her she couldn't invent excuses not to see him. Anxious to embrace his daughter, he entertained the fugitive hope that time might have healed their wounds. He also wanted to get on the same wavelength with her before he took any action against Anna.

When the door swung open, he stepped forward with extended arms. And juddered to a stop. Jessica stood across the threshold, her lips split open in a blinding grin of enormous white teeth.

"Well," she urged. "Say something."

"It's... it's great to see you."

"I mean about my teeth."

She smiled wider, flaunting her incisors like a game show hostess.

"Great to see them too," he said. "I was just going to tell you. They're spectacular. Really..." He struggled for the word.

"Awesome," she said.

"That's it. Awesome. Let me come in and take a better look."

Before he could hug her, she turned and led him across the living room toward a bookshelf, where she picked up an antique hand mirror. They stood side by side staring at her reflection in the glass. Another huge white smile.

"Really awesome," he said. Then it hit him. His voice echoed bitter hurt. "I wondered how thirty thousand dollars vanished from our account. I guess now I know."

Jessica's face went crimson. For a second he mistook her emotion as shame, but it was outrage. She stormed past him, marched into her bedroom, rattled a drawer and stormed back out bearing a three-inch thick folder labeled "Mom." She thrust it at him. He opened it and found a stack of bills. Incurred medical expenses not covered by health insurance. Co-pays, Beta-carotene supplements, equipment rental, lab tests, anesthesiologist, external dietary consultation, pain management, caregiver salaries.

"Just so you know," she said murderously, "I paid for my prosthetics out of my own pocket and a loan that's got me in debt up to my molars."

Now his own face went red and not from outrage. The bills proved that he had not only been wrong about her teeth, but that he had no idea what had been going on in his absence. He had wondered how Kathy could so suddenly contract cancer, but now he saw long months of horror unfolding in ruthless stages from minor stomach pain to surgery to metastasis to morphine injections and hospice care. Sudden and shocking for him maybe, but bleak and never-ending for Kathy and Jessica.

He apologized as many times as he could, saying that his remark had been thoughtless and cruel. He blamed it on tiredness, stupidity and anxiety over finding Kathy in such a terrible state. Finally, Jessica seemed to relent. She picked up the mirror again.

"Besides," she said, "whatever my prosthetics cost, they're worth a million. I've been waiting years and it's like a total change. They're a super-confidence builder."

"I can see that," Eric said.

She put the mirror back on the shelf and studied him.

"Your hair's turned white," she said, "and you've lost a lot of it."

"Well, I've been gone almost a year."

"And you're thinner. Too thin, if you ask me."

She sat on the sofa and he took the armchair. Her ragdoll cat Raggy wandered out of the kitchen, sniffed at Eric's pant cuff and hopped up onto the back of the sofa, where he purred next to Jessica's ear. Eric supposed that Jessica's prosthetics were normal sized but her beaming smile distracted him. She had always thrust a hand in front of any sunny expression.

"It's wonderful to see you, hon," he said sincerely. "And wonderful to be back. Despite what you might think, Mom was glad to see me too."

Her smile vanished and her eyes welled up. Raggy stirred next to her shoulder but went on purring.

"It's been hard," Jessica said, wiping the flat of her hand over her cheek. "Those bills aren't half of it. You can't imagine. You haven't been here."

"I'm sorry for that," he replied, "sorry for a lot of things."

"That doesn't help anyone."

"But maybe it's better if I apologize than if I don't. Anyway, I'm here now and I'll do my best to help Anna."

"Help her? She said you could stay?"

"That's not her call. It's my house." He was sick of repeating the phrase.

"Your house and Mom's."

"I think I know that. Anyway, it's one of the reasons I want to talk to you. I'm not sure how much longer Anna is going to be with us."

"Why? What's wrong? What are you saying?"

"Take it easy. Just repeating what I told you on the phone. She's weird. Have you seen the kitchen counter? Herbs, dried plants, tinctures, green clay. She probably keeps a deck of Tarot cards in the fridge."

"My god, Dad, where have you been—Podunk, Nebraska? Welcome back to Ashland, Oregon. Reiki, Yoga, Vegan and energy workers on every corner. If she does any of that stuff, better for us, better for Mom."

"She also wants me to *purify* my end of the house."

"Great. You're talking about *weird*. A house chopped in half—you think that's normal?"

"All I'm saying is, let's keep our eyes open."

"Mine are open."

She meant that she saw him clearly for what he was. He recalled what Anna had said. It had irritated him at the time. Now he found it less irritating, more disturbing. *Your daughter is emotionally stunted.*

"I've still got Mom's cell," Jessica said. "Do you want it now?"

"Do you get many calls?"

"Not like before."

"You keep it then."

Raggy hopped down and settled in her lap. Jessica scratched the cat behind the ears. Kathy's cell, Eric thought, but not a single question about where he had been, what he had been doing, how he was. Maybe he hadn't effected a reconciliation and won her back, but he wanted one normal conversation before he left. His weakness, the indifference of the world.

"Do you still take your car to that mechanic guy in Medford?" he said.

She looked at him suspiciously. "Why are you asking that?"

"My car's been sitting in the garage all this time. I need the fluids changed before I try to start it. Do you have his number?"

A father and daughter talk about a day-to-day thing: cars, mechanics, brake fluid. She stood up. Raggy fell from her lap, thudded to the carpet and sprang across the room, disappearing in a flash of gray fur. Jessica hunted through a drawer, found a business card.

"He's got his own garage now," she said. "It's a few blocks from where he used to be."

"He still charges reasonable rates?"

"I guess so."

"Great. Thanks. And what about Billy. Have you heard anything from him?"

She pulled a face. "Why would I hear from him?"

"Or about him? Some news, maybe through one of his old buddies?"

"How would I know his 'old buddies'?"

That ended their normal conversation. He stepped forward to hug her goodbye. Their arms clattered together and they bumped noggins. She flashed one last smile and he left.

So he was back, but back to what? It wasn't just a matter of a bizarre homecoming, the shock of Kathy's illness and the peculiarity of Jessica's new teeth. He was back to the seductive comfort of American life. Hot showers, soft towels, a firm mattress. His Coaster Colton traditional leather armchair with its high-density, foam-padded seat. The delicate touch of his Poplin fabric dress shirts. Thick pile carpet beneath his blister-free feet. And Maker's Mark close-at-hand.

Then came the hour of purification and he swore damnation for ever agreeing to it. Curtains snapped and billowed, the tablecloth rose and fell and he lay in his king-sized bed feeling like he was still camped by the side of a road, in the ruins of some eviscerated house. Leaves and paper scraps skittered around the dark room, twirling like funnel ghosts in the shadows. Was Anna trying to purify the house of its poisoned past or purify it of him?

He awoke the next morning to crumpled leaves and papers strewn over his armchair, entangled in his hair. Throughout the day, random breezes re-scattered the mess. That evening Anna declared an end to the twenty-four-hour purge. She closed the door and windows and put a match to a wand of white sage. He watched her, his suspicion about witchcraft confirmed.

When the sage caught fire, she blew out the flames and instructed him to walk in a clockwise direction. Silently cursing her, he took the sage in his right hand and did three circuits of his end of the house. As smoke wafted onto walls and into corners, he discovered himself silently chanting his unknown prayer. Afterwards he and Anna stood out in the garden and watched the smoke curl and drift against the windows. The past up in smoke.

"It's called smudging," Anna said.

He made no reply. Twenty minutes later, back inside, the house aired out, she said, "From now on the kitchen doors stay open."

She walked down the hallway to the other end, her long stride decisive, self-assured, silver hair bobbing. Witch, he thought again. Yet in the following hours he had to admit the house seemed to take on a lighter air.

That night he kept vigil by Kathy's bedside, much as he had in Father Glenn's cell, but Kathy was no venerable priest schooled in an ancient spiritual tradition, buoyed by lifelong faith. A fitness instructor no longer fit, she was his fifty-seven-year-old ex-wife and she had undergone titanic changes in the year he had been gone, in the years since they had last spoken. Did she even want him around? For all he knew, she longed to depart existence minus his emotions on the scene. And what about Abe, her lover, the personal trainer adept at weight and cardio-workout routines? What part did he play in her leave-taking?

Bitterly, Eric wondered if this was why he had returned—for a teary soap opera, a melodramatic wait for death while chanting unknown prayers. What was he supposed to do—ask her forgiveness, make another ridiculous confession, say he was sorry for the grief he had caused, sorry for the mess they had made of their family, their children? No thanks. The death watch had only begun and he already wanted her to hurry up and die. Then he could feel relief and get on with things, get back on the road or get on with some kind of life. Get a witch out of the house.

He held Kathy's hand. "Just in case it means something," he murmured, "in case it somehow matters... I'm here."

Her hand remained limp in his. She was on the threshold of nonbeing. Afloat in a morphine cloud. Maybe she was obsessed as Anna had suggested. He had to admit that he sensed demons near at hand, as if at any moment they would cause the electric hospital bed to rise, tilt sideways, drop its chrome safety rail and send Kathy rolling into oblivion.

Through the day Anna barely said a word except to give a direction or make a request. It seemed she was pointedly ignoring him, throwing a cold shoulder of disapproval, perhaps even loathing. That or maybe she just wasn't interested. She was busy with Kathy's care, busy with a hundred chores, busy in her private world of caregiving. She was obsessed too, he thought again. Possessed by her own demons.

"I want to ask you something," he said one afternoon. "Has Kathy ever talked about me—I mean, when she could still talk? I understand that you don't want to share her dreams. That's private." How did she even know what was dream and what was morphine? "But this would help me understand what connection—if any—I still have with her."

Anna hesitated. The first time he had seen her show uncertainty. So Kathy had talked and Anna didn't want to reveal what she had said.

"It's not about holding her back," he persisted, "but about letting her go."

It was also the first time Anna's dark eyes had not gazed directly into his. She looked aside, spoke in a monotone.

"Kathy said you were a coward. She said you didn't have the guts for love. Or for anything else of value, starting with poetry." Now she looked straight at him. "She said you abandoned it and afterwards you feared and abandoned every other thing or person worth loving that came into your life. She said you had abandoned it all so that was how you had ended up. Abandoned."

Hours later, he still felt carved into small pieces. He sat in his armchair, cold and broken. He couldn't even bring his hand to take hold of the Maker's. In the end, he had been right. He had made a mistake returning to Ashland. *Back, but back to what?* Surely something more than soft towels and a fake soap opera. But if his ill-fated home held a greater view or sweeter destiny, he didn't see it.

CHAPTER THIRTY

E very few days they received a visit from the hospice nurse case manager, a short, tough woman named Carrie. She checked Kathy's blood pressure and pulse, ran through a list of items and shared a few tense words with Anna. Sometimes the tense words flared into a minor spat, showing Eric that Carrie didn't care for Anna any more than he did. So one afternoon he walked Carrie back out to her car, intent on converting her dislike into a recommendation for a better caregiver.

"Anna?" Carrie said. "She's as strange as the moon. A royal pain in the butt."

"No arguments there," he said.

"Do you know if she has any friends? Any family?"

"I thought you might tell me."

"Haven't got a clue," Carrie said. "You're the one who's with her all day."

"As far as I can see," he replied, "her social life consists of checking her cell phone once or twice a day."

Carrie glanced back at the house. "She must have family or friends somewhere."

"None ever call or come to visit. She never even takes time off to go check on her apartment or run an errand."

"They say she was a pill popper. Then she got Jesus."

"Jesus? That's hard to believe."

"Truth, Divine Light, the Buddha, whatever you call it. Doesn't matter. The ones with Jesus are always unzipped but dialed in. On it."

"You're saying she's nuts but good?"

"You can't do better. But you can sure do worse."

Exactly what he was afraid of. Anna was overbearing and off-base, maybe even despotic and psycho, but he couldn't deny her skills. Watching her meticulous work made him realize how badly he had cared for Father Glenn. He had fulfilled the basic job requirements, little more. He couldn't say if Anna was consumed by dedication, compulsion or mania, but the result was a well cared for patient. His search for a better caregiver had just hit a dead end.

Late one sleepless night he stashed the Maker's in the closet and crept down the hallway. He found Anna by Kathy's bed. He sat next to her for an hour and not a word passed between them. Looking at Kathy's ashen face, he felt stricken and useless. It hurt and he wanted to cry out. It really hurt. Every now and then, Anna reached forward and moved Kathy's body on the mattress, pulled a leg to the left a few inches. She kneaded her hands into the small of Kathy's back and Kathy exhaled strongly.

"These deep breaths are wonderful," Anna whispered to her. "Your body is releasing fear and anxiety."

"Are you doing some type of therapeutic massage?" Eric asked.

Either she didn't hear him or she ignored him, so he repeated the question.

"Just touching," she answered.

"When you say 'fear and anxiety,' do you mean 'demons'?"

No response. His questions irritated her. His presence irritated her even more. Was dislike mutual? She took Kathy's hand and whispered something he couldn't catch.

Kathy's mouth opened. He leaned forward, ears pricked, but nothing came out except another exuded breath. Anna squeezed her hand. They were the couple; he was the third wheel. One disliked him, the other seemed not to remember him. He was sure Anna had agreed to his presence—agreed to break one of her rules—only because she thought it might benefit Kathy in some way, maybe help exorcise her demons.

Every evening Anna ate alone in the living room. She said it was so she could be closer to Kathy but Eric guessed it was to be farther away from him. She ate vegetarian fare and some fruit, and usually finished off her meal with a cup of tea. One night he brought home a vegan, organic and gluten-free dish from a vegetarian restaurant on the plaza. He uncorked a bottle of wine and insisted they sit at the dining room table. They lived under the same roof and he was intent on sharing a meal together, a dinnertime conversation. Maybe he would even find out something about her pill-popping past. She watched him dish out Rainbow Pad Thai with peanuts and basil.

"This hummus is supposed to be delicious," he said, making table talk. "So is this wine. It's grown and produced just south of here in Bear Creek Valley. 'Hints of peach and honey in a fresh, bold blend'—that's what the sommelier said."

"Just a little for me," she replied.

He poured a glass and passed it across the table. She chewed her food slowly, sipped her wine judiciously. He asked questions and she gave polite answers. She had been born and raised in Louisiana. Until Oregon she had always lived in southern states: Florida, New Mexico, Arizona. She had a half-sister in Tallahassee but they weren't close, only saw each other every few years. As he watched her dip her fork into the Pad Thai, it occurred to him that he had never seen her smile. He imagined the corners of her eyes would crinkle into crow's feet, making her somewhat attractive.

He chewed his food, sipped his wine, listened to her unwilling answers. She was either secretive or as bored talking to him as she was listening to him. But he kept the picnic rolling along, chatting about his own experience in southern states. He told her about his year working for DMT in Austin. Omitting his sessions with Walt, he talked about the music scene, Texas line dancing, festivals in Zilker Park, the bats at Congress Avenue Bridge.

"Bats?" She blinked, revealing a flicker of interest. Logical, he thought. Maybe he should talk about broomsticks and black cats as well.

"Mexican free-tailed bats," he answered. "A million and a half of them. They roost under the bridge from spring to fall. Every day at dusk they zoom out over the river. Imagine the sight. A million bats on the wing. They eat twenty to thirty thousand pounds of insects per night. The largest urban bat population in the country."

"Really?"

The flicker had dimmed. They finished the Pad Thai in silence. Serving dessert—a lemon tofu cheesecake—he took a final stab at small talk and mentioned his Sadhu journey. She said she didn't know what a *sadhu* was.

"A sadhu renounces his identity in the world," he told her. "He paints his face and attends his own funeral. He dies onto himself. Then he sets off on a journey without destination."

She set her fork aside, regarded him circumspectly. "I thought you just went... away." She had been about to say "went crazy," a description she had probably picked up from Jessica, maybe Kathy along with *abandoned*. "I've never heard of them before," she said. "Are there many of these... sadhus?"

"Even more than the bats under the Congress Avenue Bridge. Somewhere between seven and nine million."

She blinked again, dark eyes lit, a dash of verve in her expression.

"But... that's not possible," she said. "There can't be seven million people just roaming around aimlessly, trying... to die onto themselves."

"Probably closer to eight or nine million. You can look it up. Google must have a page or two about them."

"And they're all... just roaming around?"

"Around India and Nepal. Until recently there was also one here in America."

He pointed his forefinger into the center of his chest. She didn't smile but for an instant her expression became more pleasant.

"Did you paint your face too?" she asked.

He nodded. He was beginning to feel self-conscious.

"Did it feel like a mask or part of your skin?"

Odd question. "I'm not sure how to answer that," he said, "but rain and sweat washed it off in a week."

"Did you feel like it was still there?"

Another odd question. "I guess I did. Maybe I still do."

"And did it—does it—feel like a death mask?"

She had gone from ignoring him to interrogating him and he had gone from trying to provoke her interest to defending himself against it.

"Why do you ask that?" he said.

"Because if you died onto yourself, then it means you've come back from the dead."

She was right. Maybe that was why he felt that he shouldn't have returned, why no destiny awaited him. She inspected his face as if discerning the colors and patterns, as if seeing the red *tilaka* still on his forehead. Her ears always remained pricked toward Kathy's bedroom but he had her attention now, so he poured more wine and went on talking. He told her about his time at Chassors, about nights in Father Glenn's cell, the Liturgy of the Hours, Abbot Paul and Grand Silence. He even described standing in Father Glenn's grave. If he continued, he thought, he would soon be telling her about his pagan confession, so he jumped forward in time to Jamie John and The Little White Chapel. She had never been to Vegas and as he talked about drive-through marriages and Elvis impersonators, she pressed her lips together. He pushed harder and described wedding chapels in hotels, restaurants and golf courses, then Jamie John in his white tux, Stetson and white limo. He was on a roll now, enjoying the meal, the wine, her budding warmth. Finally, her lips curved upward. He had guessed correctly that the corners of her eyes would crinkle, but he had never imagined a smile might render her winsome.

"And what about you?" he asked, adding a dollop of wine to her glass. "Do you live here in town... or in Medford?"

Her smile faded behind her own mask, not paint, just a thick layer of reserve. She picked up her fork, poked it into the cheesecake.

"I live where I work," she answered.

"Yes, but when you aren't working. When you have a day or a weekend off."

"When I take on a patient, I devote myself entirely to their care."

"But you must have an apartment or room somewhere."

She pointed her fork at the hallway. "Down there. When I want to go home, it's a short trip."

Was she wildly secretive or just naturally discreet about a shaded past? He couldn't tell, but he sensed that the shift in conversation had brought on another shift. She had gone from enjoying his table talk to recalling that she didn't want him in the house. They had finished off the wine and were into a second bottle. He was doing most of the drinking but her cheeks had flushed. She was far from tipsy but also no longer her sober and regal self.

"Did you study for a career?" he asked.

"What do you mean?"

"Junior college or university."

"I didn't go to university."

"But you must have studied something, even on your own. I don't know why but I imagine you studied history. Something in the Humanities."

She pushed her wine glass forward and rose to her feet. "I study my patients," she said. "It's what I should be doing now. Thank you for dinner. It was delicious."

Chapter Thirty-one

From that night on, Eric turned cautious around Anna. Whenever he passed her in the hall or stepped near her in the kitchen, he prudently steered his body clear of hers. The distancing had nothing to do with dislike or ceding polite social space. He had become more aware of her as a woman.

Either she didn't notice or chose not to comment. When their paths crossed she was usually absorbed in some task anyway. She barely uttered a word. He even wondered if he had somehow offended her. Then, on Thursday evening when he was going over bills at his end, she brought in two glasses of wine, set one on his desk and sat in the armchair. He couldn't hide his surprise.

"Tell me again about your Sadhu journey," she said.

He pushed the bills aside, nodded thanks for the wine.

"How do you mean?" he said. "Repeat what I told you the other night?"

She shook her silver hair. "Whatever you didn't tell me. I don't know. For instance, how long did it take you to walk from here to Redding?"

"About three weeks."

"Did you have blisters?"

"Lots."

"So tell me."

She sat erect and motionless as usual but her eyes appeared more open and alert, her thoughts more accessible.

He felt encouraged to speak and it might later encourage her to tell her tale.

"Lots of blisters," he repeated. "I also had cramps in my legs and pains shooting through my whole aching body, especially at night when I was stretched out on some piece of cold ground. Doubts bothered me even more than blisters. In India they say that a sadhu is a ghost living between the gods and humanity. Many times I was sure it meant a sadhu is someone who's gone bonkers."

"Everything must have changed when you started working at that restaurant."

"Donny's Diner. I guess it did."

"How did it feel?"

He remembered exactly how it had felt. "Wonderful. The land of the free and home of the healthy. A shower, a bed, great burgers. I was thankful for all of it, thankful to give my blisters a rest." He hesitated and then added: "But I also remember thinking that the jewel of my solitude hadn't sparkled for very long."

She spoke quietly, as if to herself. "Keeping it polished isn't easy." She looked at her wine glass, then again at him. "But I don't mean the relief. What was it like having a job and friends again... being back in society?"

He supposed she meant no longer feeling *abandoned*. Coming from her, the question had added depth. She was seldom in any semblance of society. She lived with people removed from the general public, people about to exit the world.

"Not so different from life at DMT Worldwide," he said.

"The same day-to-day chitchat. Sports, current events, families, families, families. Did I mention families?"

"I think you did. Did you feel you were back to being you?"

He pinched the stem of his wine glass. "Not really. I still felt like a ghost."

"And now, sitting here?"

"I don't feel alone because I'm with you and Kathy. I don't feel hungry because I've just had a good meal. And I'm in my home, so I don't feel homeless."

She regarded him closely. "I still don't understand why you came back."

"You say it the same way you said it the other night, as if I've returned from the dead."

"That's the way you described it, so that's what I see. A man who died onto himself and then returned. That's why I ask."

He swiveled sideways until he faced her directly. Her eyes were still wide open, her expression reserved yet curious, the most receptive he had seen her.

"I thought I knew," he said. "I thought I was sure beyond any doubt. That's what it felt like at the time. I had gone too far to turn back on a whim. Or put differently, I was too far gone. But weeks after the fact, it's a hard question for anyone to answer about anything. *Why did I do what I did?* I'm not sure we ever know the answer to that one. Time and memory mesh in funny ways and their version of the past isn't always pinpoint accurate. Also, when I made the decision I wasn't a portrait of prime mental health. I was at the end of my rope. The last thread on the rope. Dizzy, sun-hammered, dust and grit covered. After talking with Jessica, I felt hunted by my own demons." He paused. "And haunted by Kathy. Now, back home, I wonder if she even wants me here. Does she?"

His voice must have sounded a forlorn note because she swallowed as if her wine had turned to vinegar.

"I think she knows you're giving your best."

"Come on," he said. "You can do better than that."

Her eyes narrowed on her glass. "I think if she's one of the reasons you returned and if there's something you want to tell her, now's the time. You won't get another chance."

"You said not to hold her back."

"I meant don't drown her in emotion, don't confuse her by pretending you still have a relationship, by inflating feelings to resemble love, by pretending the self you remember is the self you are, by pretending she's who she was, the person you knew. That'll hold her back. Truth and honesty won't. It'll help her go."

She spoke with experience and authority and he wondered how many other times she had given the same advice to the relatives of terminal patients. She kept death daily before her eyes, he thought, but her next words caught him off guard.

"What about poetry?" she asked. "What Kathy told me— that you used to write it. She said you published a book."

"A chapbook. A long time ago." He felt a stirring of anger. "Why do you ask? Do you write poetry?"

She shook her head. "Usually I don't even understand

it. But I read to my patients. Not all of them, of course, but some have a favorite poem they want to hear. Others just want to listen to something different. It gives comfort. I've learned to enjoy reading out loud. The rhythms, the—"

"Did you read to Kathy?" he cut in.

"A few times but then it became hard for her to follow."

She spoke artlessly, he thought, but she had to know she was digging into him. He hid his irritation. "What did you read?"

"She asked me to read Jane Hirschfield. I'd never heard of her before but Kathy said—"

"I know what Kathy said."

He left the room in a fury or maybe just suffocated by emotion, he couldn't tell which. I didn't come back for this, he thought. But there it was, the past pulled out of him like a sword from a stone. Kathy had adored Hirschfield's verse and had once insisted they drive up to Portland to attend a reading at Powell's, but he had refused to share her adoration, refused even to offer mild interest. Decades later, the sword was still sharp.

Late that night he entered Kathy's room. Anna had just finished brushing what was left of Kathy's hair and had settled her head back onto the pillow. Kathy's eyes were open—her baby blues—but didn't register his presence. He stepped carefully around Anna and placed his hand on Kathy's frail shoulder. She was in limbo, he thought. Beyond poetry. Pain and morphine land. Why didn't she die—what was taking so long? He was caught between mumbling prayers and urging her to go. He would run through the streets howling, mad with rage like everyone else.

Anna left the room and he sat by the bed, lowering the chrome safety rail. He leaned forward until his face was only inches from Kathy's. Her lost and fragile gaze awoke tenderness in him. Every breath sounded like her last. Did he want to confess to her as he had to Father Glenn? Hardly. The ugly truth was, he just wanted her to get it over with. No more dragging through day after day. So he sat there paralyzed and mute, thinking nothing except that he had once made love to her. He had made love to her hail and robust body, now frail and disappearing. Finally, he rose to his feet and went down to his end.

He looked through the window at the partially moonlit garden. He knew Anna was right. Any sensible person would say the same. Time was running out. Speak now or forever regret it. He remembered Brother Huy once telling him it didn't matter how far gone a person was. Whether in limbo or not, there was a part that could always be reached by the familiar voice of a loved one.

Once in bed, Eric slipped into a pleasant dream. He and Kathy were young lovers holding hands in an unknown countryside. A foreign land, not India, not anywhere he knew, but exotic, lush green. He awoke briefly and somehow the dream merged into a memory of a long-ago night when he had arrived home from a brutal day at DMT. He had agonized over the grim economy, troubled clients, his failures, when suddenly Kathy had said, "Let's just make love!" And they had, so ardently and even crazily that the troubles of the day dissolved against their sweaty flesh.

He fell back into the same dream minus the anxiety.

He couldn't tell what bedroom or house they were in but they were still making love. Kathy's hair was longer as she bounced and rode him. He reached upward to move her hair aside. He wanted to see her nostrils flared in pleasure, wanted to take his own pleasure from the sight of her parted lips, wanted to see her blue eyes blazing. Finally, he yanked her hair back on both sides, perhaps too violently but she only rode him harder. Then he saw that her hair was silver and a white scar ran beneath her jaw.

With an electric jolt he sat straight up, his body bathed in sweat. He had a tremendous erection. The sheet was damp, the pillow crumpled in a heap. Trying to calm himself, he suddenly sensed a presence in the room. "Hello?" he said. For an instant he thought he was still in the dream. "Is someone there?" Why did he say *someone* when it could only be one person? No answer came. The room was pitch black. He peered into the darkness. Nothing, or at least nothing he could see, but his pulse was racing. Then a faint sound came from near the door, as of a foot brushing the carpet piling. He started to swing his body over the edge of the bed but his left leg became entangled in the sheet. He pulled free and stepped onto the floor. He hurried over to the door. As he reached it, he glimpsed a shadow vanish into the shadows at the other end of the house. Or thought he did. Standing there squinting without his glasses, he couldn't be sure. He turned back toward the room, feeling the air for some fluctuation, some trace of what he had sensed. A chill moved up his backbone. He looked down the hallway again. Silent, catlike, he crept forward. He passed the kitchen. Everything appeared in order. He came to a stop near the threshold leading to both Anna and Kathy's rooms. He remained there standing still, alert to any sound. The house creaked and a breeze clattered through the branches of the tree out by the front porch. No other sound came. Finally, he turned and went back to bed.

CHAPTER THIRTY-TWO

Carrie, the hospice nurse case manager, had agreed to watch Kathy for an hour while Eric drove Anna into town. As he steered the car away from the curb, he glanced at Anna in the passenger seat.

"Did you have trouble sleeping last night?" he asked.

She turned toward him. "Not at all."

"I thought I heard you moving around."

"I got up to check on Kathy a couple of times."

"Maybe that was it."

Or maybe not. In any case, it was the first time she had been out of the house since he had arrived in Ashland and he was curious to see her in the real world. He parked near the herbalist's shop on 2nd St. and lingered by the car as she headed down the block. He wasn't sure what he expected to see. Except for her height and a flash of morning sunlight on her silver hair, little distinguished her from other pedestrians. When she disappeared into the pharmacy, he entered the herbalist's and slid a list Anna had drawn up across the polished wooden counter. The herbalist ran his eyes down over the carefully printed letters. Blinking behind thick spectacles, he began putting together bags, sachets and oils. A small pile accumulated on the counter.

"What's all this for?" Eric asked.

"Depends on what you're being treated for," the herbalist answered, removing his spectacles. "Bad breath, snakebite, kidney failure?"

"It's not for me. It's for... a friend."

"Is your friend being treated by an energy healer, a body-worker, a shaman?"

"I'm not sure."

The man put his spectacles back on. "Well, sir, then I'm not sure either."

So much for that. Eric paid, returned to the car and killed time on his cell phone. Clicking onto the Chassors website, he found a photo of Father Glenn from younger days and a modest biography. There was also the text of a eulogy Abbot Paul had delivered at the funeral, which Eric couldn't bring himself to read. Instead, he entered the Little White Chapel website, which he hadn't looked at since Vegas. He was pleased to see that Jamie John had incorporated some of his suggested changes. Eric had already transferred the money he owed and now he sent an overdue message: "Hope all's well in Vegas. Made it home safe and sound thanks to you."

Was he safe and sound? An unknown woman creeping around his house at night, Kathy dying, Jessica flaunting a hideous grin. Not the homecoming he had imagined. Down the street, Anna exited the pharmacy and entered Parson's Gift Shop next door. Fifteen minutes later she came out, carrying a rectangular box wrapped in brown shipping paper. She was dressed in a skirt, dark and silky, and as she crossed the street, the breeze set it against her legs. When she got into the car, he started the engine.

"One more stop," she said. "The post office."

Eric managed to get a look at the destination on her

box—Tallahassee, Florida—and it rekindled his resolve to find out more about her.

"Two more," he replied. "Let's repeat that veggie meal."

So that evening he served the same Pad Thai and Bear Creek wine. Anna sat across the table like a wide-awake statue. He could imagine a gossamer thread running through her, attached to her skull, bearing aloft her weight. Toward the end of the meal, she said:

"Tell me again about your Sadhu journey."

It was the only thing about him that seemed to interest her, except for poetry which was the last subject on his list of table talk.

"I've told you everything," he said. "It's your turn to tell me."

"Tell you what?"

"What you hold back. Your story."

She frowned. "You wouldn't care and if you did, you wouldn't believe it anyway."

"Try me. I might be more caring and believing than you think."

She seemed to search for words, then gave up and said: "I made a pact."

"What do you mean?"

"I mean I made a pact."

"Okay, but what kind? You make it sound like you met the devil at the crossroads."

"Maybe I did."

"You made a pact with the devil?"

"Him, the angels, local bunny rabbits, the universe—I don't know. I only know I made it."

He stopped his questions and let her tell her tale. It turned out that Carrie had been right. A teenaged pill popper. "Not a full-fledged hophead," Anna said, "but close." She had run with a group of "screwed-up kids, all some type of head—crackhead, pothead, methhead," and one night they had been in a gruesome car accident. A girl and a boy were killed while Anna and her best friend Sally survived with "moderate to serious injuries." She lifted her hair off the left side of her face and showed him the white scar along her jawline.

In the two years following the accident, she said, her friend Sally had suffered bouts of survivor's guilt and PTSD. On the second anniversary of the accident, she committed suicide by driving her car off a cliff. From that day on, Anna's own anguish became unbearable. "Months passed and I held on to the cliff edge Sally had gone over. Then one night I went over too. I gulped down a handful of greenies, but instead of landing where I wanted—oblivion—I ended up in the ER."

"Where you found Jesus."

"Where I realized I didn't want to die. Once you open the suicide door—and I mean seriously open it—you either stay suicidal or you get Jesus. There's no other choice, no other way out. I was fortunate. A woman at a crisis center recognized something in me. She called it a 'gift.' I called her 'batty.' At first, because I didn't understand what she was talking about. She was eccentric and probably half senile but very talented. She became my primary mentor. Later there were two others."

"Mentor for what?"

"A century's old tradition of caregiving."

"Does it have a name?"

"You don't graduate from a school or get a diploma."

"But you must call it something."

"It's called 'caregiving.' The training is imparted by direct transmission. One mentor, one aspirant. You're selected and instructed over a period of years."

"Instructed in what?"

"Some Naturopathy. Reiki-like techniques, meridians, massage, anointing. The use of herbs and poultices. You undergo periods of testing, including a few spells in the Mexican desert."

"I've read about that," Eric said. "Vision quest."

"Not that, but like it."

"Did you have a vision?"

"Anybody who spends enough time in the desert will start to see things."

He couldn't argue with that. Stumbling into the Mojave, he had seen Billy in the Alaskan wilderness, hunted by Kodiak bears. In the heat haze and emptiness, he had discerned a mirage-like figure tramping toward him, skeletal and haggard. His ghost self, the sadhu in reverse. Then a cowboy archangel in a white tuxedo and silk Stetson had appeared. So he knew a thing or two about desert visions.

"Tell me about the pact."

"It was very simple. If I cared for those about to leave, I could remain."

"It still sounds vague and mystical."

"As mystical as mud. You've seen reality. Mopping up lots of sweat and urine."

He observed her closely. "You were the driver of the car, weren't you?"

She looked down at her hands, nodded.

"But the accident happened twenty-five or thirty years ago," he went on. "It's terrible, of course, but you... must have forgiven yourself by now."

"Every day of the week," she said. "That's the care I give myself. The pact didn't come with an expiration date." She shrugged. "I said you wouldn't believe me."

But he did believe her. And her witch's pact confirmed that he had guessed right. She had been a student. She had spent thirty years studying death. It was why she always wore black, he thought. She existed in a state of perpetual mourning.

"You said Kathy would die soon," he said.

"I said her light was fading. She'll go like anyone else. When she's ready."

His tone became accusatory. "How many people have you seen die?"

She drew back. "I'm not sure. By the time I arrive to a patient, they're already far into the process. So a great many."

"Twenty? Thirty?"

"I said I'm not sure. I don't keep count."

"Fifty?"

"Eighty, ninety. I don't know."

"And with someone like Kathy, for example, can you use

these techniques you've learned..." He spluttered, growing angry. "I mean can you really use them to...?"

"They're just techniques, Eric," she replied quietly. "Not superpowers. I can lessen some pain, maybe calm agitated emotions, but I'm not a miracle worker who cures cancer, if that's what you're asking."

He wasn't just angry, he realized. He was fed up with her. Did she ever veer off course onto anything unconnected to darkness and demise? Yes, she asked about his Sadhu journey, but only because she wanted to know if he had died onto himself. More death. When Kathy died, she would leave to care for another man's dying ex-wife. Did she ever talk about anything else—the price of bread, a cloud in the sky?

"What do you think about the state of the nation?" he asked.

She blinked twice. "What?"

"You must have some opinion," he pressed. "Everybody does. Relations with China, immigration, racism, gun control, terrorism, climate change, unemployment. Do you even know who the president is? What about the vice-president?"

"I don't understand why you're talking like this. Why are you asking me these things?"

"I want to hear what you think. I want to hear your opinion. You must think something. Look around. What do you see? A bipolar godless culture, epidemic loneliness, torture by television, anxiety for breakfast, phobias for lunch, murder everywhere in a schizoid media-controlled nation..."

He ran out of breath and vehemence. She observed him as if he had a bomb strapped to his chest.

"Everything you describe," she said slowly, "is an illness."

Of course, he thought. How else would she see it all? He said good night and left the table. Down at his end he was still in a tantrum, though now he felt the first burn of shame. There were times when he forgot the pathetic state he was in. Then he realized he was still looking into a plate glass window, still disintegrating. Yet somehow this woman gave him strength. For an instant he fantasized that they would travel together, hunt in dark forests, sleep in parks in far-off cities. Or wake up to find that the entire universe had changed... and the world, though still the same, would caress them gently.

He stepped out into the garden, stood by the barbecue grill, still half-buried in dirt. A breeze moved through the branches, ruffling dry leaves. A cat meowed. He gulped in the fresh air. He walked down the driveway, walked down Barbara Street, turned onto Tolman Creek Road. Car headlights flashed over him. Then nothing but darkness. He passed Saratoga Lane, Grizzly Drive, Mistletoe Road. The same path he had taken at the start of his Sadhu journey. Farewell sick world. Off to join the circus. He hadn't been in a hurry to get anywhere. He had thought he had all the time in the world to get nowhere. Now time was running out. *You won't get another chance.* That was his real anger, admit it or not.

The night was silent and still and he marched on for

another ten minutes before calming down. Back at the house, he listened for Anna but not a peep came from the opposite end. He lay awake, still scorched by shame. He would apologize to her in the morning but somehow the heated exchange had left him feeling closer to her, physically closer as well. He could almost smell the fragrance of her body oil. Then he realized he could. It wasn't imagination. He sat up and lifted the pillow to his nose, sniffed the pillowcase once, twice. The scent was unmistakable. While he had been out walking, she had come in and stretched out on his bed. She had hugged his pillow.

Chapter Thirty-three

Two nights later he stirred awake out of a melancholic dream. The night was moonless, the room pitch dark. He was about to reach for the lamp when a footfall sounded in the hallway, so faint it could have been backwash from his dream. He sensed movement, a presence passing over the threshold into the room.

In the darkness no one could have seen his open eyes, but he closed them anyway to better feign sleep. He had no plan, only an instinctive urge to let the scene play to the full before he made a move. Eyes shut, he waited motionless. He remembered feigning sleep in front of Mole and Tattoo, the crackling fire, his mounting fear. No other sound came, but he knew he was no longer alone in the room. He lay on his back, waiting. Then the sheet and coverlet rose off the edge of the bed, off his body.

"I know you're awake," Anna whispered.

She slipped between the sheets and lay next to him. Startled, he fumbled for words: "But... how do you know?"

"The sound of your breathing."

He wore only his pajama bottoms. The fabric was thin cotton and he felt the brush of her thigh against his leg. Instinctively, he moved away from her, but she nestled in closer, setting her head against his naked chest. He felt the brush of her thick hair.

"Hold me," she whispered.

Another of her commands, but one he couldn't resist.

His arm came up around her before he even considered the danger of an embrace. Her breath on his chest, the curve of her breasts against his ribs. Some instinct made him raise his hand and brush her hair off her cheek. They lay still for a long while. He became aware of moisture on his chest. He used the border of the sheet to wipe her tears.

"Thank you," she murmured, and kissed his chest.

It was a kiss of gratitude, a small kiss for a small kindness, nothing more, but he could still feel her breasts against his ribs and, small kiss or not, her lips had just pressed onto his flesh. He began to get an erection and not just any erection. It felt like a year in the making, growing fast and hard.

She whispered again: "I'd love to read your chapbook sometime."

A charge ran from his groin up through his torso. "I told you that was a long time ago. It doesn't exist anymore."

She gave a soft laugh. "I don't believe you, Eric. Nobody would publish a book and not save a copy for posterity. Especially you. Never mind, I don't want to trouble you."

Then what was she doing in his bed? He was full of troubles. His throbbing erection caused him to fidget, to twist and shift positions. When she snuggled in closer, her thigh grazed his erection. They both remained still. Then she said: "I'll please you, if you want."

Please him? He had thought she was erratic and deranged. Now he knew it for sure. "What? No, I— I don't want that." What kind of maniac world did she live in? "I want you to leave. Right now. You shouldn't be here. Not with Kathy down the hall. It—it's not right."

Her whisper had turned sleepy. "Why is it wrong?"

"Because it is."

She went on in the same voice, not arguing in the least, just stating drowsy facts. He sensed she had been in the grip of some terrible emotion but, letting it go, she had drifted into exhaustion.

"You've been separated for years," she said. "She told me your marriage and your feelings for each other ended a long time ago. You said the same."

"It doesn't matter."

She seemed to yawn. He was verging on explosion and she was falling asleep.

"Besides," she mumbled, "what difference does it make if she's down the hall or down in Mexico?"

"That's not the point." Did she think he was as wacky as she was? "Do I have to remind you that she's dying? You're her caregiver, for Chrissake. She might need you right now."

"I'll know if she does."

"You can't hear anything down here."

"I'll know."

Her languid tone was maddening. "It's just not right," he insisted.

"Kathy wouldn't care."

"You don't know that."

"Yes, I do."

He had the feeling she might start snoring at any moment.

"It's still not right," he said forcefully.

"Okay, okay." She yawned again. "We don't have to do anything we don't want to do."

"Then please leave," he said.

But he said it lamely, without a shred of conviction. He didn't want her to leave. He wanted her body next to his, her breath on his chest, wanted to rejoice in his erection no matter how its throbbing drove him mad. She must have sensed it because she made no move to leave. Or maybe she really had fallen asleep.

Bolts of desire and confusion traversed him. She wore some type of negligee. The fabric felt like satin. He stroked her hair. She had come to have a cry, he thought, and to be held. Did she know he had wanted to run his fingers through her silver locks from the first day at the front door? He thought of Kathy down the hall. He didn't have to ask himself how Anna could possibly know that she was sleeping peacefully, because he knew it as well, knew she was deep in morphine limbo. But it still troubled him and his troubled thoughts began to invent nightmare scenarios. He imagined Jessica stopping by first thing in the morning. It wasn't just wild conjecture. She often passed by on her way to work. She said hello, smiled her new grin and dropped off some supplies. If she stopped by tomorrow morning, her enormous teeth wouldn't have the chance to flash a winning smile. She would discover the sordid scene of him in bed with Anna as her mother lay dying down the hall.

His ghoulish fantasies shriveled his erection. Fast asleep now, Anna exhaled onto his chest. Leaves and branches scratched against the window. A bird chirped. Was it already dawn? No light filtered in through the blinds. No sound of daylight movement. Just faint birdsong and leaves scratching glass. He hovered on the edge of sleep himself, on the edge of the abyss, his prayers still mumbled. Was he appealing to God? Later he heard the distant ring of a phone. Anna's seldom used cell. Then he slept again.

When he finally awoke, he found a pillow next to him in place of Anna. The aroma of freshly brewed coffee filled the house. It made him recall workday mornings when the automatic coffeemaker used to stir him awake for another day at DMT. DMT where he had once boasted that he held the key to every conceivable scene. He had found the big names in modern marketing and advertising laughable. He had invented colors for concepts: blue for Branding; red for Promotion. Then he had taken a long fall off his high horse while everyone laughed.

Anna usually drank a tea brew of nettles, which she infused every night in a Mason jar before bed. It meant she had made the coffee for him. He thought about her laying next to him—*Do you want me to please you?*—and he began to get another erection. He heard her hurrying in and out of her room, opening and closing drawers. What was going on? She never moved quickly and noisily, always slow and silent.

He rolled out of bed and threw himself in the shower. He shaved and splashed on aftershave. He could still hear her rushing about but he hadn't yet heard the unmistakable click of Billy's bedroom door. Something had happened and it didn't involve Kathy. He dressed in a shirt and jeans.

In the kitchen he found Anna standing behind the

counter, adding a raw stevia leaf to her tea. She wore a matching dress and jacket, black as always but with a powder blue chiffon scarf. She looked fashionable, a word he never would have used to describe her. Her hair was tied back in a bun, accentuating her troubled brow, the scar on her jaw.

"What's going on?" he said, reaching for his coffee mug.

"A family emergency," she replied. "I have to go. A taxi will be here in a minute. I'm not sure when I'll be back."

He held the mug still, gave her a look saying he might not have heard right. Her temple twitched. He sensed she was barely holding herself together.

"This isn't about last night, is it?" he asked.

"Nothing like that." Her voice broke. "It's something... unexpected."

"You can't just leave."

"I have to. It's an emergency. Look." She slid a sheet of paper across the counter. "It's Kathy's schedule. I know you know it but I've written everything down for a replacement..."

"A replacement?"

"From one of the agencies. You should get one. Don't try to do it on your own. Call 'Home Caregiver.' They're a cut above the others."

"But wait. This is crazy. I mean, nothing happened last night."

Maybe that was the problem. Nothing had happened.

"I told you," Anna said. "It's not about that."

She gathered up her things, took a quick look around. A car horn beeped out on the street.

"But maybe you could give more than two minutes' notice," Eric said sharply.

"Emergencies don't give notice."

She set off down the hall and he hurried along behind her. Royalty mode and panic at the same time. He wasn't going to get any more out of her. They came into the living room. A rolling suitcase stood by the front door, its handle raised and ready to go, a messenger bag on the carpet next to it. Anna turned into Kathy's room and made straight for the bed. He paused by the door as she leaned over the guard rail and whispered something into Kathy's ear. Kathy remained motionless, asleep or in coma. Anna kissed her long and lovingly on the forehead. Unmistakably, a goodbye kiss. Eric froze. The car horn beeped again. Anna came back toward him. He stood aside. She passed by, eyes straight ahead, making for the door. She tossed the loop of the messenger bag over her left shoulder and grabbed the handle of the suitcase.

He followed her out the door and down the path. The taxi driver popped the trunk lid, got out and bid them good morning. He hefted Anna's suitcase into the trunk. She opened the rear door of the taxi and slid onto the back seat. She started to pull the door shut but Eric stepped forward and jammed his hip against it. The driver got in the front seat and started the engine. Eric bent forward. Anna stared straight ahead, a passenger sitting in the back seat of a taxi.

"Tell me what happened," Eric said. "Who called you? Tell me where you're going. Tell me something."

"Eric, please." She looked devastated, about to crack. "Just let me go."

Eric glanced at the driver, a mustachioed man with shaggy blond hair sticking out over his frayed shirt collar. He looked uninvolved and bored, as if he witnessed identical scenes every morning of the week. Anna tugged on the door and Eric stepped back, let it thump shut. Her window was up. He couldn't hear her give the driver directions. The taxi crept away from the curb and rolled down Barbara Street. A moment later it disappeared from view.

He entered the house and looked in on Kathy. Still in morphine limbo. He stood in the living room, trembling, telling himself, "It can't be about last night."

Just then the doorbell rang. She changed her mind, he thought. But it was the neighbor from across the street, Cookie's owner.

"I just spotted you from the window," he explained, "so I thought I'd come over. I guess you heard that Cookie has gone missing."

"I'm sorry…" Eric said, "sorry to hear that."

"We put an ad in the Daily Tidings, checked at the Shelter and all. Don't know what else to do. We're thinking about raising the reward. I just wanted to tell you."

"If I see or hear anything," Eric replied, "I'll let you know right away."

"Just can't figure it. That darn Cookie never missed a meal. Well, sorry to bother you. I know you've got your own situation."

Eric said goodbye and walked straight to Anna's room. He pressed down the door handle and entered. Bed perfectly made; nightstand clear of all objects except lamp. He went to the chest of drawers by the side window. All drawers empty. He slid open the closet door. Twenty plastic coat hangers, not a piece of clothing on any. The entire room looked like it had been uninhabited for the last five years. She hadn't left a thing behind. Not one personal item, not even the scent of her body oil. Nothing.

CHAPTER THIRTY-FOUR

Anna's departure not only tripled Eric's work load, but coincided with a sudden influx of visitors. It was as if the Ashland community bulletin board had officially announced Kathy's farewell. Up until then, a friend or work colleague had rung the doorbell every few days. Anna had guided them in and ushered them out while Eric faded behind the furniture, avoiding people well schooled in his failures as a husband. Now the bell chimed two, three, four times a day. He barely recognized the faces. The girl who ran the juice bar at the Health Center, a Pilates student from nine years ago, the owner of a t-shirt shop, a gas station clerk who confided that he had always thought Kathy was "hot and cool."

Anna had screened visitors according to Kathy's state that day; the more emotions they flaunted, the quicker she had shown them the door. "They bring too many flowers," she had said, "and too many feelings." Now Eric ushered in flowers and feelings, observed tears and grief, escorted people back out to their cars. Standing by the curbside, he listened to their advice and encouragement, their own stories of sickness, loss and bereavement. Repeatedly, they uttered the word *tragedy*. "She's still so young." "There's no other word for it: tragedy." "She was always so vital." "It's such a tragedy." Some regarded him with narrowed eyes, confirming the tales they had heard. "I'll come back again," others said. "Please do," he replied, thinking *Please don't*.

Meanwhile the household chores—cooking, cleaning, dishes, the never-ending laundry—accumulated. After callers left, he should have rolled up his sleeves and labored for hours, but Kathy's well meaning well-wishers drained dry his unwell self. So he poured some Maker's, switched on the television and let clever ads benumb him. The DMT chip still in his brain automatically registered their message. Buy this object and achieve perpetual orgasm. Be eternally joyous. Shop, purchase, acquire. Then came the nightly news. Eight people gunned down in some town somewhere. Police hadn't yet discovered a motive. One lone citizen had acted bravely, saving lives. Always tack on a hero for popular consumption. We are the greatest country in the world and we are very brave. Now back to shopping.

He had hoped or believed or convinced himself that Anna would handle Kathy's demise with some witch's brew while he hovered in the background, removed from blast waves. That scenario had collapsed along with the day-to-day schedule. Death now became menacing and inescapable and the person dying wasn't some unknown priest.

He finished every evening drunk and anguished. The silence in the house magnified, turned thunderous. Grand Silence. Staring at Kathy, he told himself: "She no longer has the energy to dislike me. Me or anyone else. She's focused on her pain, on her leave-taking, on her few remaining breaths. But why is she taking so long to go?" He couldn't tell if she was in coma, asleep or drugged senseless, but he had witnessed the same final curtain with Father Glenn. Being came down to a breath and a prayer. No chorus of angels, no whisking away by Valkyrie. Tomorrow, the next day, the day after, Kathy would die and he would have to handle it alone. And where would her death leave him? Would he feel compelled to resume his Sadhu journey and finish an unfinished thing?

"I know what you want to ask," he whispered, leaning on the chrome safety rail, "and the answer is *No*. She hasn't called yet. It's been four days now. I don't know what happened or where she went, but I don't think she's coming back. We're in this alone now. You and me. Jessica will stop by every few days but she's out of her depth. She's frightened. I'm frightened too. I don't know of what. Maybe nothing." At last he had found words, but he felt like he had stepped onto a roller coaster. "I'm not sure what I'll do after you're gone. Sell the house maybe. Move somewhere else, start again. I only know I don't want any responsibilities. Remember how you used to say I took them on to prove I existed. Keep myself tied up and engaged to show I was alive but really just so I could avoid living, cover and bury existence in a clutter of activity. Remember what you used to tell me? 'Slow down, give it up, drop the fake duty, live your life.' Maybe you were right. Maybe I am a coward. I tried to let go of all that when I left and I promise I'll let it go for good when you leave." He was rambling again. He was also trespassing on terrain he had been warned to avoid. *Don't hold her back.* "No more distractions," he went on, unable to stop, "no more false cares and duties, no more self deception and maybe no more self. I'll attend my own funeral when I attend yours." Was he trying to double her agony? "Anna said you were attached to your body. You're hanging on to a fading thing and now I think you're hanging on for her to return and that isn't likely. You have to let go. We both do."

He commanded himself to shut up and let her be. In case of an emergency in the night, he now slept on the living room sofa. But nerves frayed, boozed up, ashamed of everything he had just said, he couldn't sleep. He kept thinking about the night Anna had slipped into his bed. He had told her *Please leave.* Now she had.

He also thought of Abbot Paul sprinkling holy water onto his head. Nocturnal baptism. Wouldn't that feel refreshing right now? Then he fell asleep. Pain and fear should have vanished but the highway howled through his dreams. Cars, tractor-trailers, pickups with gun racks. In the morning he felt he had spent the night tramping down a roaring interstate.

He needed help but resisted calling Home Caregiver. He was certain that if he hired a substitute, Anna would never return. So he telephoned Jessica instead and read her a list over the phone. The next day she did the shopping and unloaded everything on her way home from work. She sat with Kathy for ten minutes and then hurried out to her car.

"I'd stop by more often," she said, "but I'm so busy these days..."

"Don't worry about it," he said. "You're helping a lot."

She flashed her pearly whites, then said, "What about Anna?"

"I can't tell you any more than I have. She said it was a family emergency."

"I can't believe she'd just leave like that."

"I couldn't believe it either."

"She was happy here and she loved Mom. Taking off like that with hardly a word. It doesn't sound like her. Did you do something—maybe make a move on her?"

"What?"

"She's an attractive woman." Her gaze narrowed on him the same as Kathy's co-workers. "And I know how you are."

She drove off, leaving him by the curb. He looked up and down the block. All the tree trunks now displayed a poster with a photograph of Cookie. *Have you seen our Cookie? $200 reward for Info leading to recovery.*

A short while later Carrie arrived. Eric had forgotten about her visit. As she entered the house, her sharp eye registered the disorder. She asked where Anna was and frowned when he told her.

"That sounds like pill-popper speak for 'relapse.' Listen, Mr. Tyler, if she disappeared for some reason—any reason—don't play brave and try to go it alone. You need a hand here. Two hands. Call Home Caregiver."

Instead, after she had left, he hurried out to the garage and began digging through the boxes stacked against the rear wall. Some of the cardboard flaps were so old they felt like dishrags. Cobwebs clung to his forearms and rising dust sent him into a coughing fit as he emptied a box of photo albums. Finally, he came upon a smaller box covered in burlap sacking. He undid the burlap, opened the box and lifted out a package wrapped in maroon gift paper. He tore it open and found two copies of *Heart like a jewel,* his chapbook, carefully preserved for posterity.

He left the mess and hurried back inside to Anna's bedroom. He set both copies of the book onto the empty nightstand and stood aside, mission accomplished. A full minute passed before he summoned the sanity to ask himself what he was doing. What did he think—that his pathetic poetry would become a magnet and draw her back?

That night while cleaning up the living room, he found tears running down his cheeks. He went to the far end of the house to take his sobs away from Kathy. Wind blew through the garden and moonlight wafted through branches into his room. Shadows swayed across the walls. Like it or not, he thought, but do it.

The following morning, he sat next to Kathy's bed.

"I'm going to call Home Caregiver," he told her, "and get someone over here. We both know it won't be Anna, so let's get ready. But we can't go on like this. We can't— Wait, there's the doorbell."

A muscular figure stood on the front porch, a dozen roses shaking in his large hands. It was Abe, co-instructor at the Health Center, the personal trainer Kathy had joined for after-hours fun in the weight room. Eric had never met him and Abe immediately struck him as someone missing a few nuts in his fruitcake. Abe looked in at Kathy from the doorway of her room but couldn't force himself to enter. His flowers fell to the carpet and he hurried out of the house. On the porch he turned back around.

"I just can't..." he stammered. "...can't believe any of this. Like it isn't real. She was always so... fit. I mean, healthy. There's no other word. It's a tragedy."

He left in a rush. Eric picked up the fallen roses, carried them out back and threw them onto the compost heap. Then he called Home Caregiver and requested a 24-hour caregiver with experience. Naively, he had assumed they would immediately dispatch a savior, but another day and a half of chaos passed before they sent an elderly woman named Miss Collins. As soon as she walked in the door, he felt his burden lighten.

A few hours later, he realized that Miss Collins wasn't "elderly." She was his age, but acted twenty years older, an octogenarian granny from an Iowa farm. She was adorable and smiled charmingly and held Kathy's hand with a tender touch but it seemed Home Caregiver had sent an experienced hand-holder.

"Do you think you could prepare a little snack?" he asked. "The fridge is full of food and anything would be great. A salad perhaps?"

Miss Collins smiled, bowing her head like a shy girl. "Oh, I never step into an unknown kitchen. You can never find a darn thing. I'm at home in my own scullery. I know right where all my pots are but I'm just a guest in your house."

Half an hour later she revealed that she only worked 8 hours a day and would leave for home every evening. When he called Home Caregiver and demanded an explanation, they said no 24-hour caregivers were currently available. He confronted Miss Collins on her way out the door.

"But... what if Kathy dies tonight?"

"Good heavens!" she replied. "You shouldn't talk about such things."

The following day when he threw another flower bouquet onto the compost, Miss Collins regarded him severely.

"Those flowers are God's love expressed through a friend," she said. "To treat them like common garbage is a sin."

That evening as she was preparing to leave, she squinted at the glass in his hand and announced that she could smell alcohol.

"Miss Collins," Eric said, "let me remind you that I'm in my own home. As you yourself said, you're a guest here."

"You don't have to remind me of that, Mr. Tyler. I'm a professional and very aware of my position. No one has to explain my position to me."

"Well, then let me remind you that it's not unusual for people to have a drink in their own homes at night."

"I will not abide by whiskey drinking."

She returned the following day and again took hold of Kathy's hand. Eric suspected that she needed the hand-holding more than Kathy. Then he realized that even floating in a morphine cloud, Kathy probably couldn't bear any more of it either. That afternoon he gently informed Miss Collins that her services were no longer required. He paid her for three extra days and called a taxi. Out on the street, she pressed a perfumed hanky to her rouged cheek.

"Let's not mince words, Mr. Tyler," she said, sniffling. "You are firing me. No one has ever fired me before. Not in six dedicated years of caregiving. You have humiliated me and I will never forget this black day."

CHAPTER THIRTY-FIVE

The sound of a car door thumping shut drew Eric to the window. Dreading the arrival of another of Kathy's colleagues or, worse yet, the return of Abe or Miss Collins, he peered out at the street. A taxi sat beside the curb. The driver was opening the trunk. Eric's eye went to a shock of silver hair emerging from the rear door. Anna climbed out, pulling a package behind her. Eric turned to Kathy and said, "She's back."

By the time he got through the front door and down the path, the driver had set Anna's rolling suitcase onto the curb. If she had arrived carefree and vivacious, Eric might have danced for joy, but a glance at her pale face and haggard eyes impelled him forward into a hug. Unsteadily, she draped her arms around his shoulders. A faint sob escaped her mouth into his ear. Like the cry of an infant, he thought. He held her, told her everything would be okay, then another similar cry drew his eye downward. In the curbside grass next to her messenger bag sat the package she had pulled out of the back seat. With a start he realized that it was a baby carrier basket holding a newborn infant. He had to look twice. Was it possible she gone away to give birth?

He paid the driver and grabbed the suitcase, messenger bag and a folded stroller. Anna picked up the baby basket. Following her back up the path, he noticed her long legs wobble. Once inside, she set the baby basket onto the sofa.

"Are you ill?" he asked.

She shook her head. "Exhausted. I haven't slept in... I don't know. Days."

"Then go to bed."

"I have to feed Owen. The baby."

"I'll feed him"

"You?"

"I know how to feed a baby."

"Yes, of course. I'm sorry. I'm just so... tired." She swung a limp arm toward her suitcase. "Everything's there but you have to prepare a bottle. First you—"

"I know how to prepare a bottle. Go to bed."

She started toward her room but then took a sudden, clumsy turn into Kathy's room. Eric arrived at the doorway just as she bent over Kathy's bed. She kissed Kathy on the forehead, whispered something. Then she stumbled past him into her own room. For an instant he regretted leaving the two chapbooks on the nightstand. Anna glanced at them and collapsed onto the bed. Within five seconds she was sound asleep. He removed her shoes and examined her face. Her mouth was ajar. Except for her mop of hair, she was barely recognizable. The skin had tightened above her cheeks and thin lines now formed webs at the corners of her eyes. She had lost weight, her jowls had sunken. In an odd way she resembled Kathy's skeletal look. A shiver ran through him. They're going to die, he thought, one after the other.

It was true that he knew how to feed a baby. He had prepared bottles and fed Billy and Jessica countless times in their infancy. But that had been more than two decades ago and he hardly remembered a thing. In Anna's suitcase he found bottles, a formula milk powder and cleaning brushes. He set a kettle to boil, washed down everything in sight and opened his laptop on the kitchen counter. He typed "How to feed a baby" into Google, skimmed a half dozen pages and went out to check on Owen. Still gurgling peacefully. But his peaceful gurgles made Eric uneasy. The house of a dying woman was no place for a newborn.

He told himself not to think too much about feeding a baby, that the process would kick in automatically, like riding a bicycle. He kept air out of the bottle, allowed Owen to pull the nipple into his mouth, and paused frequently, withdrawing the bottle to imitate breast let-down patterns. Eventually, Owen drowsed off. Another face in sleep, Eric thought, though one that had no dreams or thoughts or years behind it. No yesterday, no tomorrow. He couldn't have been more than two weeks old. Eric looked for some resemblance to Anna and quickly found it: high-boned, rounded cheeks and her classical Greek nose. Maybe she really had gone off to give birth. Some women never gained weight, never showed signs. Witches, for instance.

Three hours later he fed Owen again, this time while sitting next to Kathy's bed. Kathy's eyes were half open and from some remote region she seemed to contemplate Owen in the crook of his arm, sucking milk. Owen's gaze also came from far off, but his eyes stared into that same distance as well; space and time didn't yet separate his gaze from its object. Eric had the impression that Owen's murmurs soothed Kathy. The opposite effect they had on him. He feared that Anna and Owen might now compose one package. He needed to find out where the baby had come from and where he was headed. The longer Eric held him in his arms, the greater grew his dread. No matter how sweet and soothing his rippling gurgles, Owen had to go.

Anna awoke late that evening, groggy, spiritless, still exhausted. She checked on both Owen and Kathy, showered and ate some fruit. Besides weight, she had also lost her regal air. She seemed not to notice the mess of the house. When Eric offered her a glass of wine, she said, "It'll put me back to sleep."

Even her voice sounded different, a faint quaver now in its register. Her eyes flitted about. She reminded Eric of a silver raven trapped in a cage. They sat on stools at the kitchen counter. He opened a Pinot and poured two glasses.

"I realize you're beat," he said, "but I need to know what's going on."

She sipped wine, set her glass back down, made an effort to speak

"Ten days ago in Florida my half-sister Julia died in a motorcycle accident. You remember I told you about her?"

"I remember," he said. "I'm sorry for your loss."

He wondered what phantoms the accident had awoken in her own psyche. She seemed to lose track of her words, then find them.

"I told you before that we were never close," she said. "We shared the same useless father. Nothing else." She paused again. "Julia was eight and a half months pregnant. Owen was saved by Caesarian section."

"Eight months pregnant and on a motorcycle?"

"That was Julia. Stupid, vain, predatory. I never liked her. The only reason we even maintained contact was because there were no other relatives."

"What about Owen's father?"

"Less than half a year ago he was shot dead. A drug deal that went south. Afterwards, Julia apparently drew up a will naming me Owen's legal guardian in case of her own death."

"She never said anything about it to you?"

"Not a word. It seems that little detail wasn't important to her." She winced as if her wine glass had suddenly grown heavy. "My mentor met Julia one time. By chance when we were on a street in Tallahassee. Later she told me, 'That one will bring you trouble.' I always thought she got it wrong since I never lived anywhere near Julia, never had anything to do with her. Now trouble is here."

Eric nodded. He had the exact same feeling.

"What will you do?" he asked

"What can I do?"

Again the quaver in her voice, some echo of impending defeat.

"All I know is we can't have a baby here," he said. "It's impossible."

"Then tell me what to do," she said tiredly, "and I'll do it."

Anna asking *him* what *she* should do. He was talking to a stranger.

"You've got to find a solution to your problem," he said.

They sat staring at their wine glasses, both now empty. He couldn't bring himself to reach for the bottle. Anna looked like she might collapse at any moment.

"You'll have to tell me to go," she said. "I won't leave Kathy on my own." She shook her head, shook herself awake. "I didn't want this. Believe me. I didn't want it in any way, shape or form. You can't imagine what it does to me."

She was wrong. He could imagine. Her pact with the devil had just suffered a fatal blow, not to mention her profession of full-time caregiver. Kathy would soon die— tomorrow, the next day, next week—and Anna would have to search for new employment. In the past she might have been recommended all over town but now her résumé came with a new item attached. How many families would welcome her and a crying infant into the home of a dying relative? The witch mixing herbs and potions had become a mommy cleaning up baby poo.

"Isn't there some family member who could take Owen?" Eric asked.

"None came to Julia's funeral."

"But there must be some distant relative."

"The distant relative is me."

"There has to be someone else."

"The only one I know of is a cousin who's serving time on burglary charges."

"Julia must have had some friends."

"A few who aren't in prison yet, but probably will be soon. None who would be remotely interested in fostering a newborn and none I could in good conscious give Owen to." She let out a sigh that sounded more like a moan. "I can't talk any more."

She didn't have to. He could divine her thoughts. If she wasn't a caregiver, who was she? He was sure that putting Owen up for adoption was out of the question, so he didn't even try that angle. But he had to make it clear that Barbara Street wasn't destined to become Owen's home. Likewise, she had also just made something clear to him. *I won't leave Kathy on my own.* They had arrived at an impasse.

He sipped more wine but now it tasted like a mixture of earth and stone. Maybe he should dine on air. From the living room came the sound of Owen whimpering. Anna motioned to rise but then slumped back down onto the counter.

"Please, could you this once?" she asked.

He took out the formula milk powder and set the kettle to boil. He was beginning to feel like a trapped bird himself. Unlike Anna, he was in a cage of his own making. A cage padlocked by a thousand-year-old tradition of hospitality. The bars were forged of silence, stillness, solitude. He might not want to accept the responsibility but he couldn't ignore that Owen was a gift sent by God. Eric should welcome him into his home as he would welcome the Infant Jesus Himself.

CHAPTER THIRTY-SIX

As before, Eric and Anna sat by Kathy's bed, though now he cradled a baby in his arms. Owen sucked at his bottle while Eric observed his spotless cheeks, his smooth forehead. Impossible to hold a newborn and not feel a tremor in your soul. But Eric delighted in Owen's purity of being, not his presence. He recalled the promise he had made to Kathy: to live his life. Motion and hustle were just a way of running down strength, a strain on the nerves. Other lives were due. He handed Owen over to Anna,

The house creaked, the tree beyond the window moaned. He watched Anna raise the bottle to Owen's lips. She was attentive to his purrs and snivels but disturbed by them as well. She was designed for another devotion, obsessed by a different demon. Purple shadows still drooped beneath her eyes. Not just weary, Eric thought, but transfigured, as if reprogrammed, her core self recast. She was no longer the woman who had crawled into his bed, offering to "please" him. Though some things didn't change.

"Tell me again about your Sadhu journey," she said.

"You don't give up, do you?" he replied.

"I like hearing the story."

"I've told you everything. There's nothing more to tell."

"Then tell it again. It's one of those stories like a loop. It can start anywhere."

"Where in the loop do you want to start?"

She thought for a moment. "With Jamie John. Start with

him. How did you feel when he stopped to pick you up? A giant with a handlebar mustache and a white tuxedo inviting you into his air-conditioned chariot. It sounds like a fairy tale. Didn't you feel like it—like you were entering a fairy tale?"

"More like I had fallen into a flying igloo. I hadn't moved so fast or been anywhere so cold in months."

"He told you it was your lucky day."

"He also called me 'old timer'."

"You must have looked horrible."

"Felt like it too."

"Do you miss it?"

"There's not a lot to miss. Blisters, sore feet, hot sun."

"You said the jewel of your solitude didn't sparkle very long. I thought about it when I read your poems. The title poem: *Heart like a jewel*."

He frowned. "It's an easy metaphor."

"Is an easy metaphor bad?"

"I think I even borrowed it from some Buddhist text."

"Is it bad to borrow?"

"Somebody—T.S. Eliot maybe—said it's better to steal."

"Well, I liked it anyway."

She still held Owen in the crook of her arm, the bottle at his mouth. Kathy's laborious breaths had grown louder. Inhalation, exhalation. And Owen slurping. The chorus of sounds made Eric sleepy. He felt he might nod off at any moment. Kathy's next exhalation was harsh. Then the only sound left in the room was Owen slurping.

"My hands are full," Anna whispered. "You should close her eyes."

"Do what?"

He lurched forward. Distracted by talk of poetry, his tired brain hadn't registered the reality two feet in front of him. He reached over the chrome rail and let his fingertips smooth Kathy's eyelids downward. He placed a kiss onto her still warm forehead, held the kiss there as her last warmth flooded onto his lips. My wife, he thought. Once upon a time, once upon a long time past.

After a moment, he said: "What should we do?"

"Let Owen finish his bottle," Anna answered.

Logical and appropriate. Eric folded his hands in his lap and found the mumbled mantra running through his brain. Good. The one thing of value he had brought back from his Sadhu journey. Not a *Hail Mary* or *Our Father* learned by rote. Just a sound turning a final breath into a blessing. He felt like he would fall into a coma himself and when he awoke he would continue dreaming the saddest dreams. Failure would carry him along perilous paths to the ends of the earth, the abode of shadows and dust devils. He had to travel, to shake off enchantments, forsake his heart no longer like a jewel.

Meanwhile Owen went on slurping his milk. Finally, Anna jiggled him on her shoulder and he produced a wet squawk, somewhere between a hiccup and a burp. He was asleep even before she set him into his basket.

"If you'd like," she said, "we can wash Kathy together. If you don't want to, I'll—"

"Just tell me what to do," Eric said, "but first I have to call Jessica."

He took out his cell phone thinking that Kathy's slow crossing over into death had suddenly accelerated. Had she waited for Anna to return? Almost certainly. Or maybe no matter how much you anticipated death, it always came by surprise.

Jessica arrived twenty minutes later. How often since his return to Ashland had he seen her minus her new smile? In tears, she hugged him, hugged Anna, glanced strangely at Owen. Then she told Eric that she couldn't bear to see the corpse. She sat in the living room on the sofa, grinding her teeth, mustering a determined look, Owen's basket on the cushion next to her. "I'm okay," she said. "You go ahead."

Eric went into Kathy's room and closed the door behind him. Anna stood waiting by the bed. Kathy's death had activated her automatic pilot. She seemed more alert, more herself. She had prepared water, soap, washrags, sponges and towels. She set out a plastic package containing lotus leaves and a miniature bottle of essential camphor oil. Next to it she placed a second bottle of olive oil, though when Eric bent forward and looked closer it appeared too thick to be olive oil.

"Is that to anoint her?" he asked.

"After we've washed her." She handed him a pair of blue surgical gloves. "We start with the genitals."

She mixed the lotus leaves into the water and directed him to follow behind her. She worked methodically. Assisting her, he realized how ineptly he had bathed Father Glenn's corpse. She poured water onto the right side of the body and then onto the left. Using one of the towels, he swabbed the run off over Kathy's ribs and stomach. The flesh was sallow and shrunken. Her limbs had withered to nothing but bone. No more obsessions, he thought, no more demons.

He struggled to concentrate on the ablutions, but couldn't stop thinking that he had once made love to this once gorgeous body. Two living beings had emerged from it. He had been present for both births. He recalled Kathy's pants and cries and the joy in her eyes when the midwife announced Billy's birth: "Here and happy, alive and kicking!"

Anna washed the body three times. Before the third, she added several drops of camphor to the water. A bracing fragrance of greenery, almost of rosemary, struck Eric's nostrils. Now, as he dried Kathy's body, tears ran down his cheeks. Anna lifted the second miniature bottle, wet her right thumb with its contents and pressed her thumb onto the center of Kathy's forehead. She murmured phrases he couldn't distinguish. A witch's chant, he guessed. Some ceremonial rite. Not so different from his own mumbled mantra. He may not have understood the words but he grasped their intent. Or thought he did. Hymns of transition, a song for a safe journey.

He became aware that Anna's body was shaking. Her chants and mourning grew more vibrant, more savage. Suddenly she let out a terrible wail, a shriek of lamentation that froze him. She threw herself forward onto Kathy's naked breast and lay there keening like a wild animal.

Jessica cried from out in the living room. "What is it? What's happening?"

Eric reached forward and pulled Anna back. She trembled in his embrace. His own body had begun to shake as well. He released her and stepped aside. Her dark eyes glinted fiercely. He managed to find words:

"We should call someone."

She took a slow breath. "The hospice." Her voice once again turned calm, as if she had just poured out all her pain. "There's an on-call nurse. She'll send the hearse."

CHAPTER THIRTY-SEVEN

At the reception following Kathy's funeral, Eric struggled to perform the role of stalwart ex-husband. Mercifully, Jessica turned gracious and articulate, as if she had spent years training for a career as mistress of memorial ceremonies. She employed her new smile and greeted all of Kathy's friends and even chatted to Kathy's seldom seen relatives, who came down from Portland. After the meal, Eric gave a short commemorative talk in which, unaccountably and bizarrely, he suddenly quoted Psalm 128: "Your wife will be like a fruitful vine within your house, your children will be like olive shoots around your table." Jessica stared at him thunderstruck and Anna looked as if he had just announced a bingo tournament. A few mourners reached for tissues.

It seemed that every person Kathy had ever met had shown up. Everyone including Abe, the personal trainer. Eric offered his hand but Abe stared as if it held a live snake.

"This never should have happened," he said bitterly.

Eric retracted his hand. "We're all in a state of shock."

"Never," Abe repeated.

"We'll miss her," Eric said. "All of us."

"She was always trim and toned," Abe insisted.

Many of Kathy's former co-workers seemed to share his feelings; a few even acted disgusted by Eric. A rumor ran around that he had met Anna on his Sadhu journey, they had engaged in an illicit affair and Owen, their love child, was the scandalous result. Others were less judgmental. The girl who ran the juice bar at the Health Center said she was "anguished and heartbroken" and felt sorry for him.

Mabel Shoemaker gave Eric a warm hug and told him to be "strong." He replied that he would be, but he was so dazed and wearied he could have quoted a psalm to her as well. He just wanted to get out of there and get home. Meanwhile Anna stood apart, tending to Owen in his basket. Her black garb had become fitting, Eric thought, just when her work as a caregiver was ending.

Two former DMT colleagues appeared out of nowhere. Eric recognized their voices and faces, even remembered the shape of their offices in the Medford headquarters, but their names escaped him. Life at DMT. Like a memory of childhood. The open road under all skies, he thought, and one man perfectly sober, more reticent than the finest beggar, proud to have no home, no friends. What junk. Still, their sincere condolences made him wonder if he had returned for this: to bury his ex-wife with an appearance of dignity, to bury the past with her.

A familiar face materialized in front of him. It was Tony, one of his former best friends and Saturday morning golf buddies. They stammered at each other and Tony tried to express his condolences. "What we did was wrong," he suddenly blubbered. "Earl and Pete and me, we turned against you for... for nothing, and it was wrong. If—if you ever want to play a few holes..."

Finally, the affair ended. Back home, Eric poured a drink and sat by the rear window, watching trees and plants out in the moonlit garden. Anna put Owen to bed and made herbal tea. He couldn't suppress the notion that Kathy was still in the house. He resolved to clear out her things the following day. Then he went to bed. In the middle of the night he dreamed he was about to make love to a woman who was half Kathy, half Anna.

In the morning, he called the medical equipment rental company and two men came to remove Kathy's hospital bed and wheelchair. Over the following days Eric collected all the other articles of her illness—crutches, drip stand, commode chair, humidifier, sitz bath—and dropped them off at a Medford charity. He gave her clothes, including 20 pairs of tennis and track shoes, to the Goodwill Retail Store on Tolman Creek Road. Then he scrubbed down her room from ceiling to floorboards and re-installed Billy's old bed, night stand and dresser. As he was laying a rug across the slatted wood floor, Anna looked in.

"Shouldn't we do the smudging again?" he asked. "Especially in here?"

"We will," she said listlessly.

She had gone from tireless female caregiver to tired female in need of care. Days had passed and neither of them had mentioned the obvious. Anna's employment and purpose in the house had officially ended. She and Owen had to leave, but it was as if Kathy were still nearby, still in need of care.

"Let's go out for dinner," he suggested. "We can talk and then take a walk by the river."

At a downtown restaurant they talked very little. They

each had a salad and an eggplant-hummus burger while Owen burbled in his basket, much to the delight of the waiter, who complimented them on their "lovely child." Toward the end of the meal Anna said:

"Are you very... disquieted over Kathy's death?"

Her usual odd way of putting things, he thought. But precise all the same. His 'quiet' had been removed. They walked into Lithia Park and strolled along the creek. At Black Swan Lake they watched three ducks paddle along the shore. Other walkers were out. They smiled at Owen in his stroller. Then a woman who had been at the funeral passed by, one of Kathy's work colleagues. She glared at Eric. He guessed it had something to do with his "illicit affair."

"Let's head back," he said.

At the house, he unlocked the front door and Anna carried Owen inside. He followed behind her. Midway across the living room she suddenly stopped, her tall body tense.

"Somebody's here," she whispered.

"What?"

"Here in the house. A presence."

Eric stood stock still, peered down the length of the hall, ears pricked. Everything was quiet, no sound except the distant hum of the fridge. He reached for Anna's free arm and gently pulled her back outside and down the front path. Near his car he took out his cell phone and started to dial 911 but then stopped.

"Wait here," he said.

She held Owen close to her breast. "Where're you going? What're you going to do?"

"I'll be right back."

He hurried around the side of the house, glancing through parted curtains at the interior. Nothing broken and no sign of entry. The garden was quiet, the rear door locked. He double-checked every window. Back out front, he found Anna and Owen still by the curb.

"What did you mean when you said 'a presence'?" he asked. "A ghost? Kathy's spirit?"

"Don't be ridiculous," she said, still in a whisper. "I meant a man."

"But you didn't see anyone?"

She shook her head.

"So you're saying you felt a strange vibration or a—"

"I smelled body sweat and I'm calling the police."

"No, you're not." It was a voice she had never heard. DMT Chief Strategy Officer. Important boss. Her hand froze reaching into her purse. He continued in a whisper but kept a commanding tone. "The cops already think I'm the neighborhood nutcase. Just wait a damn minute."

He told her to take Owen to the other side of the street. If something happened, she should call the neighbors. He waited until she and Owen were safely on the opposite curb and then he returned to the front door. He opened it and left it wide open. Anna might be imagining things—her nerves were on edge the same as his—but he could guess the presence she might have detected. Abe. Eric hadn't forgotten his first impression, shaking hands or not. A strange guy with frayed wires.

He started a slow, room-by-room search through the length of the house. No sign of anyone, no scent of anything. When he reached his room at the rear, he opened the top drawer to his dresser. A little pile of bills and loose change sat inside, untouched. He started back through the house, calmer now, inspecting every corner. He opened the fridge, glanced around the bathroom, peeked in the hall closet. At the front door he signaled for Anna to come back across the street. When she arrived, he asked if she could still smell anything.

"You had the door open the whole time," she said. "You aired the place out."

"Or maybe you imagined it," he replied. "Either way there's no one here. Nothing's broken or stolen or even moved an inch."

She looked around uncertainly. "I guess not..."

"We've had a rough few days," he said. "We need a break." He gestured toward Owen's basket. "Why don't you feed him and put him to bed and I'll pour some wine."

"I don't want wine."

He poured her a glass anyway. He carried it to the living room along with a bowl of chips and arranged everything on the coffee table. She came out a few minutes later. They sat on the sofa.

"Everything okay?" he asked.

She fixed an eye on him. "Are you asking about Owen or still asking if I think there's a ghost in the house?"

"Only asking. But we'll lock up tight tonight."

Maybe she hadn't imagined anything, he thought. Maybe

she had invented it. Cast a little spell to create a diversion. Avoid the issue at hand.

After a moment she kicked off her shoes and lifted her feet up onto the cushion. It was an easy, relaxed motion, but it made him realize he had never before paid any attention to her feet. They were narrow and slightly flat. The lack of an arch made them appear longer than they were; her toes were thin and delicate, unusual for a tall woman. He had to check an impulse to set his wine onto the coffee table and offer a massage.

They were quiet for a while. A police or ambulance siren wailed out in the night. He could feel each of them at a loss for something to say. Yet why force idle talk onto silence? They had enough with the wine and chips, the sofa, each other. The simple truth: the issue was now at hand and it wasn't just a matter of Anna and Owen leaving. Ghost or not, presence or not, Kathy was gone and the barrier she had represented—at least to him—was also gone.

Finally, he stood up and said goodnight. Anna made no reply, simply stared as if expecting him to say more. He hesitated, then walked down to his end. In the bathroom he washed his face, thinking that he should have said more. But what? He caught himself scrubbing hard, trying to rub away the web patterns near his temples. He looked at his sunken eyes and the loose skin over his cheek bones, once as tight and smooth as bound vellum. He had never regretted the passage of time, the withering of flesh, but he found himself thinking of his retirement, his children grown into young adulthood, Kathy dying at such a young age. The years passed whether he regretted them or not.

He walked out of the bathroom but then turned back down the hall. When he arrived at the kitchen, Anna stood by the open fridge door, setting a Tupperware onto a middle shelf. She swung the door inward and it thudded shut. She looked at him. The same quizzical look she had given him a minute ago in the living room. Now he stared back with a look of his own.

"What?" she said.

He reached out and took her hand.

"Come with me," he said.

She pulled back slightly. "What about Owen?"

"He'll be okay. If he wakes up, we'll hear him. Come with me."

<h1 style="text-align:center">Chapter Thirty-eight</h1>

They made love over the following days. Owen's naps provided the opportunity and Owen napped a lot. As soon as he started to snooze, Eric and Anna hit the bedroom, peeled off clothes, pulled back sheets. By the third day, they had moved all of Anna's belongings down to his end and located Owen and all baby paraphernalia in the guest room within easy earshot.

Eric had believed he would never again make love. Now it seemed he would never stop. At first, his caresses were clumsy, as if he wore oven mitts, but an ardor verging on anguish propelled both of them into each other's arms again and again. He caressed a new, previously unknown Anna. She remained secretive and injured but somehow made love as if making merry, as if making mischief. A witch delighting in dark forces? He didn't know and didn't care. The more they made love, the more he frolicked in passion's domain. *Do you want me to please you?* Yes, *please.* He had never imagined he would come back this way.

He wondered how he and Kathy had ever let themselves abandon tenderness. Exchanging elation for apathy, splitting their home in half. Careful, he warned himself. Don't embark on a pleasure cruise away from turmoil. Lose one treasure, but not two.

"We have to talk," he said.

He watched her dark eyes lock onto his, felt her reading his thoughts. She knew exactly what he meant, spoke as if he had just outlined the subject in detail.

"Technically," she said, "the state of Florida is still searching for a possible parent."

"You mean in Owen's extended family? You don't sound hopeful."

"Not even slightly. It's a formality. Paperwork pushed from desk to desk. If someone existed, I'd already know about them."

"I don't want to rush either of us," he said, "but I also don't want to confuse Owen's situation with wherever our relationship is going, if it's going." He noted a faint spark in her gaze. "Just so you know: I'm thinking about selling the house. Or renting it and moving into a smaller place, maybe an apartment downtown. I still need to figure all that out. I'm also thinking I might... leave again. Right now the only thing I know for sure is that Owen can't be here."

"I can't be here either," she replied. "Like I told you before, my pact didn't come with an expiration date."

What he had guessed she might say. "Are you going to look for another placement?"

"I've been looking."

That surprised him. "Any luck?"

"So far not a nibble. No one around here wants a baby. They won't even listen to the idea."

"Maybe you need to consider a different line of work."

"I tried that once before. I got fed up with sickness and suffering, death and dying, caring for cadavers. I wanted my own life, wanted to feel alive, vital, fresh. So I broke my pact."

"And?"

"And I won't make that mistake again."

Another stalemate, except this time he was left with the phrase, "No one around here." She didn't mean "around here" on Barbara Street or "around" the neighborhood. She meant around the greater Ashland-Medford area. She had exhausted her possibilities and was searching farther afield, maybe even out of state.

He had said his piece and had nothing to add. So he softened his tone and backed off, which was easy to do because it meant going back to making love, to being pleased and pleasing. One morning, raking leaves in the garden, he found himself whistling. As far as he could remember, he had never whistled in his life. He hadn't even been aware that he knew how to whistle. It wasn't any recognizable tune, just cheery song, another backyard bird flitting among the flowers. Even though he might soon be humming a different tune.

On Thursday morning, he met Jessica at the Bright Day Café. Mabel served them each a latte at a window table. He observed his daughter grinding her teeth.

"What's wrong?" he said.

"Nothing."

"Are you mad at me about something?"

"Not mad. I wouldn't call it that."

"What would you call it?"

Dragging it out of her word by word, he learned that a friend of hers had seen him walking with Anna and Owen in Lithia Park. According to the friend's account, he and Anna had stopped near a central duck pond and engaged in a "sexy kiss."

"God, Dad," Jessica said, lowering her voice. "What

are you into—some kind of fake happy family scene? It's perverse."

"Fake family? Perverse?"

"She's like fifteen years younger than you."

"So who cares about that?"

"You should, for one. You're making a fool of yourself."

"Why don't you let me worry about that?"

"And right after Mom dies."

"Let me worry about that too."

"It's pathetic," she said. "Even you have to admit it."

Once again she was telling him he was pathetic and crazy and that he should get hold of himself. The only difference was that this time he had changed from Jesus crossing a desert into a pervert. When he arrived back home, he made the mistake of telling Anna about his talk with Jessica. She was busy feeding Owen and immediately made a face. A kiss by a duck pond? Who had they offended—the ducklings? He shrugged and mentioned Jessica's concerns about their age difference. Anna drew the bottle away from Owen's mouth, looked at him: "And who cares about that?"

She put Owen to sleep and they went to bed. She lay her head on his chest and drifted off into dreams. He was slow to follow. He still had the sound of Jessica's teeth grinding in his head.

Hours later he awoke with a start. Something was wrong. Anna sat on the edge of the bed, her long torso naked in the dim moonlight, the plated mass of her hair bunched across her shoulders. She was reaching for her robe. Eric sat up. She leaned back, put her lips against his ear.

"Somebody's here," she whispered. "In the house."

"Wha—?" He stiffened, leaned forward, ears pricked. He was about to say he didn't hear anything but then he did: the distinct sound of the living room floor creaking. "But... I bolted the security lock," he murmured.

"They came in through a window. Kathy's room."

He yanked the sheet aside. "Call the Police," he whispered urgently.

She grabbed his wrist. "Don't go down there."

"Get Owen," he said, freeing himself. "Call 911. Hide in the bathroom. Lock it."

She said something else but he had already pulled on his pajama bottoms and was halfway across the room. As he crept out into the hall, he glimpsed a large masculine form down at the other end. Minus his glasses, he saw only a blur and then the blur was gone. He couldn't be sure he had actually seen anyone. He took soundless steps forward, aware that no childhood baseball bat remained in the house. When he came to the kitchen, he reached across the counter and slipped a carving knife out of its wooden holder. He hefted it in his right hand, ears still pricked toward the living room. No other sound came. He knew that if Anna and Owen hadn't been in the house, he would have spun on his heel and raced straight out the back door. He also knew he couldn't stab anyone, no matter what, so he slipped the knife back into the holder and grabbed a cast iron skillet, small but solid and heavy enough to knock anyone flat.

He crept down the hall, now dark and empty. A noise came from Kathy's room and he regretted not taking the knife. He hesitated, caught at the point of charging forward or retreating back to the kitchen. Finally, he turned the knob on Kathy's door and pushed it open. The bedside lamp was on, the window wide open. A naked man stood near the bed, large and muscular, his back to Eric. A hideous tattoo covered his shoulder blades: black and red daggers, flames and gargoyles. Across his lower back in old English print appeared the word *KAOS!* Eric gasped and the man spun around, his bearded, sullen features twisted into a grimace.

"Billy..." Eric said.

Billy's dilated eyes went to Eric's right hand, to the frying pan. He let out a cackle. "Hey, Dad, what's cookin'?"

He pronounced the word *Dad* with hostility and repugnance. Eric stammered. "You can't... just walk in here in the middle of the night. My God, Billy, wh— what're you doing?"

"What's it look like?" Billy snapped back. "I'm going to bed. Now get the fuck outa my room."

He reached down and yanked the sheet off the pillow. His movements were ham-handed, thuggish. He was drunk or drugged, maybe both. He had gained forty pounds since Eric had last seen him, half muscle, half fat. Flame and dagger tattoos covered his chest and stomach. His penis swung between burly thighs. His green eyes had a far-off, brutal gaze. Eric was aware of Anna coming up behind him, looking over his shoulder. Just then three police cars pulled into the frame of the open window. Uniformed officers jumped out onto Barbara Street and came running toward the house, guns drawn.

"Now what?" Billy said, sneering.

An officer appeared in the window frame, took a quick

look into the room and holstered his revolver. "Everything okay here, sir?" he asked Eric, noting the skillet.

"Will be as soon as you leave," Billy said, and laughed out loud.

"Billy, shut up," Eric said.

Billy let out another laugh and tumbled into bed, oozing drunken disdain. The officer watched him for a moment and then spoke again to Eric.

"Sir, would you mind stepping out your front door?"

Turning, Eric met Anna's gaze. He glanced downward. She gripped the carving knife in her right hand. "Hide that," he snapped.

On the way through the living room he dropped the frying pan onto the sofa. By the time he got to the door, the other officers had returned to their squad cars. As radios crackled and car doors shut, house lights flicked on across the street. Silhouetted forms appeared in windows. The officer listened impassively as Eric spluttered through an explanation.

"...I apologize... it's just that my son... came home unexpectedly and... decided not to knock..."

The officer's expression remained blank. "Sir, it looks like the lock on that bedroom window has been tampered with. But you're saying that's your son in there?"

"Yes, that's correct. He's my son."

"And you're telling me everything's okay here in your house?"

"Yes, it's fine. Thank you. I'm sorry... very sorry about all this. I—— I apologize."

"And there's a baby on the premises?"

"A...?"

"That's the report we received. An endangered baby."

"Yes..." He glanced back at Anna. "Yes, we have a baby here."

"May I see the baby, sir."

"Yes, of course."

Anna hurried down the hall. Eric remained at the door, struggling to keep his mouth shut. He had already apologized enough. Anna must have said "endangered baby" to get rapid results. And she had: three squad cars in a matter of minutes. She reappeared with Owen in her arms, wrapped in a light blue baby blanket, sound asleep. The officer peered down at him.

"Cute little guy," he said. "Good night, folks."

After he left, Anna carried Owen back down the hall and Eric went into Billy's room. Billy was fast asleep, snoring noisily into the pillow. Jeans, underwear and a t-shirt lay scattered about the floor. Eric closed the window. On the way back out, he paused by the door, his hand on the light switch. He stared at his son's face. Years since he had seen him. Billy's features were swollen, marred by untold abuse. He didn't merely look tattooed and horrible. He was dirty; he needed a bath.

Eric was about to turn off the light when a glint of metal from under the bed caught his eye. He bent down and looked at the floor. There was a cracked leather rifle scabbard, a rifle, a handgun, and a large hunting knife with a gut hook.

CHAPTER THIRTY-NINE

The following morning Eric and Anna drank coffee in his study.

"I need to know what you're going to do," she said.

"First, I have to talk to him," he replied.

"He shouldn't be in Kathy's room."

"He's Kathy's son. My son. The room belongs to him."

"He shouldn't even be in the house."

"It's his home."

"He's dangerous."

"You don't know that."

"I've seen him. He's not well. He's…" He was sure she was about to say *a pill popper*. Instead she said, "…diseased."

He wondered if she had seen the guns. He should have told her about them then and there but he knew it would propel her out the door. So he justified a quick detour around the truth. Billy had lived in Alaska, a state where gun ownership was the norm. More people owned firearms than didn't. He would talk with Billy, get the guns out of the house and then tell her.

"I won't ask him to leave until he gives me a reason," he said.

"Then I'm taking Owen and moving into a motel."

He clunked the coffee mug down onto his desk.

"Wait a damn minute. He isn't some stranger. He's my son. I know him. And I won't let anything happen to Owen. We'll take care of Owen and we'll take care of each other."

She seemed to relent, or at least that's how he chose to interpret her silence. Drinking a second coffee in the kitchen, he rehearsed a paternal speech while Anna busied herself with laundry. Like him, she stayed alert to every sound from the front of the house. He already regretted not telling her about the guns but that would be top priority in his speech. Besides, what he had said was true. He knew Billy. Knew his son.

He cleaned the kitchen and took out trash. Then he worked in the garden but never strayed far from the back door. He lifted the barbecue grill out of the dirt and washed it down. He raked leaves. As the morning passed, he began to suspect that Billy had left the house the same way he had entered, through the window. Shortly after noon, Eric cracked open the bedroom door. Billy had barely moved an inch. Or he had moved a great deal and had ended up in the same position, mouth ajar, dirty face pressed against the pillow. Eric observed his unkempt hair, the long lines abuse had carved down his cheeks. He felt overwhelmed by both tenderness and dread. He also felt compelled to recall how he had looked upon arrival at Chassors. The guns were still beneath the bed.

The shopping needed to be done but he didn't want to leave Anna and Owen alone. No matter how he had argued against Anna or how fervently he longed to welcome Billy home, he couldn't fool himself into thinking he trusted him. Billy was his son all right and he was Billy's father; nothing could ever change that. His son's homecoming, however crude and brutal, had sent paternal tremors surging through him. His own life was frayed; maybe Billy's was too. Maybe the real penance was his delinquent son, not his ex-wife. But Billy was uninvited, an interloper who had broken into the house in the middle of the night. Even snoring, he emanated threat.

So Eric put off the shopping until later, but he knew what it implied. He could never leave Anna and Owen alone as long as Billy stayed in the house.

He threw together a late lunch of pasta and salad, setting aside an extra portion. He and Anna ate quietly. He sensed her working on her own options. If he took one course of action, she would take another. Then the sound of Billy stirring came from the front end. Anna looked at Eric as if to say, "Well, let's see how this goes." She carried Owen to his room.

Five minutes later Billy lumbered into the kitchen. He was dressed in an "Aus Rotten" t-shirt and camouflage pants corkscrewed to his ankles. He was barefoot. Large, dirt-caked toes. Ignoring Eric, he yanked open the fridge door, ripped off the tab on a can of beer, slurped a jet of foam. Then he threw the plate of pasta into the microwave, fired it up and stood nearby muttering, "...fuck... fuck..." until the bell rang. He sat down and shoveled a forkful of pasta into his mouth, then another, chewing robot-like, still cold-shouldering Eric, who watched from the other side of the counter.

Yes, Eric thought, he's my son. Same ticks and quirks. Same spray of blackheads across his nose. The false crassness and bluster came straight out of adolescence, but there were whole new layers of aberrance. Billy acted unnatural and deviant, on a collision course with any obstacle in his path. If the obstacle wasn't there, he would create it. He pushed his plate aside, burped loudly, threw a grimace across the counter.

Eric spoke in a calm voice:

"We should talk about things. It's been a long time since we've been together. I guess you know your mother just died."

Billy pulled an exasperated look, as if Eric had referred to an event so trivial it wasn't worth mentioning. "So, bye-bye, toodle-oo," he said.

"Billy, I'm talking about your mother, the person who brought you into this life."

"Yeah, well I didn't ask for that, did I? And I didn't ask you to fuck her to make it happen. So like I said: bye-bye and fuck you too. Fuck both of you for bringing me into this shithole game."

He was exactly what Anna had said: *diseased*. Not at ease, lacking ease, and out to make everyone else ill at ease as well.

"Anyway, I'm glad to see you," Eric went on amiably, "glad to welcome you home. Are you here on a visit or here to stay?"

Billy snorted. "I'm here—that's all you got to know."

Eric remained impervious to the belligerence but inserted a note of authority into his tone. "If you plan on staying longer than today, I need to know quite a bit more. I also want your cell number in case I have to get hold of you at any time."

Billy smirked as if the notion was so absurd and uncool as to be hilarious. He pushed up off the counter and reached into the fridge for another beer. He took two pills out of his pocket, tossed them into his mouth and put on a show of swilling down half the beer.

"You gave this place up," he said. "You said you didn't want it, said you were going away forever and ever, said all kinds of shit. Maybe you thought I didn't know but I heard, all right. You got religion or some bullshit in your fucked-up brain and went for a walk in the clouds. Then Mom dies and now you're back and you got a chick and a kid and you need a place to crash, but that ain't my itch. Mom died and I'm the oldest so the house goes to me. Now it's mine."

So that was it, Eric thought. Billy hadn't dropped through the window out of nowhere. Word had reached him and he figured he had hit the lottery. He had memorized some half-baked chatter and come to collect his winning ticket. Free roof over his dirty head, free drugs and booze till the end of time. Even sitting across the counter, Eric could feel rage coming off his son's large frame like swelter from a blast furnace.

"You mean now you're going to pay the taxes and insurance?" Eric said.

Billy pulled the beer can away from his mouth. "What?"

"This house is in my name. It doesn't matter if I got religion or bullshit in my brain. I'm still the owner."

Billy stared at him. Eric no longer knew him well enough to tell how much stupidity he was acting out and how much had become ingrained after years of acting stupid.

"I won't turn you out, son," he said, watching Billy flinch at the word *son*, "but I will lay down rules. If you're going to stay, you'll have to obey them."

Billy twisted his mouth into another smirk and scoffed victoriously, as if he had gotten exactly what he was after. "Make all the rules you want. You were always good at that."

"Then pay attention. First rule is no guns in the house. I don't care if they're registered and legit or not. Get them out now or I call the cops."

Billy inhaled the rest of the beer, crushed the can in his fist. "Hey, you got thirty... forty bucks to slide me? I'm a little short. I'll get it back soon as I get paid..."

Eric sat still for a long moment, making Billy twitch impatiently. Finally, he reached into his wallet, took out a twenty-dollar bill and set it on the counter, pinning it under his fingers.

"Second rule: this end of the house is off limits to you. The kitchen door stays locked and you stay down at your end. Got it?"

"Whatever. Hey, I said thirty or forty."

"Next, you keep away from Anna and the baby. You don't even say good morning."

Billy rolled his eyes, scowled.

"Next, your friends aren't welcome at any time for any reason. Not even a one-minute visit. Not any of them."

"For fuck's sake, just gimme the money."

"Next, your drugs aren't welcome here either. No meth, no weed, no—"

Suddenly Billy jumped forward, batted Eric's hand

aside and snatched the twenty-dollar bill. "Fuckin' A," he muttered, pocketing the bill.

Eric's hand stung from the blow. He resisted the urge to rub it.

"Remember what I said," he warned, but Billy was already plodding down the hall.

A few minutes later the front door opened and shut. Eric arrived at the bay window in time to see an old Buick driving off. He opened the door to Billy's room and peered under the bed. The guns were gone. Maybe because he had ordered it or maybe because Billy carried them around wherever he went. But they were out of the house now and Eric no longer felt obliged to tell Anna.

He glanced around the room. Underwear still on the floor, the night stand lamp tipped onto its side, the bed unmade and soiled. He felt anxious but also morally cornered and it wasn't just a matter of penance. How could he forbid his prodigal son from returning home when he, the prodigal father, had just done the same? My poor sweet soul, he thought, I might have to forego eternity.

Back in the kitchen he picked up Billy's plate and fork, threw the beer cans into the trash and wiped down the counter. His hand still stung. Billy had knocked it aside to get the twenty dollars but also to let Eric feel his strength. Surly, defiant teen sneering in the face of upright, dogmatic Dad. How quickly they had slipped into their roles of a decade ago. Dad who set down rules, parceled out allowance money. Except that now the teen was way past adolescence. He was twenty-five-years old, a young adult supposedly finding his way in the world.

More like losing it, Eric thought. He recognized his son's voice, his blackheads, some long ago expression on his grimy face, but not much else. Maybe Billy had fallen through the bedroom window and crash-landed in his old bed because he needed Eric to recognize him. Or maybe he had returned, as he had implied, to exact revenge for ever being born, for being brought into "this shithole game."

When Eric locked the kitchen door, a sick feeling came over him. He showed Anna the key. "I laid down the law," he told her. "He breaks it and he's out. I promise you that."

"What does he want here?"

Eric shook his head. "I really don't know."

"He must want something."

"He's lost." Eric said. "Really lost, so I suppose he wants the same thing we all want. To find his way." Or maybe he just wanted to stay lost. "Come on, let's go for a walk."

Strings of burnt sienna clouds drifted across the eastern horizon above the Siskiyous. Owen fell asleep in his stroller before they even reached the bike path. Eric guessed Anna was still weighing options. He imagined that looking at Billy, she had caught a glimpse of her own pill-popping past. As for himself, instead of enjoying a pleasant evening stroll, he was sweating furiously. What was happening back at the house? Had Billy returned yet and, if so, what trouble had he brought with him? Eric thought about his car keys, Kathy's jewelry, the money in his dresser drawer. When they got back from their stroll, what would he have to deal with—a request for another loan that would never be repaid, or something more sinister?

CHAPTER FORTY

Two days passed and Billy didn't return.

"Maybe he found somewhere else to crash," Eric said. "Or maybe he went back to Alaska."

"I still don't understand why he came in the first place," Anna said.

Eric could only make a guess. "Home is where you go when you can't take it anymore."

Every time a car door slammed out on the street, his intestines twisted into tight knots. He stopped washing dishes or preparing Owen's bottle and readied himself for his son, drunk or drugged, stumbling through the front door. Then the car drove off or a neighbor entered a house. To drown out street noise and create some calm, Eric turned on the radio. A local station with national news and small-town advertising. ("Ashland Candy welcomes your sweet tooth!") Whenever he ran errands in town, he took Anna and Owen with him.

"He might or might not show up," Anna said. "Might or might not do something ugly. Meanwhile we tremble every time a bird chirps."

"Just give it a bit more time," Eric said. "It'll work out."

Brave words but he couldn't deny the danger, real or imagined, couldn't deny it split him down the middle just like his house. He tried to convince himself that Billy could never sink so far beneath his tattoos that he wouldn't recognize him, but Billy was no longer a bubblegum kid riding his skateboard down Barbara Street.

The indeterminate threat mixed badly with Owen's care and turned Anna back into her bossy self. She angered over trivialities and their state of new lover's bliss withered on the vine of hurtful argument. It was as if she wanted to annoy him so he would explode and throw her out, making her decision for her. The pact that had kept her vital and engaged disintegrated with each passing day. She needed a new patient, someone in pain and dying and desperate for her skills. But Billy had put everything on hold.

On Thursday afternoon Eric dropped Anna and Owen off at the pediatric clinic in town and drove to Safeway. As he was climbing out of the car, he spotted Billy across the parking lot, talking to a red-headed girl. He was dressed in the same t-shirt and camouflage pants. He caught sight of Eric, left the girl and came hurrying across the lot. He pulled up abruptly, irises dilated, pupils ashen.

"I need fifty bucks," he said.

"Why don't you try starting with 'Hi, Dad'?" Eric replied.

"Fifty bucks."

"You still owe me twenty. Remember?"

Billy grimaced. "Gimme a break. We both knew I was never going to pay you back so why pretend?"

"That means you won't pay this back either so why lend?"

"Cuz it'll make you feel better, like a great Dad. You pick the reason. Just give me the fucking money."

He leaned so far forward Eric could have counted every blackhead on his nose. Then Billy gripped Eric's arm. He made it look like a friendly touch but his powerful fingers began to squeeze. Eric threw a quick glance around the parking lot. Shoppers were getting in and out of cars. The red-headed girl had disappeared. A security guard stood by the automatic door at the store entrance.

"I could smash you right here and now," Billy said.

"Get your hand off me," Eric snapped. "What's wrong with you? I'm your father for Chrissake." His heart clenched. Billy looked flawed, savage, shot to pieces. "It's not even craziness or rage," Eric thought. "It's spite for being born. Malice."

He yanked his arm free, stepped back, took out his wallet. He extracted a twenty-dollar bill.

"I want to know if you plan on coming to the house," he said, "and I want your cell number."

Billy rolled his frazzled eyes, looked about to spit.

"Then this is it," Eric said. "No more charity."

Billy snatched the bill out of his hand. "We'll see about that."

He marched off toward town. His steps were uniform and sure, no trace of a wobble. He was at full manic tilt, on his way to a liquor store or a dealer. Watching him go, Eric realized Anna wasn't the only one who needed a pact. He had betrayed both poetry and fatherhood and now he felt a father's poetic anguish. You see your child's wound and you can't heal it. Where had he read it? *The three wise men: the heart, the soul, the mind.* Billy blustered and raced around berserk, leaving anarchic thoughts in his wake—"I'm nobody. Nothing. I don't exist."—like the mantra engraved on his back. *KAOS!*

Eric wondered about his own mantra. When had his mumbled prayers last resounded in his head? It was as if he had buried them along with Kathy. Then the joy of making love to Anna followed by the torment of Billy's arrival. Pleasure and pain, and no need for spiritual claptrap. How quick the return to the pagan past.

When he picked up Anna, he didn't mention running into Billy. Again he reproached himself for the omission. Later that afternoon he was straightening a pile of papers on the dining room cabinet and came across a pamphlet entitled, "Open Adoption: Finding your child a Quality Home." So he wasn't the only one with secrets. He scanned a few paragraphs. They covered topics such as "temporary guardianship" and "kinship embracement." The title of the final section was, "How to embrace adoption as a loving choice."

At the dinner table Anna looked like she had just fallen down a flight of stairs. Dark shadows again hung beneath her red eyes. Eric wondered if she had visited the adoption agency that afternoon instead of the pediatric clinic. Later he was listening to the radio again—an "up-close and pooch friendly" interview with a local dog trainer—when Jessica called. Her teeth clattered loudly and she said, "Billy's back. I ran into him outside that Irish pub. He's worse than ever."

Eric replied with knee-jerk father talk: "He's your brother."

"My brother would've come to Mom's funeral. My brother wouldn't rob me blind like some methhead mugger."

"What do you mean—rob you?"

"He didn't even say *hi*. Just grabbed my purse and took all my cash. Shoved it back at me like he was pissed I didn't have more."

When Eric told her Billy had stayed in the house, her teeth stopped clattering.

"Dad, if you let him live there, you really have lost it."

Later he watched Anna bathe Owen. She supported the head and torso with her forearm, using a soap-free washcloth and damp cotton balls for his eyelids. Eric had once bathed Billy the same way. As she poured warm water down the short length of Owen's spine, he recalled Billy's back before tattoos. Anna wrapped Owen in a towel and patted him dry.

Eric sipped some Makers while listening to Part Two of the interview with the dog trainer. The combination of whiskey and radio eventually sent him to bed. Later, much later, he heard Anna whispering his name. Hazily, he recalled turning off the light, crawling under the sheet, fluffing his pillow. He sensed that hours had passed. Anna sat in the dim light, looking at him worriedly, Owen in her arms. There was a racket of laughter and music.

"What's going on?" he said, sitting up.

"He's back. He's brought a bunch of people with him. They barged in a minute ago. They're having some kind of party."

Eric looked at the alarm. 3:17 AM. He swung his legs out of bed, paused to let the world fall into place. Then he reached for shirt, pants, shoes, pulled them on, raked his fingers through his hair.

"Don't go down there," Anna said. "They're drunk. Call the police."

"And do what—report a party in my own house?"

"Don't go."

"The neighbors have probably already called them anyway."

He headed down the hall. As he approached the kitchen door, the racket grew louder. He recognized the music from Billy's adolescence. Megadeath and AC/DC played at the same time, the same volume. The door was locked. He tried his key but it was bolted from the other side. He knocked with his knuckles, then banged with his fist, kicked, shouted Billy's name into the roar of heavy metal. Finally, he headed back down the hall. On his way through the bedroom he snatched his cell phone off the nightstand. Anna stood near the bed, Owen still in her arms.

"Lock this behind me," Eric said, and hurried out the back door into the garden.

CHAPTER FORTY-ONE

Cars and pickups were parked on the front lawn. Lights glowed in two houses across the street. Passing the bay window, Eric glimpsed twenty people in his living room, mostly men, a few women. He had expected to find an older, tougher crowd—skulls and bones and black leather—but it was a bizarre mix of lowlife hipsters and drop outs, Ashland punks and Oregon farm boys in from the sticks. Three hipsters stood by the porch, each with a hand wrapped around a can of beer.

"Who are *you*?" one said as he walked past into the house.

By the time he reached the center of the living room, his eyes stung from the smoke. The deafening roar of heavy metal charged out of two boom boxes on the mantle. Joints and cigarettes had been ground out on the marble coffee table around Kathy's favorite serving bowl which now held a pile of pastel-colored tablets, some white capsules and what looked like plant fertilizer pellets. A half naked couple were entwined on the floor near the fireplace. Eric peered through the smoke for some sign of Billy. Dull, confused eyes stared back. Pausing by the sofa, he spotted a large stain on the center cushion. A man in black overalls had passed out near the end table.

Billy was in his bedroom, pawing at a woman sprawled across his bed. The same red-haired woman from the Safeway parking lot. She was down to her bra while Billy groped at the buckle of her jeans. He was shirtless; the flame and dagger tattoos twitched on his chest and stomach. She giggled, batting his hand aside. He looked up, saw Eric, glared.

"Get your friends out of here now," Eric said.

"How 'bout you get outa here," Billy replied drunkenly.

He reached out to grab Eric but Eric stepped aside and Billy fumbled at air. "I'm gonna beat your fuckin' ass," he slurred, and fell out of bed onto the floor. The woman laughed. "I'll beat yours too," he told her from the floor.

Eric turned back into the living room, headed straight for the boom boxes and pulled both plugs. The music died and every voice in the room stopped. He spoke loudly.

"The neighbors have called the police," he announced. "You can get out before they get here but you've only got a minute. So grab the dope and go!"

A few people stood frozen, staring at him unsurely, angrily. Others pushed for the door or snatched at the pills on the coffee table. "Wait," somebody yelled. "He ain't nobody. He's talkin' shit." A sudden rush and scattering drowned him out. The hipsters shouted out jokes about "blowing the scene" or "blowing anything in sight." Two men scuffled over the boom boxes. A woman called them "punk losers." Someone pushed Eric aside and he fell into the sofa. The man who had passed out near the end table stumbled to his feet, grabbing a handful of fertilizer pellets.

Outside, car engines roared into life. Eric exited the front door just as a pickup reversed across the front lawn, tearing up grass like a buzz saw. The driver let out a rebel yell. "Wahoo! Party time!" The guy riding shotgun heaved a beer bottle over the cab roof like a grenade. It crashed on the porch at Eric's feet. Cars sped away in both directions. Within minutes the street grew quiet. Lights switched off in the houses across the way. Back inside, Eric searched for Billy. Either he had vanished in the stampede or he had again slipped out his bedroom window, which was now open. Eric shut it and checked under the bed. Nothing but a rug.

He locked the front door and turned off the lights. A moment later a police squad car came down the street. Its spotlight passed over the house on the left. Then the beam flooded through the bay window, illuminating the living room in an eerie glow. Like a convict on the run, Eric stood stock-still behind the door. Thirty years in Ashland and one visit from the police on a windy night. Now they showed up every night, windy or not.

He went down to the kitchen and unbolted the center doors. Anna came in and stood by the counter.

"Owen and I are leaving," she said.

"It's going to stop tonight," Eric replied. "Right now. I'm throwing him out. As soon as he walks in the door or falls through the window."

She observed him without reaction. Then she left to put Owen back to sleep. Ten minutes later she and Eric were in bed. She fell asleep immediately while he lay awake, raging. Worry and irritation were only part of it. The other part was what Anna had described: every time a bird chirped. He was imprisoned in his own house. His half of the house.

Incarcerated by his belief that his son could be redeemed. Yet again his thoughts raced off down strange paths. What price lipstick for a Judas kiss? Why yearn for an eternal sun if on a quest for divine light?

He slept for three hours, took a shower, drank coffee. He had half a mind to make Billy clean up the mess, but he might not show up again for days, maybe weeks. So Eric started collecting bottles and cigarette butts. He found a crystal bowl in shards behind the sofa. A macramé wall hanging, a wine decanter and several knickknacks were missing, probably stolen. He took a garbage bag out the front door and picked up the bottles and cans strewn across the lawn. The buzz-saw gouge had dragged dirt and grass onto the sidewalk.

Then he noticed a commotion halfway down the street beyond the Cookie posters still flapping on tree trunks. An ambulance, a police car, a small crowd of neighbors. The sight sent a perverse thrill through him—so he wasn't the only guy on the block with troubles—but then two people in the crowd turned and pointed and their forefingers were aimed at him.

Ten minutes later he sat in the back of the ambulance next to a stretcher bearing Billy. A neighbor had found him sprawled across her backyard patio. Caked in mud, he had an ugly gash across his forehead and was moaning incoherently. "Classic case," an ambulance attendant had muttered to a cop. "OD, trip, conk your noodle."

Eric spent the rest of the morning at the hospital. Eventually a doctor explained that a concussion had been ruled out and that small dosage shots of Narcan were taking effect and Billy would be all right. Later Eric listened to the same doctor give the same explanation to Billy, who muttered, "Who gives a fuck?" Looking bored, the doctor left the room.

Billy passed out again. Eric sat by his bed, trembling. Now more than ever he needed his mumbled mantra to maintain some calm. Though if he was praying, truth was, he couldn't say for what. Erratic thoughts sprouted in all directions, imagination and memory, his fame as an ad exec and marketing king. As if he had invented new flowers, new stars. A magus, an angel above morality. Now back on solid earth, a peasant, a farmer, a clod of dirt.

Later Billy awoke slowly and painfully, an uncomprehending expression on his unshaven face. "Am I dead or what?"

"You're going to be okay," Eric answered. "You're in a hospital. They're taking care of you."

Billy finally seemed to register Eric's presence. "Get the fuck outa here."

"How about if I go for a cup of coffee," Eric replied, "and you take a minute to wake up."

"Fuck you. I'm gonna hurt you deep."

Just drug talk, Eric told himself as he left the room, but a spiteful laugh chased him down the hall, chilling his insides. In the cafeteria he called Jessica and left a message, compressing the night into a grim nutshell. Then he called Anna. She listened to his explanations without comment but he could read her thoughts loud and clear. *Cut him loose.* She had been there herself; beyond the verge. She knew Billy needed Jesus; nothing else was going to save him. Had he been somebody else's son, Eric would have been the first to agree. He felt in his bones—feared in his bones—Billy would drag him down into the same black pit he inhabited. Eric didn't think he could stop it, didn't know how any father could. Even the phrase *I'm going to hurt you deep* would not hit home until he was actually hurt deep.

When he got back to the room, Billy was gone. He checked at the nursing station down the hall. The nurse assistants had just changed shifts and the one on duty had left. The new nurse studied her computer, then called the assistant and left a message. Eric went back to Billy's room, opened the closet door. His clothes were gone. His hospital gown was crumpled on the floor. Within thirty minutes the hospital staff had exhausted every possibility. The senior nurse told Eric it was obvious that Billy had walked. Eric asked if she had any suggestions.

"Check with his dealer," she said. "Sometimes they go from here straight back to source."

Eric had no idea who that distinguished person might be. He also had no idea who Billy's friends were, if he had any, so he went home. He stood in the garden, listening to birds chirp. After a while Anna came out. She looked beaten to a frazzle. We're all going down, he thought. They went inside together. He rinsed off plates, put them in the dishwasher. Then the hallway caught his eye. He had forgotten about the mess.

In the living room, he inspected the stained sofa, the

beer bottles on the carpet, the shattered crystal bowl, a burn mark on the armchair he hadn't noticed before, the filth and emptiness of Billy's room. He got the vacuum cleaner, a duster, mop, bucket and broom and set to work. Two hours later he had the party mess cleaned but he kept at it. He wanted to scrub every square inch of the place, eliminate every germ, microbe, dust mote. He removed the curtains and wiped down the bay window. He shampooed the fireplace rug and the interior mat by the front door. I'll throw him out in one clean sweep, he thought.

He removed the sheets from Billy's bed and washed them along with the sofa's antimacassars and the end table cloth covers. He wiped out the drawers, dusted every shelf, vacuumed every room a second time. He used a screwdriver to remove the security bolts on the kitchen doors. Anna watched him work. He reminded her that he wasn't going to allow Billy back into the house. She looked at him as if he were talking about something that didn't involve her.

"As soon as I fix it with him," he emphasized, "I'm going to do the smudging again. We should have done it after Kathy died." She still had a faraway look. "What is it?"

"I've decided to put Owen into foster care," she said.

He set the screwdriver aside, wiped his hands on a towel. "Then what?"

"Right now I can't see beyond foster care. It's a pile of paperwork and legalities."

"Come and talk for a minute," he said.

"I have to finish something first."

Finish packing, she meant. It was the beginning of

farewell. He saw it as plainly as if she had just hung a good-bye banner on the fridge. He washed up, poured a shot of Makers and took it down to the front end. He pulled the armchair to the corner of the living room and positioned it so he had a view of both the front door and Billy's bedroom window. Then he turned on the radio. Part Three of the interview with the dog trainer was just being announced. In this episode the trainer would offer tips on "a complete and balanced diet." Eric took a sip of Makers and began to wait. Whatever Anna did, his course of action remained the same. Cut loose his prodigal son.

CHAPTER FORTY-TWO

The interview with the dog trainer changed to an hour of classical music, followed by local news and then a talk show discussing the relationship between video games and children's nightmares. It reminded Eric of the gruesome dreams that had plagued Billy in his boyhood. Horror and cold sweat at the hour of the wolf. He or Kathy would wake Billy up and soothe him, but he rarely fell back asleep unless one parent remained nearby.

Listening to Owen cry down the hall, Eric also recalled Billy's first infant fever. Inexperienced parents, he and Kathy had struggled mightily over administering a few drops of acetaminophen from an oral syringe. They couldn't bear the thought of putting any kind of drug into their child's immaculate body. Depressing the plunger, they feared they had squirted one driblet too many onto his tiny tongue. In mutual panic they had raced off to the ER and given a seasoned pediatrician a good chuckle.

The local news came on again. There had been an eight car pile-up on Interstate 5 near the California border. State police blamed low visibility caused by unusually thick fog. A second story described a recent change in the schedule of Ashland city council meetings. Next came an editorial on permit applications for medical marijuana dispensaries. Every now and then Eric drifted off and forgot why he was sitting there, forgot what he was waiting for. Then he clutched and became alert, cautioned himself to stay resolute, forceful, detached.

Anna brought in a breakfast tray of toast, orange juice, coffee and a cheese and avocado omelet. He told her he wasn't hungry. She set the tray on a fold-out table. Her movements, her silence, even the shape of the omelet convinced him she was packed and ready to go.

"You can hear the door open from the other end," she said. "You don't have to stay chained to this chair."

"I want to be here when he comes in."

He guessed she hadn't yet left because she feared for his safety and didn't want to leave him to face Billy alone. Or she had other plans and needed more time. As they sat there looking at each other, a UPS truck parked in front of the house across the street. The brown-clad driver got out carrying a small package and his handheld computer. He passed out of the frame of the bay window and returned a minute later without the package. They watched as he paused by the door of his truck, reached in and brought out a plastic water bottle. He set a pill into his mouth and washed it down.

"I wonder what he just took," Eric said. "Aspirin, Vitamin C, prescription med?"

"No way of telling," Anna said. "Maybe he has a headache or maybe he's a head."

"What kind do you think Billy takes?"

"No way of telling that either."

"What would you guess?"

"I'd guess he takes anything within reach."

Eric imagined the house without her, the emptiness. The aroma of the coffee and toast finally got to him. He reached for the tray and finished off the omelet within minutes. He drank the orange juice and then sipped coffee.

"Delicious," he said and meant it, but his voice lacked conviction.

The sound of a car engine came from down the street. A door opened and shut. He peered out the corner of the bay window. Anna remained seated but he sensed her growing tense. Three houses away a man with a handbag and suitcase tiredly climbed his front steps. "It's just some neighbor," Eric said. He didn't know the guy but, watching him enter his house, he thought of the many times he had arrived home from Austin, pummeled comatose by some onerous DMT project. He felt a pang of sorrow. Sensing loneliness and heartache, he also felt as if his last desires were vanishing. Thirst, hunger, his longing for peace. *What do you seek?* Nothing. Nothing at all.

"When I left here a year ago," he murmured, "I thought the past would recede into a void and the future would cease to exist. But it doesn't work that way. Even when you're dead onto yourself, the stars still retreat and advance."

Anna looked at him closely. Meanwhile, Part Seven of the Dog Trainer Interview—a discussion on "furry friends and pet parents"—droned on. The Trainer described his preferred disciplinary methods, which involved reward-based techniques rather than asserting dominance by physical punishment. The broadcast was momentarily interrupted by a garbled announcement describing a serious situation in Medford. Another few minutes of the interview followed and then another interruption. This time the newscaster's voice cracked with both static and nerves. Urgently, he stated that initial reports had been confirmed. An active shooter had entered an office building near the historic district of Medford. Shots had been fired and at least three people had been injured, perhaps critically. Police were on the scene, including a tactical unit specialized in terror control. Whether terrorist attack or multiple shooting was not yet known. A spokesman urged residents to stay clear of the area until further notice. Authorities were now evacuating nearby office buildings. Eric was about to comment that he couldn't remember a similar situation occurring in the area, then he suddenly sat forward.

"My god," he said. "It can't be what I think."

"What do you mean?" Anna replied.

"DMT is there. That exact neighborhood." He lost his voice for a second. "Th—there's something I didn't tell you before. Billy has... has..." He couldn't bring himself to pronounce the word *guns*.

"I know what you didn't tell me. Does he know DMT is there?"

Eric nodded anxiously. "I used to take him for visits when he was a boy. But it's crazy to even think..." He raked his fingers through his hair, ran his palms over his face. "Maybe I should go... just in case."

"They just said to stay away."

"At least I should call."

His nerves had gotten the better of him but the number of the DMT marketing department was still hard to forget—541-770-7700—and this time he remembered the receptionist's name, Cindy. A moment later her voice came on the line but it was the answering machine, the recorded message for afterhours and weekends.

"This isn't right," he said. "It's the middle of the morning. If all the lines are busy, it should be the daytime message telling callers to 'Please hold.' Something's wrong."

Ignoring Anna's protests, he scooped up his car keys and wallet.

"Call the police," he told her shakily. "Tell them who I am and that I'm on my way."

He hurried out the door, got in the car and drove off, leaving behind a screech of rubber. Why had he told Anna to call if he could do it himself? He was rattled. "I'm overreacting," he thought. "I'm thinking crazy, acting crazy..."

On the road out of Ashland he had to remind himself where he was going, how to get there. It was as if he had never been to Medford, as if he hadn't traveled the same route a thousand times in the past. He turned on the radio. All the local channels carried the story. Cub reporters who had never reported anything except high school football scores sounded hysterical while veterans struggled to pronounce difficult phrases. Now there was a possible hostage situation. The shooter had been identified as a young white male dressed in tactical gear. More shots had been fired. It was not yet clear who had discharged weapons, the shooter or the police.

Eric dialed 911 on his cell phone. He got a recorded

message saying he should state his emergency, leave his number and someone would get back to him as soon as possible. He hung up and called four more times and got the same recording. He became aware that he was drenched in sweat. He commanded himself to leave a message. His voice broke.

"This... this is an emergency. My name is Eric Tyler. I live in Ashland. I'm a retired businessman... a former employee of DMT Worldwide. DMT has an office building in... the area where... where you just reported an active shooter. I believe... I think I may have... could have important information. I'm in my car on my way there now. Please call me if you get this. I... I'll be there soon."

He had forgotten his glasses and the road was a blur. He blinked a half dozen times, wiped his eyes. He dialed back and forth over radio stations repeating the same story. He felt nauseous, as if he was back on the desert's edge, walking in a trance, the sun pounding his skull. He could feel leg cramps, foot pain, almost see his skeletal face reflected in plate glass.

In an effort to fill time or give a semblance of an updated story, one of the radio stations featured two local experts engaged in editorial debate on the "still active situation."

"FBI data ranks Medford as the most dangerous city in Oregon," said one expert. "Let's not forget that."

"We can't forget since you remind us so often," countered the other, "but any American city experiencing rapid growth will witness a spike in crime. Besides, this has nothing to do with that."

"You may use the term 'spike' but I refer to an obvious link between methamphetamine use and arms ownership, not only in Oregon but across our nation. We face a grave—"

"Gentlemen, please," said a moderator, "your comments must remain pertinent to the still active situation."

In Medford Eric was forced to park five blocks from the DMT office. He got out of the car and trotted through traffic jams and groups of distressed pedestrians toward the historic district. A police chopper hovered overhead, blades whacking and thumping. A block from DMT he came upon a tangle of squad cars, ambulances and fire trucks. Officers shouted for onlookers to "Move back!" Eric got the attention of a female officer.

"I think I know the shooter," he told her. "I mean it can't be but there's a chance that it could..."

"Come with me," she said.

She led him into a cordoned area and made him sit on a fold out chair beside an armored vehicle. Police ran past shouting to each other. A gleam of sunlight appeared on the roof of a building down the street. Eric caught a glimpse of a rifle barrel and then it vanished behind a stone parapet. "Please, no," he thought. "Please, no." Where was his mantra when he needed it? He closed his eyes and saw darkness, saw the word *KAOS!* He verged on screaming.

An eruption of gunfire froze him and everyone around him. The entire street seemed to paralyze except for a bevy of pigeons shooting upward off a sidewalk. It sounded like there had been a half dozen shots. Eric couldn't be sure. There were still echoes. He felt as if he had swallowed his scream and was now underwater gasping for breath. He became aware that an officer stood next to him. Medical personnel and firemen ran back and forth, giving and receiving orders. Four Jehovah's Witnesses prayed aloud near the entrance to a coffee shop. Onlookers pressed forward. Two policemen cleared a path. An ambulance drove off. Eric couldn't tell if a siren wailed or if the noise only sounded in his head.

Three people approached him, one in uniform. He tried to concentrate as they explained a "process of identification." One man introduced himself as a psychologist specialized in grief counseling. He would remain available in any way that Eric might need. They led Eric past two women who were weeping. A newspaper reporter cried out, saying he wanted an interview. The uniformed cop muttered, "Get that bozo out of here." Someone had hold of Eric's arm and he realized it was the psychologist helping him walk, making sure he didn't keel over. He was still thinking, "Please, no." He had been thinking it all the time he was underwater. Off to the right he heard a troubled voice: "Four down, including... one of ours."

They stopped near a gurney bearing the corpse of the shooter. Eric tried to clear his still blurred vision. He distinguished a nearby medical technician with blood on her sleeve. The officer said something and then repeated it and finally Eric understood he had to look at the corpse. Steeling himself, he pulled his arm free from the psychologist's grip. Then he gazed down at the face, pale and bloodless, of a young man he had never before seen.

CHAPTER FORTY-THREE

It hit Eric then. Billy was gone as surely as if he had been the corpse. The prodigal son had made good his threat. He had refused to become Jesus and be welcomed home.

That didn't stop Eric from hoping he might be wrong, so he spent days driving around Ashland and Medford, crawling up one street and down another, inspecting alleys and dead-end lanes. He went out early every morning. He checked in with the police, the ER and every homeless shelter and service in the Rogue Valley. He stopped by liquor stores and marijuana outlets, gun shops and firearms dealers, detox clinics and the Irish pub. He showed people an old cell phone photo of Billy and described how he looked older now. He felt like he was acting in a detective film, though each day his role became harder to play. The clerk at Bard Liquor told him about his estranged daughter, how the girl had gotten caught up in a bad crowd, how she had become addicted to crack cocaine and committed crimes. The clerk encouraged Eric to keep looking and never give up. Then he admitted he himself had given up years ago.

In the evenings when Eric arrived home, he and Anna exchanged looks and sometimes he told her about things he had seen during the day—table talk again—but she rarely had much to say. "She has no pact," he thought.

The multiple killings left a shadow on Ashland streets. Everyone seemed to know someone connected to the incident, a friend or relative who worked nearby or had passed close to the area only minutes before the slaughter. Eric learned that the DMT answering machine had been on because the police had evacuated the premises. The shooter had taken hostages in a nearby building. Trundling along in the car, Eric listened to radio broadcasts conjecturing on the killer's motive or lack of motive, interviews with his family and acquaintances. Finally, he turned the radio off. He didn't care if reports described an introverted young man or a maladjusted outcast.

One afternoon while driving through Medford's northern neighborhoods, he parked near Rogue Valley International-Medford Airport and watched planes take off and land. He tried to estimate how many times he had flown out on missions for DMT. Every Sunday bound for Austin only for starters and many more flights on many more missions. That's what the DMT hierarchy used to call a business flight. A mission. As if it turned an executive into a missionary.

Just then he spotted a dilapidated Buick traveling in the opposite direction on Bullock Road. He caught a glimpse of Billy in profile. His hand fumbled at the key. He spun the wheel, pulled into a screeching U-turn and tromped on the accelerator. Within minutes he had chased the Buick down and pulled up next to it at a stop sign. Behind the wheel sat a bespectacled seventy-year-old woman. She looked at him fearfully, as if at a stalker or madman. On the way back to Ashland he had to turn off onto Wildcat Lane. He sat trembling in the car and remained there for thirty minutes. In the end, he thought, there was only one prayer. *I'm lost and helpless. I don't know anything. I have no hope. Please take me home.*

As soon as he arrived, he entered Anna's bedroom, went to the night stand and picked up the two copies of *Heart like a jewel*. He carried them out the back door into the garden. He could not even remember how he had written the poems. Could blood flow when there was no wound? Methodically, he tore out page after page and tossed the crumpled paper into the bowl of the barbecue grill. He sprayed charcoal lighter fluid over the torn pages and lit several scraps. Flames spread. Staring into the fire, he forgave himself for everything: for betraying the poems, for burning them now, for carrying them in his psyche like ghosts in a ruined mansion. Afterwards, he threw the ashes onto the compost heap.

Anna watched him from the back door. He went inside and asked her to take a seat in his armchair. He sat on the edge of the bed, facing her.

"I can drive around for the next year," he said, "but I'm not going to find him. He's gone. If he was strung out on meth or booze, I might come across him in some alley or detox center. But he had a plan."

Her voice was low. "To hurt you like he said?"

"I thought the obvious, that he would try to hurt me physically. Pound me flat or wring my neck. Instead, he robbed me of any chance at the past."

"You mean he left you... nothing."

"Unintentionally, he left me clarity." He leaned forward, took her hand. He felt his chest constricting. Clarity didn't mean pain free. "I thought I'd have to sell the house and move into a smaller place. Then I even thought I'd have to start all over, start walking. Leave for good again. But I was wrong." He paused, swallowed. "You're the one who has to go."

She looked down at the floor, nodded. She knew exactly what he meant. "You have to tell me how," she said.

"You already know. You've listened enough, at least enough to know it's just a different kind of pact, that's all."

"Tell me anyway."

"Take underwear, socks, good shoes. Some toothpaste, a toothbrush. Fifty or sixty dollars. You'll need it at the start. Everything else will come in time."

Her eyes were large, sparked by fear or determination, maybe both. "Should I have a funeral?"

"Let's have a farewell drink instead."

"You're sure about Owen?"

"He's my end of the pact. Like I said, I'm clear. So you should be too. Don't carry it with you."

He took two wine glasses and a bottle of Pinot. They toasted, sipped wine.

"I'm going to shave my head," Anna said. "Will you paint my face?"

He painted a gold, blue and green trigram onto her forehead. In the center he dabbed on a red *tilaka*. Her freshly shaved skull bore several razor nicks. How strange she looked minus her mop of silver hair. He streaked her cheeks in light brown, her jaws in gray, taking care to cover the white scar. Impassively, she watched him paint. He saw her mask take shape, saw her transform, saw her become invisible. Suddenly, he became afraid.

"Wait," he said. "This is wrong. I don't know what I was thinking. It's just not a good idea. I mean, this isn't India. My god, it's America, land of the free to be crazy. It's not the same for a woman. The dangers, the nuts out there. It was bad enough for me. A woman can't just wander around aimlessly."

"I'm not going to," she said. "I know exactly where I'm going. I've been there before. I'll be fine." She gave a soft laugh. "Maybe I'll even have a vision."

He stared at her uncomprehendingly. Then it struck. Unlike him, she had a pilgrimage route to follow, a sacred shrine to visit. She was going back to her point zero, back to the desert.

He went to Owen's room. He was sound asleep. Eric picked him up and lay him on his shoulder, felt him murmur into his neck. The low purr penetrated him like a whisper of fear: legal hurdles would be endless, duties eternal, the burden unbearable. One step at a time, he warned himself, love and serve. Then he took the first steps down the length of the house. Anna was at the front door. She kissed Owen, who let out a whimper.

"I won't be back," she said.

Eric nodded and she kissed him full on the lips. He returned the kiss, whispered *goodbye*.

Barbara Street was empty. He held Owen and watched Anna head along the sidewalk, pulling her small rolling suitcase behind her. She came to Tolman Creek Road. He had a last look at her wildly painted face and then she vanished around the corner.

Chapter Forty-four

Over the next two weeks Eric bought a crib, some crib bars, dangling toys and baby clothes. He selected a permanent pediatrician and interviewed possible babysitters. Until he found one, Jessica sat with Owen on her off hours while he ran around town on errands.

One evening he stopped by Safeway and picked up some chicken and noodles, shaving cream and disposable diapers. Waiting in the checkout line, he watched the young woman operating the scanner and cash register. She was dressed in the standard issue short sleeve, black polo all the employees sported. She had dark hair mousse-styled into a slicked back look.

"Hey," Eric said. "We know each other."

The woman stopped dragging his bag of noodles across the scanner. "What?"

"You were at my house. On Barbara Street. There was a party."

Her nose wrinkled. "I don't know what you're talking about, mister."

"Remember, you and Billy were in the bedroom and I walked in."

She glanced nervously down the nearest aisle. "Come on, mister, I can't get in any more trouble. I need this job. I don't know any guy named Bill."

The woman in line behind Eric began to tsk. He ignored her.

"You used to have red hair," he insisted. "You remember Billy. He's tall with a scraggly mustache and a tattoo on his back. Flames and daggers and it says 'KAOS!'"

She did a double take, looked at him closely.

"You mean Alaska."

Now it was his turn for the double take. "I guess maybe I do."

"That's what everybody calls him," she said. "I didn't know his name was Bill. Are you his Dad or something?" When he said he was, she added: "I always knew he'd go back."

"He went back to Alaska?"

"That's all he ever talked about. He hated it here."

"Do you know where exactly he went?"

"What I just said: Alaska."

"I mean, what town or city."

She shook her head, glanced again at the aisle. The woman behind Eric let out another loud tsk and pushed her cart to the neighboring line.

"What about his cell number or email?" Eric asked. "Do you have that?"

She regarded him suspiciously. "You sure you're Alaska's dad?"

He pulled out his driver's license and showed it to her. Since she didn't even know Billy's name, it didn't prove much, but she leaned forward and inspected it anyway.

"His real name is Billy," Eric explained uselessly. "William Tyler. You see I'm Eric Tyler, his dad. My middle name is William." She looked up at him, still unsure, so he added: "Anything you could tell me would help a lot."

She shrugged. "Nothing to tell. Alaska is like total anti-tech."

"Anti-tech?"

"Totally. Ask anybody."

"I didn't know that..."

"Like off the grid," she said.

He paid for his groceries and carried them out to the parking lot. For a long while he sat in his car, tempted to go on waiting until the store closed for the night and she came out. He wanted to ask her more. More about his son, whose name he didn't know. His son, Alaska, who was anti-tech. Maybe she could describe what he was like. Had she considered him a good boyfriend, a good guy who had treated her well? Maybe he hadn't been her boyfriend at all, just a guy she knew, someone to drop a few pills with and have some fun. Or maybe anything. Eric reached for the key. The engine started and he drove home.

He parked in front of the house. Jessica came walking down the path, hair still pulled back in her official go-to-work ponytail, her large incisors gnawing at her bottom lip.

"You're late," she said.

"Sorry, hon, I got held up at Safeway."

"So text."

"Everything okay?"

"Fine. All the stuff for his bottle is on the kitchen counter. He's in his room, but I still think this whole thing is weird. It's like you're going senile or something. You've got to get it together."

"I'm trying, believe me."

She drove off and he went into the house and finished preparing Owen's bottle. He took everything out to the garden and sat on a lawn chair with Owen on his lap. A breeze sifted through the branches of the eucalyptus. He tilted the bottle and set the nipple onto Owen's lips. Owen pulled it into his mouth and began to suck contentedly. He drank most of the bottle, Eric burped him and held him in the crook of his arm. He gazed at the newborn features, the unshaven face. On the verge of sleep, Owen burbled gently and Eric listened to the sound, a chain of bubbles softly breaking one after another. More than a gurgle, it sounded like an evolving murmur of ease, a worship deep and endless.